This book is dedicated to Orna, with love.

SWEET SWEAT

Justine Frank
Roee Rosen

Translated from Hebrew by the author
Published by Sternberg Press

Contents

Preface

The halls of culture have sealed cellars, dim depots that are the final destination of people and artworks relegated to oblivion. Most of these people and objects were discarded because they are inconsequential and dull, but some are buried because confronting them, even with an intervening buffer of time, is disturbing and threatening. Occasionally there is a recovery mission: a well-equipped troupe, directed by an enthusiastic scholar or cultural flâneur, digs its way to a forgotten grave and excavates an esoteric article, a secret event, a shady life story. Most often these discoveries are merely embarrassing aberrations, suited for oblivion. But sometimes they are illuminating, reminders that it is not only the present that is hectic and fluctuating; the past, too, is a bustling battle zone. The past evolves. New discoveries might redecorate rooms in the halls of culture; sometimes they might even re-perfume the bed linen.

Justine Frank, the forgotten Jewish Belgian painter and writer, defies an easy assessment, both aesthetically and ethically. Frank's rediscovered paintings and writing scandalously juxtapose explicit erotica with Jewish tropes. In Frank's paintings this odd union of Judaism and sensuality has a capricious, carnivalesque character: an elegant, sinister criminal clad as a rabbi exposes his large, feminine breasts; menorahs become insects and bats; the Hebrew alphabet metamorphoses into an orgy of fornicating figures. Even the artist's numerous self-portraits commingle Judaism and smut. For example, in many of her images the artist's profile features an overgrown, hooked nose with a distinctly phallic form, echoing both anti-Semitic and pornographic caricatures.

Sweet Sweat (*Sueur Douce*), the pornographic novel Frank published in 1931, might be considered even more of an embarrassment. The book is extreme in its perversions, and signs of Judaism recur throughout. Should *Sweet Sweat* be read as a juvenile provocation or worthy literature? Is the book an assault on religion, a blasphemous farce, a somewhat twisted expression of mysticism, or, perhaps, a daring secular model of Jewish identity, an atheistic claim for – and appropriation of – Jewish heritage? In Frank's novel, carnal desire is excessive and raucous – but a loud voice is no guarantee of clear speech. The book offers no unequivocal answers, and the reader's encounter with Frank is never soothing. She does not offer cookies and tea, and there is no sweet talk or apologies. Frank is dead, but she is a possessive, polemical ghost, bent on vulgarity.

Frank's biography only exacerbates the uncertainty and unease stirred up by the novel. Her alliance with the French Surrealist circle and her intimate relationship with controversial author Georges Bataille plant her at the heart of one of the twentieth century's most riveting cultural scenes – yet even in that colorful company, in which scandals were a veritable trademark, Frank went a step too far.

In the mid-1930s Frank immigrated to Palestine. The destination seems so unsuitable that it raises the possibility that she was driven by self-destruction. Her clash with the local Jewish community, her existence as a social outcast throughout the ensuing years, and the grim circumstances of her death all reinforce the conclusion that she willfully played the part of heretic in her life and art – both in relation to the European avant-garde and to the emerging Zionist society in Israel.

The first part of this volume is a biography of Justine Frank, but as information about her life is scarce, the fog surrounding her oeuvre is not lifted there. Besides the few bits of documentation – for instance, a relatively detailed description of the infamous 1942 episode that ended with Frank's arrest – there is hardly any firsthand testimony about the artist. The dearth of data is a result not only of Frank's status as a social pariah, but also of the fact that – her exhibitionism, profligacy, and belligerence notwithstanding – she was a jealously private person, almost secretive when it came to her past.

I was able to locate and interview only one person who had known Frank personally: Tamar Biniamini, daughter of Fanja Hissin. Hissin, a widow who owned one of the first small variety shops in Tel Aviv, was Frank's most intimate friend, and the artist lived her last year in Hissin's apartment. Biniamini, the custodian of Frank's estate, was able to provide singular descriptions and insights, but her testimony regarding several episodes in Frank's life squarely contradicts the established chronology. Yet if Frank is to be judged by history, the prosecution has ample reasons to demand Biniamini's dismissal. Her stories betray an unconditional love for Frank. Moreover, her understandable need to defend the much-maligned artist has also to do with preserving – perhaps doctoring – her mother's legacy. And, in addition, there is the simple fact that Biniamini was only three years old when Frank immigrated to Palestine and twelve when the artist passed away. Her account is limited by the confines of a child's perception and there is the natural difficulty of divining her authentic recollections from what her mother later told her.

Frank was ostracized. Her work was almost never exhibited. Her book was hardly read. Her name was omitted from most art-historical chronicles and from the annals of the Jewish community in Palestine. The repulsion she inspired might have been the result of societal trepidation in the face of her assertion of a female identity incongruous with contemporary preconceptions. And Frank herself can be blamed for her rejection. The antagonism she provoked, in any case, still persists. While spending several years researching Frank's life and assembling the first retrospective exhibition of her work, I came up against walls of hostility and resentment that have not yet crumbled. And yet, the first buds of a Frank renaissance are emerging. In January 2000 Italian philosopher Antonio Somaini initiated an interdisciplinary international conference about her. This symposium brought curators, artists, and scholars from varied fields to the Fondazione Querini-Stampalia in Venice, among them French theorist Jean Baudrillard, American artist Joseph Kosuth, and French anthropologist Alain Caillé. The fascinating exchange of ideas it stimulated suggests that Frank's work addresses the present with even more urgency and relevance than her own time. Hopefully, the growing interest in Frank will contribute to a better understanding of her work and also unearth more concrete evidence about her life – I expect that the flawed biography that makes up the first part of this volume will eventually be dismissed and replaced by a worthier work. In the following pages I have attempted to avoid unsubstantiated speculations and to tell Frank's story as straightforwardly as I could.

At the heart of this volume is Justine Frank's only novel, *Sweet Sweat*. It tells the story of Rachel, a girl who grows up in a shtetl ludicrously located in southern France. At age twelve Rachel is kidnapped by the libertine Count Urdukas (the name pays homage to Isidore Ducasse, or Comte de Lautréamont [1846–1870], a writer whom the Surrealists hailed as a forefather). Urdukas intends to rape and murder the girl, but he is suddenly dissuaded from committing these crimes by the sweet smell of her sweat, which strikes him as a revelation. From Urdukas's viewpoint, Rachel's body odor proves she is a prodigy, her gift being an extraordinary talent for all things criminal, obscene, licentious, and abject. Similar to a talent for music, Urdukas feels, this inborn genius will flourish only through laborious exercises, the development of coordination and technique, the refinement of the senses, and – no less important – the study of criminal classics. Urdukas, a connoisseur of the perverse, takes her education as his calling. He makes Rachel his mistress and leads her down a winding road of fornication and crime. But the pupil outstrips her mentor. The count gradually subjects himself to Rachel's excessive whims, and she conjures up the fantasies they realize, including the last and most horrendous: a grotesque wedding in which Rachel's old religious father is coerced into marrying his own daughter, who then rapes and murders him.

In some ways *Sweet Sweat* is an offspring of the novels of the Marquis de Sade; it is part of the smut genealogy of the French avant-garde, alongside texts by Guillaume Apollinaire, Louis Aragon, Georges Bataille, and, later, Pauline Réage. Yet, its precursors notwithstanding, *Sweet Sweat* is unique in several ways. First, French pornography is deeply rooted in Catholic culture, and Catholicism resonates in these books far beyond their paradigmatic stance of sacrilege and profanity. *Sweet Sweat*, on the other hand, posits Judaism as its religious trope, resulting in a marked difference in both cultural repercussions and literary style. Second, the pornographic sphere in Frank's era, for authors and readers alike, was almost exclusively masculine; *Sweet Sweat* is distinguished by the writer's gender. Third, *Sweet Sweat* endows its heroines with magic powers, which they employ to fulfill perverse desires; magic, as a rule, is foreign to the various pornographic genres.

Sweet Sweat was privately printed under the pseudonym Gregoir Coque two and a half years after Bataille issued his most famous pornographic text, *Story of the Eye*. Presumably, Bataille's circle of friends financed *Sweet Sweat's* single edition of around thirty copies. A complete version of the novel is unavailable, unfortunately, and so the version in this volume is abridged. When I decided in 1996 to devote some time to a study of Frank, I located three copies of *Sweet Sweat*: two at the Collection de l'Enfer at the Bibliothèque nationale de France in Paris and one in Tamar Biniamini's library in Tel Aviv. One of the Paris copies was vandalized; most of the pages containing explicit sex scenes – and these are the bulk of the slim volume – had been torn out. The other copy, in mint condition, was stolen from the library in January 1999 (and I had neglected to back up my preparatory notes with a full photocopy of the book). It seems that not only Frank's foes but her admirers as well are set to deny her a place in history. Ironically, Biniamini's copy was "vandalized" by none other than Justine Frank herself. The book was a gift from the author to Fanja Hissin, and many of its pages are filled with ink and pencil drawings. Frank used other pages for personal commentary, in her thorny, frantic, barely legible handwriting. Some of these comments are phrased with intentionally exaggerated professorial pomposity – part annotation, part self-mockery; most of them are affectionate and intimate notes to Hissin. These writings and drawings run over the printed text, making the Biniamini copy a fascinating study object but only a partial version of the novel. The fragments assembled here are all we can confidently restore from the two remaining copies and from the few sections I had photocopied from the stolen Paris copy. The fragments are complemented in this edition by descriptions of the narrative's missing parts. Frank's book was never translated into English; Anne Kastorp's seminal essay (Kastorp 1993) includes excerpts in the original French. I am confident that the republication of *Sweet Sweat* will lead to the recovery of more copies and the unabridged novel will again be available.

Though this book is intended for a general reading audience, Frank's multifaceted persona and her complex work pose problems that cannot be tackled through a biography alone. Therefore, in order not to overburden Frank's life story, I have relegated my more elaborate reflections to a concluding essay. *Sweet Sweat* engenders a scholarly octopus whose eight tentacles interlace: Surrealist art, feminist theory, Jewish mysticism, a genealogy of the figure of the Jew in the Christian literary canon and in Western psychiatry, nationalist ideology, radical transgression, moral criteria applied to pornography, and the experiential pleasure of pornographic material. All of these issues are not only crammed into the scholarly locus they were allotted – but they threaten to overshadow the source from which they were originally secreted: the hyperactive glands of *Sweet Sweat*. The essay, therefore, follows an eclectic, frenetic array of bifurcations, each of which points down a different path, reflecting the fact that Justine Frank's story is itself one of entanglement, self-contradiction, and multiple meanings.

Stained Portfolio

On the Life and Work of Justine Frank

Roee Rosen

1. A PRESENT WITHOUT A PAST: ANTWERP 1900–1925

Very little is known of the early chapters of Justine Frank's life, between her birth in Antwerp in 1900, and 1925, when she settled in Paris. The municipal archive of Antwerp lists five Frank families residing in the city at the turn of the century, but none of them is registered as having a daughter named Justine. The chronologically closest recorded birth of a baby girl is that of Christine Frank, on November 4, 1898. It stands to reason that this girl was, indeed, Justine Frank; such a revision of name and birth date accords with what we know of Frank's character. If Justine is Christine, then she was born to Judith and Leopold Frank. There is almost no information about her father's life or family history, except that he was a watchmaker. A little more is known about Judith's family. She was the daughter of Jacob Kahn, who before he went bankrupt was one of the most prominent and affluent cobblers in the Jewish leather industry that flourished in Antwerp beginning in the mid-nineteenth century. Judith Frank's paternal family tree attests that in 1830, when Belgium won its independence, her grandfather was granted full citizen's rights in accordance with the new equality laws. It is likely that on her maternal great-grandfather's side, Christine Frank was a descendant of the large community of Portuguese Marranos (Jews who were forced to convert to Catholicism, but secretly kept their faith) that settled in the city in the early sixteenth century. Christine was an only child; a sister, Hannah, born in 1894, had died of influenza at the age of two. This fact solidifies somewhat the hypothesis that Christine was Justine: Frank, who vehemently refused to talk of her family and of her childhood even to an intimate friend such as Fanja Hissin, did nevertheless mention several times that she had a sister "whose traces were lost," and Tamar Biniamini, Hissin's daughter, recalls her mother's futile attempts to track down Frank's sister in the early 1950s. No further information about Judith, Leopold, or Christine Frank's family is filed in Antwerp's municipal archive or in other pertinent archives, such as those at Beth Hatefutsoth, the Diaspora Research Center in Tel Aviv, or the United States Holocaust Memorial Museum in Washington DC. Even the dates of their deaths are unknown. It is likely that the family left Belgium and even likelier that all members perished in the Holocaust.

If Justine was indeed Leopold and Judith's daughter, she was raised in the modest, stable comfort of a petit bourgeois family on the brink of assimilation. The proposition that Justine was *not* Christine should not be ruled out (it may be that her birth was not recorded in Antwerp simply because she was delivered elsewhere); it does seem certain, at any rate, that she was reared in a well-off household. Her rounded education, the art classes she doubtlessly attended, and her command of both French and English are sound indications that her parents did not suffer serious financial hardships; in fact, it is possible that she was of a class higher than that of a watchmaker and a cobbler's daughter.

Frank spoke some Yiddish, but with a limited vocabulary and an odd accent. Biniamini recalls that Frank used the Jewish dialect to amuse her mother, for whom Yiddish was one of two native tongues (daily communication between the two was in English). Frank's broken Yiddish may be an indication that her ancestors had wandered to Belgium from Eastern Europe and settled in the city during the great immigration wave of the 1880s (as did the vast majority of the local Jewry); she could have picked up Yiddish from her grandparents.

Whether Frank was raised in a lower- or upper-middle-class home, Yiddish was almost certainly considered by her immediate family to be an embarrassment, a mark of a lowly past that was best kept hidden. Yiddish was widely considered to be an inferior German dialect, degenerated not only in a linguistic and cultural sense, but genetically and physically as well. The widespread opinion throughout Europe, enhanced by contemporary science, was that "Jewish" speech – *mauscheln* – was a result of Jews' malformed jaw structure. Yiddish was classified as yet another symptom (along with flat feet, for example) of the Jew's indelible difference (Gilman 1991). This belief was so strongly held both in the popular imagination and in scientific and cultural circles that many Western European Jews, such as Zionist leader Theodor Herzl, adopted it as well – with one significant adjustment: they connected *mauscheln* (and other anti-Semitic attributes of Jewishness) only to Eastern European Jews, whom they despised.

Yiddish was one of many signifiers of Judaism that Frank tackled in her work. When her paintings co-opt marks of Jewish inferiority (some of which, perhaps, were repellent to her), it is a troubled appropriation, with an unresolved tension between the symptomatology of the attributes of the Jew in European culture and the internalization of these very syndromes by Jews themselves. The single appearance of Yiddish in Frank's obscene novel is dichotomous as well: a sentence uttered by the Jewish protagonist, Rachel, in "the language of the Jews," was intentionally mistranslated in French by the author. There, dialect plays a role in a covert swindle that breaches the fundamental trust between a book and its reader. In this scenario Yiddish is a linguistic territory of exclusivity: the French reader is denied the privilege of comprehension, a reverse discrimination of sorts.

Yiddish, then, links the young Belgian artist to the Eastern European diaspora. In relation to this, recent scholarship has raised a provocative theory concerning both the artist's family history and the hidden meaning of her oeuvre. According to Professor Anne Kastorp of Brown College in East Orange, New Jersey, Frank is the descendent of none other than Jacob Frank, the infamous Sabbetaian mystic whom Gershom Scholem called "the most hideous and uncanny figure in the whole history of Jewish Messianism" (Kastorp 1997; Scholem 1974, 308). This hypothesis provides a comprehensive, if rather fantastic, explanation for Frank's bizarre life story as well as keys to the interpretation of her work. It is a truly dramatic elucidation, since Kastorp postulates not merely a familial relation but the survival of a small enclave of the Frankist sect and Justine Frank as an active member.

If indeed Frank was a Frankist, then her pornographic novel, which includes a parricide scene, could be read according to the blasphemous logic of the dictum "redemption through sin," the radical and paradoxical logic that propelled Frankists to intentionally commit extreme acts of transgression. To follow this daring stipulation further, the family's assimilation into gentile Belgian society must have been a deception, a cunning cover for the radical spiritual sect that was persecuted to near extinction. And if Frank was a Frankist, then her tempestuous life, laden with secrets and lies, was a programmatic continuation of an esoteric, centuries-old faith, which had found a new, deceitful incarnation in modernity. The artist's licentious, lawless, and capricious behavior is clarified, according to Kastorp's theory, as a willful and calculated personal mystical practice disguised as an artistic pursuit and a secular lifestyle, and intended, in fact, to do no less than hasten a messianic Third Coming (after those of Sabbetai Zevi and Jacob Frank himself). And yet, though Kastorp is indisputably the world's leading scholarly authority on Frank's work, and her far-reaching theory is difficult to dismiss offhand, it should be confronted with caution and reserve. It is important to emphasize that Kastorp's stipulations are based entirely on clues culled from Frank's own paintings and writings, without any historical or factual foundation. There is an immense chasm between Kastorp's assertions and the views of most Frank scholars (myself included), which is especially ironic considering that these scholars' views – one and all – are premised on Kastorp's earlier, seminal work about the artist (Kastorp 1993).

Casting Frank as a violent messianic mystic entails devastating damage to the Surrealist artist's prestige. Kastorp herself, once a bona fide Frank enthusiast, now condemns her as a veritable moral hazard. Precisely because of this drastic change of heart, and in order to emphasize that Kastorp's recent postulations hinge on speculation rather than fact, I have decided to present a detailed (and critical) account of her theory only in my concluding essay. Justine Frank persistently employs Jewish symbols and images, but she does so as a secular, indeed epicurean, women who lived outside any communal or religious Jewish framework. Hence it is plausible that Frank was neither well-versed in Halachic nor Kabbalistic Judaism; she may have been, in other words, ignorant of the rich history and polemics tied with Jewish self-definition and was very likely set on asserting this ignorance precisely to demonstrate that the sovereign air of such self-definition is always, necessarily, a fallacy.

A supplementary piece of evidence concerning the young Justine Frank was unearthed by art historian Roger Rothman: Frank arrived in Paris armed with a recommendation letter by Belgian Surrealist poet Camille Goemans, a copy of which Rothman recovered in Goemans's literary estate. The document has a generic address, "To whom it may concern," and testifies that "the young lady is an artist and a colleague, well worthy of any form of support (Rothman 2008)." It is impossible to determine on the basis of this letter whether Goemans and Frank had a meaningful rapport or whether it was a simple gesture of goodwill on Goemans's part (or, perhaps, a nominal act to rid himself of a nuisance). In any case, this letter must have won Frank a cordial welcome among the French Surrealists, and it is the only indication that young Frank had had some relations with artists and poets before her arrival in Paris and that she had connections to Brussels's avant-garde circles. In addition, from the fact that she solicited such a letter, we can infer that she was ambitious and determined to shed her provincial past as quickly as possible.

Beyond the few facts narrated above, there is no information about Frank's family. However, there was someone in Belgium, possibly a family member, who kept in contact with her and supported her financially. According to Tamar Biniamini, from the day she left Antwerp and until 1936, Frank received a bimonthly cash allowance in brown envelopes addressed first to Paris and later to Tel Aviv. This accounts for Frank's sustenance. She did not work on a regular basis, and employment was held in disregard by members of her Parisian cultural milieu. André Breton frequently voiced his desire to rid himself of the debasing need to work, and Marcel Duchamp expressed pride on several occasions for successfully realizing this wish throughout his entire life. Like Duchamp, Frank was professionally unemployed.

A portrait of Frank as a young woman on the eve of her departure to Paris seems to materialize from thin air – a present without a past. And the portrait is quite astonishing: an impoverished young woman who seeks no income; a painter and an author without academic training whose draftsmanship will prove polished and whose prose attests to familiarity with several fields of knowledge. This paradox – of a distinct yet obfuscated figure – seems to have found expression in Frank's external appearance as well. She was a tall woman, thin to the verge of emaciation, yet her posture and demeanor projected force and resilience. Her remarkable beauty was cut almost to the clichéd measures of the pre-Raphaelite ideal – replete with a thick mane of black hair, extraordinarily large black eyes sunk deep in their sockets, and a sharp contrast between the dark contours of her features and her pale, tubercular complexion – but her almost aggressive grimness had nothing in common with that fantasized model of feminine frailty. It seems that her entire defiant being sought an impossible state of existence: autonomy without territory.

2. "INNOVATIVE SMOKE": PARIS, 1925–1928

Frank became acquainted with members of the Surrealist movement soon after her arrival in Paris in autumn 1925. For Surrealists it was a thrilling period of transition. In spring 1924 André Breton had published the "Manifesto of Surrealism," in which he called for a new awareness of dreams and the unconscious as well as revolutionary challenges to the reign of reason in art and in life (Breton 1972a). For some time before that, Breton had idolized the Dada leader Tristan Tzara, and when Tzara arrived in Paris, Breton and his friends Louis Aragon and Philippe Soupault had collaborated with him in a series well-orchestrated theatrical scandals. Soon, however, Breton had grown dissatisfied with the anarchic, intently callous spirit of Dada and aspired to replace it with a new spiritual agenda: Surrealism. (Ideological issues aside, Breton's disavowal of Tzara had a lot to do with the former's tendency to anoint cultural idols and later tar and feather them as erring traitors.) When Frank and Breton crossed paths, he was the indisputable leader of the new Surrealist epoch.

In the early 1920s Surrealism was primarily a literary movement. At the time of the publication of the Surrealist manifesto, Breton had several years of experimentation behind him with automatic writing, early Surrealism's key technique. In *The Magnetic Fields*, a book he had coauthored with Soupault in 1921, he attempted to free writing from the restraints of conscious control and self-censorship by predetermining the speed of writing and by the convergence of two authorial psyches (Breton and Soupault 1997). But Breton had an exceptional eye for art and mundane objects, and he was a brilliant essayist on art; he had already collaborated with artists such as Francis Picabia, Marcel Duchamp, and Man Ray. It was mainly at his initiative that Surrealism soon enfolded visual art and cinema.

The Surrealists enacted an array of experiments meant to liberate the subconscious. Among those was the séance, performed not to communicate with the dead but to encourage "sleeping fits," trance states resulting in eccentric behavior and spectacular verbal outbursts. The authenticity of these trances is disputable; the most accomplished performers were young authors Robert Desnos and René Crevel (who made no secret of their competition for Breton's attention). Crevel almost succeeded in convincing a group of hypnotized Surrealists to commit collective suicide (he attained that goal several years later, alone). Desnos, for his part, attributed the virtuoso word games he effortlessly orated while "asleep" to telepathic contact with Duchamp, who was living in New York. (Duchamp, not sharing Breton's enthusiasm for trances, denied Desnos's claims with laconic irony.)

Frank's early years in Paris were the only period in her life unmarred by social and personal conflicts. On the contrary: she joined the Surrealist circle as a welcome, if marginal, player. She participated in automatic-writing games and was present at several meetings in Breton's legendary rue Fontaine home. The apartment, where he would stay for the rest of his life, dazzled its guests with an almost phantasmagoric ensemble of art, "primitive" masks, sculpture, and fetishistic objects culled from street markets. Frank later told Fanja Hissin that she had witnessed one of the last Surrealist experiments with hypnosis – the infamous session during which Desnos, knife in hand, chased Paul Éluard into the latter's garden in an attempt to stab him. (Desnos's fondness for knives persisted in his waking state; he later attended a dinner party in honor of Ezra Pound intending to stab Jean Cocteau and be rid, once and for all, of the hated artist-poet) (Breton 1993, 70). Hissin could not have known it, but Frank had lied to her about witnessing Desnos's assault on Éluard: the Surrealists had stopped tinkering with hypnosis a year before her arrival in Paris.

Frank truly was witness to a different scandalous scene, one she found highly amusing. In May 1926 she waited at a nearby café with several other women close to the Surrealists while Breton, Aragon, Éluard, and Benjamin Péret broke into the offices of *Les Nouvelles littéraires*, from their vantage point a "bourgeois" journal, in response to a mention of Aragon in its pages. While Aragon chased the editor upstairs, pounding him with his walking stick, the other three threw furniture out of the office window until they were all arrested by the police. Such extravagant actions were characteristic of Surrealism, which mixed radical ambitions and petty personal grudges, revolutionary creativity and juvenile pranks.

Unknown photographer, Justine Frank, *1928*

Among the few photographs of Justine Frank is a studio portrait taken at that period. The anonymous photographer captured the artist with eyes rolling upward and lips slightly open – in the history of iconography, clear marks of a sexual or religious ecstatic state – an expression reminiscent of the women in Salvador Dalí's famous photocollage *The Phenomenon of Ecstasy* (1933). The portrait, like Dalí's work, emphasizes with little subtlety a multifaceted association dear to the Surrealists between orgasmic self-abandon, the convergence of wakefulness and dreaming, spiritual ecstasy, and madness (several of the photographs Dalí incorporated were appropriated from the psychiatric archive of the nineteenth-century neurologist Jean-

Martin Charcot). In the picture Frank's hair, unfurling like a fan, is the dominant erotic and fetishistic element. This, as well as the solarization of the photograph, betrays the anonymous artist's unabashed emulation of Man Ray's more original and polished works.

This picture of Frank is immersed in Surrealism's predilections and style, but even at this early stage it seems that rather than truly belonging to the group, she was playing a role. In her first years in Paris Frank neither exhibited her paintings nor showed them to her colleagues. Some critics suggest that this was a period of patient artistic evolution for her, but Frank was far from being a model of modest labor. Another, more plausible possibility is that she avoided exposing her identity as an ambitious artist as a survival tactic within Surrealism's politics and power struggles.

Breton's goal was to assemble a group of artists who would confer prestige upon Surrealist art, and he was especially proud of securing Pablo Picasso's participation in the first Surrealist exhibition. Frank correctly sensed that women had no place in this setup, particularly an odd figure such as her, a foreigner with predilections ranging from scatology to Judaism. She, for her part, was an individualist, a loner, sensitive to the verge of paranoia to any hint of disregard. Though her casting as a mere extra on the set of Surrealism was incommensurate with her talents, she knew that she needed contact with the group for her own nourishment; suppressing her artistry paradoxically ensured her stable status among the Surrealists.

Furthermore, it is likely that at heart Frank felt detached from the volatile politics that agitated the group. By 1926 Surrealists were as preoccupied with chance and the subconscious as with Breton's knotty attempt to reconcile that agenda with doctrinaire communism. In the 1930s Breton would unflinchingly condemn the horrors of Stalinism (while French communists expressed their absolute and blind acceptance of Soviet dogma in a psalm of praise to the leader) and pay a heavy price for it in the defeat of his efforts to win partisan approval for Surrealism. But in the second half of the 1920s Breton still acted like a fanatical, righteous, aggressive commissar, coercing his colleagues into total loyalty to communism. For Frank partisan complicity was incompatible with a radical psychological and parapsychological art practice; Walter Benjamin also pointed out the contradiction between Surrealism's indulgence of the supernatural and a materialistic worldview (Benjamin 1986).

In addition, Frank observed with irony and repugnance Breton's trials of Surrealists whose art was suspected of inadequately serving working-class interests. Among the outcasts were Philippe Soupault and – even harder for Frank – Antonin Artaud, the author, actor, and director whose work's violent passion, moral quandaries, and ritualistic elements fascinated her. However, Frank was prepared to ignore a certain malodor. She waited patiently off court until Breton's ill-fated attempt to subjugate Surrealism to communism ran its course.

There was yet another dimension to Frank's hesitance to expose herself to her new colleagues. In his novel *Nadja* (1928) Breton mythologized his real-life romantic flirtation with a mentally unstable young woman, picturing femininity on the verge of madness as inspiring and sublime. Frank knew full well, however, that the commitment of the real Nadja to a mental ward had led to Breton's desertion of her (Polizzotti 1995, 284–85). Feminine madness as an erotic, antibourgeois muse for Surrealist men was one thing; coping with the suffering of a real woman was quite another. Frank was as disinclined to fit a prefabricated mold of mystifying madness as she was cynical about the link between feminine sensuality and hysterical fits that Surrealists were very fond of establishing.

In *Sweet Sweat* Frank describes Rachel's licentious excitement at the sight of the gas mask her lover is compelled to wear in defense against an overpowering feminine bodily odor. The intermingling of combative defense device with human flesh is captured in Rachel's address to her lover: "The air of your breath, acetone fumes; the air of your winds, innovative smoke." In Fanja Hissin's copy of the book, Frank underlined this sentence, scribbling at the margins, "A portrait of André Breton, drawn from life." Thus Frank mocks both Breton's fondness for fetishistic objects (such as gas masks) and his praise for chance meetings (a sewing machine with an umbrella; a face with a mask; Breton, himself, with Nadja). The flammable breath in these lines may refer to Breton's poisonous attacks on his colleagues; the "innovative smoke" of the Surrealist revolution is degraded to the toilet in an echo of Artaud's infuriated denigration of the Surrealists, after his expulsion, as "toilet paper revolutionaries" (Artaud 1976b, 161). Frank, like Georges Bataille and Dalí, abhorred the Surrealists' daily gatherings at a café, recognizing them as means to enhance Breton's authority. For many of the younger Surrealists these were frightening compulsory sessions with the tyrannical leader. The margins of Hissin's copy of *Sweet Sweat* contain several other insulting comments about Breton (Frank calls him, for example, "a sponge lion"), and Tamar Biniamini recollects her mother quoting Frank's numerous acidic snipes about the Surrealists and their leader.

And yet Frank's attitude toward Breton was not unequivocal: her contempt and criticism were mixed with intellectual deference and, most likely, dread and a sense of inferiority. Breton's charisma might have even evoked in Frank a measure of romantic attraction against her better judgment. In any case, the fact that he persistently ignored her was a constant reminder that she was merely feminine adornment of sorts, not a full-fledged member of the group. Frank was lonely throughout her life, but in Paris her loneliness was underscored by the fact that most of the other women in the circle were wives or lovers of the active, masculine members. The extraordinary beauty of the young Belgian surely did not go unnoticed, yet rather than attracting scores of suitors it was seen as off-putting, even intimidating. For a sensual and tempestuous woman, this romantic indifference was humiliating and withering.

Frank's earliest extant work is a dossier of drawings known as The Stained Portfolio (1927–28), featuring well over a hundred sketches that were never shown during her lifetime. All of these drawings are stained by a material that has not yet been chemically analyzed; most likely it is black ink that has discolored into reddish-brown blots. It has been suggested that the stains were caused by accident or negligence (Kastorp 1993, 260), but this should be dismissed, in my opinion, for two reasons. First, even though the stains shrink as one leafs forward through the sheets (as they would if the ink had been spilt on the front page), a close inspection reveals that on certain sheets the stains wander slightly and new stains appear in the middle of the dossier. And while it is possible that a large amount of ink was spilled on the sketches as they were spread on Frank's studio floor in several separate groups or that the artist had several such accidents, staining the pages on different occasions, these explanations are, to me, farfetched. Frank might have been a disorderly and tempestuous woman, but her work is marked by caution, technical rigor, and even a degree of pedantry.

Second, many of the stains are clearly figurative, and it is the sort of figuration, moreover, that is characteristic of Frank's work: hybrids of animal and human forms, oversized genitalia secreting or squirting jets of liquid, and other such grotesqueries. Some claim that these images exist only in the eye of the beholder; others suggest that Frank was beguiled by the visual randomness of accidental stains and transformed them into smutty caricatures. These explanations leave me unconvinced. Deliberate staining, on the other hand, makes sense in relation to Frank's tendency toward illusion, invention, falsehood, and deceit, her interest in compulsive sexual indulgence and bodily secretions, and – finally – her self-destructiveness, which may have found an extreme outlet in vandalizing such an exceptionally labor-intensive project as this portfolio of drawings.

The stains are not the only peculiarities of the work. Unlike any other sketchbook in the history of art, Frank's portfolio contains preparatory drawings for virtually every painting she would ever execute as well as drafts for works which have either been lost or were never realized. If the dating of the portfolio to the 1920s is to be believed, it follows that Frank devised her entire artistic development in advance, to the last detail.

If so the artist's oeuvre (and, in fact, her whole life) could be understood as a single, gigantic artwork – a labyrinthine, almost monstrously excessive *Gesamtkunstwerk*.

If the dossier is indeed such a macro plan, then Frank's lifework is a compulsive, all-encompassing parody; it is a travesty of preconceived (modernist) notions regarding artistic inspiration, aspiration, and progression. Furthermore, the prefabrication of an entire career directly contradicts the conception of life as a linear continuum of growth and maturation. This is especially disorienting in relation to Frank's work, because her style changed over time and there seem to be clear causal links between the circumstances of her life and the emergence of certain motifs in her paintings.

Justine Frank, from The Stained Portfolio *(10), 1927–28*

Justine Frank, from The Stained Portfolio *(11), 1927–28*

Justine Frank, from The Stained Portfolio *(43), 1927–28*

Justine Frank, from The Stained Portfolio *(44), 1927–28*

Perhaps Frank doctored the dates on the pages (even as late as the eve of her disappearance in 1943). There are several famous cases of artists retroactively redating their work; Russian Suprematist Kazimir Malevich and Italian proto-Surrealist Giorgio de Chirico are known to have done this. Such falsification may be intended to inflate the work's price or present the artist's aesthetic innovations as earlier and thus more visionary. And yet if Frank adjusted the dates of The Stained Portfolio she was certainly not motivated by greed. Throughout her life her paintings – early and late – had no monetary value whatsoever. Such a fabrication, then, would have to be explained on the basis of artistic intention and personal character – deception, in other words, as a value in itself. In Belgium the local Surrealist group was highly influenced by Paul Valéry, for whom deceit and fakery were essential to art – although, as Roger Rothman has written, Valéry's poetic stance ironically disavowed Bretonian Surrealism's search for subjective authenticity and sincerity (Rothman 2000, 150–62). Deceit was undoubtedly characteristic of Frank; but should falsity in this case be construed as an echo of Valéry's poetics, a swindle with unique spiritual or intellectual intentions, or simply the habitual behavior of a pathological liar?

The problem of the dates and the enigma of the stains complement the work in the Portfolio, especially its plethora of self-portraits. Frank rendered herself in numerous disguises (sometimes as nine different characters on a single sheet) in an orgiastic masquerade in which she is simultaneously a great crowd and a single soul. The Portfolio also includes quasicinematic sequences, reminiscent of animation cells, that evolve gradually from one page to the next. One such subgroup renders a lugubrious landscape that belongs stylistically to late German Romanticism. Nature's sublimity is debased when nooks in the horizon line are revealed to be female genitalia, smoke curling from a volcano to be wind escaping buttocks, and branches of a withered tree to be the candlesticks of a menorah. Two hovering moons double as a pair of eyes, and the landscape becomes a convulsive, elastic entity: on one level, a ludicrous portrait, on another, a vulgarization of the traditional analogy between the human body and nature, and, on yet another level, a staple Frankist variation on Jewish themes. Behind these aspects spreads the vast, orgiastic, undulating, and baffling valley of Justine Frank, the person. The stained sheets of the Portfolio, in which every Frankist theme is rendered, are a traveler's edition of sorts; an entire artistic career shrunk to fit in a suitcase.

Frank was finally included in a Surrealist group exhibition in 1928. She presented a series of ten colorful gouaches titled Physiognomies, and surprisingly the reaction was, by and large, positive. She won not only accolades but even a client – and not a common collector: three of the gouaches were purchased by renowned New York gallerist Julien Levy, who played a pioneering role in delivering the Surrealist gospel to America both through his gallery exhibitions and by editing the first American anthology of Surrealist art and writings.

Characteristically, Frank did not fully enjoy her success; she felt overshadowed by the rising new star of Surrealism, Salvador Dalí. Years later, in her conversations with Fanja Hissin, Frank was unable to measure her own achievements without bitterly comparing them to his greater ones. She felt, it seemed, that she was in a private competition with Dalí, one she was destined to lose, given his charisma, behavior, verbal virtuosity, and extraordinary talent. The Spaniard's success was especially irksome because there was so much in common between his early paintings and her own work – except that he had crystallized these qualities into sharper, more seductive finished products. Frank dedicated considerable artistic effort to the articulation of images with double and triple meanings (a landscape that is also a face that is also a body), but Dalí realized iconographic metamorphoses in a much more fluent, seductive, and painterly manner. In addition, in a number of brilliant texts he anchored his work in a coherent theory, one that ambitiously appropriated Freudian ideas: what he called "critical paranoia" (Dalí 1998c, 1998d).

Soon Dalí would expose his megalomaniac intention to oust Breton, "the Pope of Surrealism," and take his place; he would enrage the French circle with the unabashed commercialism of his work and with his guiltless pleasure at the stardom bestowed upon him in the United States (at a time when Bretonian Surrealism, unwieldy, taxing, and decidedly anticapitalistic, was unknown in America); he would poke fun at Breton's politics; and he would embarrass the Surrealists by sensationally professing his attraction to Nazi and Fascist luster and pomp (his infamous musings on Adolph Hitler as a sexual object were a mixture of intentional provocation, vulgar humor, and an unabashed fascination with power). All these thorny qualities would lead to yet another of Breton's trials and to Dalí's expulsion from the group. (In fact, Breton was so outraged at Dalí that he attempted on one occasion to publicly destroy a painting by the artist.)

But upon Dalí's initial arrival in Paris in the late 1920s, Breton had been all too eager to embrace him. To Frank's Physiognomies, on the other hand, Breton responded with a chilling silence. Nevertheless, the generally positive reception in general and Levy's support in particular were truly encouraging. Had Frank been less conceited, competitive, and inclined to pessimism and depression, she might have been able to gradually solidify her minor success. But the recognition won by the Physiognomies remains the greatest public achievement of her life. The whereabouts of the gouaches Levy purchased, perhaps for his New York gallery, has been unknown since 1930. They may have been sold in an unrecorded transaction, or simply lost.

In Frank's Physiognomies, animals and objects – a fish, a butterfly, an umbrella, a fork, a menorah – are combined and doubled by simple mirror symmetry to produce a small archive of animated faces. The portfolio's title points to the picture archives of sciences and pseudosciences such as eugenics and physiognomy – those that attempt to classify by facial features – creating a morbid undertone. It reminds us that during those very years, the period of European anti-Semitism's most disastrous fermentation, such archives were employed not only to identify criminals and the mentally ill but to support racial theories, as well.

The Physiognomies are also visual contemplations of the portrait. The tradition of portraiture is founded on the belief that external appearance reflects the soul, or the psyche; that Rembrandt's visage in a self-portrait, for example, mirrors his character and inner being. But Frank's paintings mask the face and emphasize the impossibility of such penetration to the point of collapsing the distinction between surface and depth. The Physiognomies ridicule the ambition to read the face, but it is ambivalent ridicule. The works have a strong affinity to some of *Sweet Sweat*'s most intense paragraphs, those in which Frank applies the percepts of physiognomic analysis not to the faces of her protagonists but to their genitalia and buttocks, as if the "nether lips" were as much a reflection of the soul as the upper ones.

Justine Frank, from The Stained Portfolio *(26), 1927–28*

Left: Four Male Idiots, *from* Physiognomische Fragmente, *by J. G. Lavater, 1797*
Right: Justine Frank, from The Stained Portfolio *(46), 1927–28*

Following her success in 1928, Frank participated in two more Surrealist group shows. Toward the end of 1929 she presented two landscapes on canvas in the vein of the perverted Jewish sublime landscapes she first articulated in The Stained Portfolio. These works drew no special attention, but they at least did not cause her any damage. In April 1930, however, she dared tackle a motif dear to the hearts of the Surrealists and, furthermore, did so in an audacious manner that stirred antagonism and anger: she painted her own versions of the literary character Fantômas, the hero/criminal, nocturnal dandy, and powerful master of disguises.

Left: Cover of Fantômas, *by Pierre Souvestre and Marcel Alain, 1911*
Right: Justine Frank, Frankomas, *1930*

In the series of pulp novels and films that bore his name, Fantômas excelled in spectacularly cruel and creative murders. The books, authored by Pierre Souvestre and Marcel Alain and first published in 1911, were unprecedented in their cheap, speedy production, enormous mass appeal, and incredibly fantastic storylines (Walz 2000, 42–75). The Surrealist circle was a veritable Fantômas fan club. Robert Desnos dedicated a poem to the arch-criminal, which he read in a live broadcast on French radio in 1933, and Breton concluded his prose-poem "Soluble Fish" (appended to the Surrealist manifesto) by identifying himself with Fantômas: "The walls of Paris [. . .] had been covered with posters showing a man masked with a black domino, holding in his left hand the key of the fields: this man was myself" (Breton 1972b, 109).

Among the artists who paid homage to Fantômas in their work is a Belgian Surrealist much more famous than Justine Frank: René Magritte. Like Frank, Magritte based his rendition of the character on the cover illustration of the first novel in the series, with one change: his Fantômas holds a rose instead of a knife. In Frank's paintings the fictive criminal, renamed Frankomas, has undergone both a religious conversion and a sex change. A hat such as those worn by religious Jews augments his elegant coat, and his face is the artist's. Frankomas holds neither a rose nor a knife and certainly not Breton's poetic "key of the fields;" instead Frank's androgyne clenches an odd object that reappears in several of her paintings: a shriveled carrot, perhaps, or a fecal mass.

It would be an understatement to say that Breton and his friends disliked the soiling of Fantômas's dandyish glove with dung – for even as they championed sexual perversion, scatology appalled them. Dalí, himself avidly immersed in all matters coprophilic, recalled later that "[the Surrealists] did not like anuses! I tried to trick them by giving them lots of anuses, carefully dissimulated, and preferably Machiavellian ones" (Dalí 1965, 24). Both Dalí and Frank detected the conservative streak hidden behind Surrealism's radicalism. For the Surrealists, perversion and crime had a heroically revolutionary resonance, but real secretions remained repulsive.

As repelled as they were by dung, the Surrealists were even more infuriated by the exchange of Fantômas's glorious disguises for traditional religious attire. Surrealist artists often incorporated Catholic iconography into their work – invariably from a position of sacrilegious defiance toward the system in which most of them grew up. Breton's disgust with religion was especially vehement, and he loathed being called the Pope of Surrealism. Once, during a dinner party at his home, Breton noticed that Georgette Magritte, René's wife, was wearing a cross on a necklace, and he took the jewelry as a personal affront. The fierce argument that followed brought about a split between the two artists (Polizzotti 1995, 335). It is easy to understand, then, the aversion Frank's paintings provoked. Her "Jewification" of Fantômas was not perceived as critical of religion but rather as the desecration of an antireligious icon. The Frankomas paintings turned Frank from a marginal, somewhat exotic and eccentric foreigner into a real persona, of the "non grata" kind; "vulgar – but in bad taste," Kastorp puts it (Kastorp 1993, 255). The Frankomas paintings mark the end of Frank's career as an exhibiting artist. It is hard to overstate the disparity between the fleeting moment of recognition she won and the abundance of her artistic production. During twenty-six years of intensive work, the window of opportunity was open only during for that brief period.

Victor Brauner's painting *The Surrealist* (1947), presently in the Peggy Guggenheim Collection, Venice, is almost certainly Frank's portrait. As such, it is conspicuous against the backdrop of Frank's marginalization within Surrealism. Brauner's painting pictures a woman with big brown eyes whose long hair stands on end and unfurls, fanlike (perhaps a painterly allusion to the 1928 photographic portrait). The Hebrew letter *aleph* hovers in front of the hair, above a double loop symbolizing eternity. (In Frank's gouache *Homage to Goya* [1927], an *aleph* appears on the forehead of a monstrous cat.) Brauner's Surrealist poses behind a table shaped like a winged fish (an animal that also appears in Frank's work), next to which stands a semi-animalistic, semi-vegetative entity whose stemlike neck issues from a flower.

Victor Brauner, The Surrealist, *1947*

This entity has two gigantic eyes, like holes (perhaps echoing the bizarre double-holed guillotines in Frank's paintings). The mystical air of the work attests to Brauner's interpretation of Frank's Jewish idioms as a kind of Kabbalistic expression. The general atmosphere of the painting is emphatic and reverential; it shows that despite Breton's animosity and the general contempt Frank suffered, she did make a lasting impression. There are no other traces of Frank in Brauner's estate, and the question of the nature of their relationship must be added to the long list of puzzles remaining in the artist's life.

3. THE EYE AND THE SWEAT: PARIS, 1929–1934

Frank became acquainted with George Bataille as early as 1926. Mutual affection was immediate, but their relationship turned intimate only in 1929. Perhaps this was a result the publication of Bataille's pornographic novel *Story of the Eye* in 1928; Frank responded to the book with great enthusiasm. For the first time in her life, it seems, she found an authoritative figure with whom she could identify. They shared a broad range of tendencies and interests: a persistent exploration of the connections between sexuality and violence; an investment in base materialism (Bataille's coinage) in defiance of humanist idealism; an intense attraction toward the darker aspects of the religious impulse; an inclination to seek spiritual illumination and revolutionary potential in the abject, the repressed, and the impure; and a strong emphasis on scatological aspects of eroticism.

Bataille's relationship to violence, irrationalism, and revolution were all significantly different than Breton's. Even at his most provocative, Breton's aspirations were premised on relatively traditional moral grounds. In the "Second Manifesto of Surrealism" he explicitly names his ultimate goals: revolutionary liberty and pure love (Breton 1972c). Bataille considered Breton's endeavor and his values naive, even timid. For Bataille, ecstatic immersion in corporeal decomposition and in nature's excessive abundance was tied to what he termed "atheology:" a religious passion after the death of God, sparked within the body, that would lead to transgression and the unmaking of societal order.

Bataille shares with Frank a shrouded early history. He wrote about his childhood in brief, hallucinatory, and frenzied fragments that include a description of himself, as a teenager, and his mother abandoning his blind, violent, and syphilitic father to his death during World War I. This sensationalist antibiographical literary miniature jumps abruptly from the author's infancy to his young adulthood, a period of religious passion in which he planned to join the priesthood (Bataille 1987b). In addition to his tempestuous relation with his father, Bataille's writings and his biography have led several scholars to suggest that he had an incestuous relation with his mother (or, at least, such a desire). Bataille's erotic story "My Mother" (Bataille 1995a) is a first-person narrative of carnal desire between mother and son, and elsewhere Bataille portrays himself masturbating in front of his mother's corpse on the day of her death in 1930 (Champagne 1998, 106n16). With Bataille as with Frank, it is difficult to divine fact from fiction – self-depiction is sabotaged even as it is performed – and like Frank, Bataille, it seems, was attempting to foster a personal myth and simultaneously thwart any conventional, coherent notion of himself, as a self, a subject.

Bataille became disillusioned with his religious calling around 1920. In the mid-1920s, while working in numismatics at the Bibliothèque nationale de France in Paris, he lived in extreme, almost programmatic libertinage. He married Sylvia Maklès in 1928, and their daughter, Laurence, was born in 1930. (When the two divorced, in 1947, Maklès wed psychoanalyst Jacques Lacan). There is almost no doubt that his sexual-romantic affair with Frank began after the publication of *Story of the Eye*. And even though Bataille was relentlessly dissolute, it seems he put an end to their affair after two years, in 1931, out of romantic love – not for his wife, but for Colette Peignot. Peignot, better known as Laure (her nom-de-plume, which Bataille used for her posthumously published writings as well, of which he was editor), was Bataille's true mate in a search for extreme experiences. She was also the only woman to be admitted to Bataille's secret society, Acéphale, the guiding principles of which included the aspirations to be free from guilt and to fulfill perverse desires and an acknowledgment of the positive role of decay, and which featured secret rituals including the slaughter of goats (Champagne 1998, 15). Bataille's love affair with Laure lasted until her death from tuberculosis in 1938, which left him heartbroken.

Knowing Bataille's sexual predilections, Frank could not have expected their affair to last, but she was shaken by the abrupt manner in which she was thrown back to her stifling seclusion. Her pain was probably all the more searing because Laure obviously had a genuine intimacy with Bataille, the sort that Frank had not thought possible for him. Frank and Bataille maintained an intense relationship on other levels for another year. There is no doubt that Bataille was first reader of her book's several drafts and that his comments left their mark on *Sweet Sweat*. It is also almost certain that their encounters during that period often deteriorated into violent rows and that gradually the relations between the two caused Frank more pain than happiness.

However, evidence about Frank's life is scarce, and it is important to stress that although a sexual affair between her and Bataille is probable, such a hypothesis is compromised by the ambiguity of Frank's sexual preferences in general. Frank's most significant and intimate friend was a woman: Fanja Hissin. Frank and Hissin first met when the latter visited Paris, accompanied by her husband, in December 1930. And while it might be misleading to call it love at first sight, this meeting was the foundation of a resilient friendship that would play a determining role in Frank's decision to immigrate to Palestine four years later. Hissin, seven years her friend's junior, shared her bed with Frank during the last year of the artist's life. After Frank's death Hissin spoke of her daily to her daughter, in a private memorial of sorts. But Hissin carefully cropped out of her repertoire any mention of the bedchamber.

Like Surrealist photographer Claude Cahun, Frank often depicted herself in her work as a masculine or androgynous figure. Both Cahun and Frank focused on sexually charged self-representation with an undercurrent of humor and both produced noteworthy literary texts. Cahun's work *Heroines* (Cahun 1999) is a series of monologues delivered by powerful historical or mythological women. Yet while Cahun's text openly asserts her homosexuality, it is impossible to assign either to Frank's visual art or to *Sweet Sweat* any revelatory role in relation to her sexual preferences. Her work may be read as hinting at a same-sex predilection, it may be perceived as a travesty of heterosexual stereotypes, or it may be construed as an attempt to deny sexual difference offering a more anarchic, fluid, and diverse model of sexual performance. Frank's entire oeuvre attests to her compulsive preoccupation with sexuality, but fantasies do not necessarily correspond to reality. And here is the crux of the Frank enigma: her entire artistic production deals with sexual desire, but her own sexuality remains utterly obscure.

My belief is that Frank's relations with both Hissin and Bataille were, indeed, of an erotic nature. A perverse libertinism was mixed, in Frank, with romantic yearning, though both aspects were overshadowed by her highly flawed social skills. But even if Frank and Bataille's friendship was not romantic, it was undoubtedly characterized by extreme emotional involvement, high tension, and instability – and its end was a bitter blow for Frank.

The depth of the rupture between the two is evident from the latter's complete disregard of Frank's art after her immigration to Palestine. In 1961, on his deathbed, Bataille published his last book, *Tears of Eros*, an expansive compendium of visual images showing cultural intersections between sexuality and violence (Bataille 1989). The book features Rembrandt's erotic drawings next to medieval images of tortured martyrs and photographic documentation of sacrificial voodoo ceremonies alongside paintings by André Masson. It includes work by a number of Surrealist women artists (such as Leonor Fini) but, although her art is highly pertinent to the book, not even a single work by Justine Frank. Furthermore, there were neither original paintings nor reproductions of Frank's work in Bataille's estate, even though she almost certainly gave him at least one painting (a sketch of this work, in which Frank exercised her staple facial manipulations on Bataille's features, is presently in Tamar Biniamini's collection). Could it be that Frank enraged Bataille so much that he destroyed her artworks? Or did he banish them out of guilt over their affair, after Laure's death?

The end of their relationship, in 1931, was no doubt unconventional. Both Frank and Bataille roamed the twilight zone between decency and obscenity, and neither was known for their mental stability. Perhaps Frank cut off contact between them, despite her taxing isolation, because even her radical sensibility was affronted by his work. Even an avid admirer of the depth and daring of Bataille's writing would have found his extremism, which would peak in the late 1930s, hard to stomach. According to the testimony of several Acéphale members, Bataille had become dissatisfied with rituals of animal slaughter and wished instead to stage a human sacrifice, to create a "real modern myth." While there is some debate about the details of this episode (and the seriousness of the protagonist), the incident was recalled by such trustworthy figures as Roger Caillois (Bataille et al. 1995, 15–16). *Tears of Eros* concludes with a horrifying sequence of nineteenth-century photographs documenting the Chinese execution method known as "death of hundred cuts," during which the condemned's body is gradually chopped to pieces. (The pictures were first shown to Bataille by his psychoanalyst, Adrien Borel, as part of his therapy, and in 1925 the analyst presented them as a gift.) In the book Bataille suggests that the dying man's expression and his standing hair attest not only to extreme suffering but also to ecstasy (Bataille 1989, 204–6).

Or perhaps Frank was repelled by the ambiguous and complex attitude toward fascism Bataille expressed in his 1934 essay "The Psychological Structure of Fascism" (Bataille 1985g) and in the writings he and others published within the circle of the *Contre-Attaque*, which he founded in 1935 with none other than Breton; Bataille himself later admitted that these reflected a "paradoxical fascist tendency" (Stoekl 1985, XVIII). Regardless, as unconventional as Frank was, her own scandalous attitude toward the meeting point of eroticism and violence was always characterized by fantasy and irony, and she surely found Bataille's reflections disagreeable.

Frank's affiliation with Bataille's circle was anathema to Breton, but he contained himself as long as their association was discreet. The publication of *Sweet Sweat* in 1931 brought about the final breach between Frank and the Surrealists. Even though the volume contained no information about publisher, editor, or patron, Bataille's involvement was likely conspicuous. In this sense the book was a public statement of alliance – and the timing could not have been worse. In 1931 the mutual public badmouthing between Bataille and Breton was reaching its most vile and violent peaks. Breton had reserved a large part of the second Surrealist manifesto, in 1929, for an assault on Bataille, in which he renders Bataille as a moral hazard and a cynical, destructive, and unnerving thinker (Breton 1972c). The bulk of the second manifesto, in fact, is dedicated to personal attacks on Bataille that are nothing but elucidations of a predetermined verdict: expulsion from the Surrealist movement. But Breton's slander of Bataille in the early 1930s was harsh even by this standard. But Bataille, never a member of Surrealism, was all too eager to do battle. In addition to a vicious unpublished essay smearing Breton ("The Old Mole" [1929–30]), he was a principal collaborator on "A Corpse," [1930] an exceedingly brutal pamphlet on Breton; the majority of the writers were expelled ex-Surrealists seeking vengeance. The authors of "A Corpse" did not settle for a hearty serving of verbal venom and public debasement but also stalked Breton, pestering him with a variety of cruel pranks for months.

Justine Frank did not win the dubious honor of being addressed in the "Second Manifesto of Surrealism" – she was unceremoniously ignored as a negligible offshoot of Bataille – but the dispute was much more aggravating and all-encompassing for her than for Bataille. The zeal with which Breton smeared his victims rarely stopped him from later resuming contact with them, as he did with Dalí, Magritte, Artaud, and Soupault; the exception was Aragon, once Breton's closest friend, whose defection from the Surrealist camp to become a partisan communist poet Breton never forgave. The sanctions Breton applied against Bataille neither interfered with the latter's work nor lowered his status in the surrounding cultural milieu, and the two would reconcile and join forces later, as war erupted. But Frank, not perceived as a worthy enemy to begin with, could hardly have expected a similar absolution. She, who had never won exceptional honors, now found even the few doors that had recently opened for her beginning to shut, and at a time when she was creating some of her most ambitious works. And as if the complete paralysis of her career were not enough, with it came the swift collapse of her relations with Bataille. Save for her epistolary connection with Fanja Hissin, Frank found herself in total isolation.

Her loneliness casts a bitter light on a popular subject of her works of that period: group self-portraits. In the painting *Frank's Guild* (1933), for example, the artist depicts four

Justine Frank, from The Stained Portfolio *(41), 1927–28*

different characters: Justine as a maiden clad in black; Justine as a veiled figure, leaning forward, with only her eyes and lips visible through slits in her hood (perhaps a hangman, a criminal, or a ghost); Justine as a whiskered young yeshiva *bucher*; and Justine as a thick-bearded rabbi whose tight, purple-striped shirt offsets muscular shoulders and ample breasts. The still life on the table behind which this macabre company is assembled features a bowl holding a pair of blushed apples and a heap of those carrots/dung lumps/shorn phalluses that the artist was so fond of. Next to the bowl stands a miniature tombstone carved with a Star of David and the artist's initials; it is a memento mori devoid of subtlety, lugubrious rather than humorous. A few months after this morose painting was completed, Frank packed a suitcase and left for Palestine.

4. A PRIVATE WORLD WAR: TEL AVIV, 1934–1940

It is odd that Justine Frank chose to immigrate to Palestine, of all places. Most likely she opted for Tel Aviv because of her friendship with Fanja Hissin; and she may have avoided moving to another European city because she foresaw the horrors looming over European Jewry. (Many of her works reflect her penetrating awareness of anti-Semitism's stronghold in European culture.) In any case, Frank certainly was not carried to the Holy Land through Zionist zeal; in fact, once in Palestine her distaste for nationalist ideology grew into outright hostility. In both her art and her private life Frank defiled and defied local dictums, and it seemed that she did her best to antagonize her new compatriots. She harshly disavowed the local culture and contemptuously dismissed its artists.

Frank's refusal to speak Hebrew was especially offensive. Already before the establishment of the state of Israel, Hebrew had been the mainstay of Jewish identity in the region. The revival of the language – after two thousand years of diaspora in which it was used exclusively for ceremonial purposes – was an essential aspect of the Zionist enterprise and, arguably, the most important instrument in fabricating and propagating a national identity. Thus, for new immigrants to Palestine, speaking exclusively Hebrew was literally a requirement (in fact, after the state had been established, immigrants working in the public sector had to change their names to new, Hebrew ones), and much has been written about the heavy price this dogma exacted. Diasporic Jews – whether from Eastern Europe or North Africa – faced public scorn, ridicule, and humiliation if they held onto their mother tongues. Jewish immigrants were meant to disavow their cultural heritage and private history and vanish into the Zionist melting pot.

That imperative – *Israeli, speak Hebrew* – enraged Frank. Two years before her immigration she had painted four small gouaches on paper, *Alchemical Boards For the Study of Hebrew,* telling precursors of her response to the ethos of spoken Hebrew in Palestine. The *Boards'*s grounds are a trompe l'oeil wood veneer meticulously executed with a thin brush. On an upper corner of each work Frank painted a combination of three Hebrew letters. The pedagogic pretense and faux childishness of these study cards are exposed as the letters are transformed, in the center of each composition, into hallucinatory animated entities. Some of these are figures with chopped limbs and swollen genitals; others are hybrids of sexual organs, pubic hair, machine parts, torture devices, and animals, while the letter י (*yod*) is nothing but a hooked lump of dung. When the letters are combined, creating words, a miniature orgy is engendered. Thus, for instance, the letter נ (*noon*), a headless, limbless masculine torso, anally violates the letter מ (*mem*), a forward-leaning figure positioned sideways to accommodate intercourse. A page from The Stained Portfolio presents the entire obscene alphabet Frank designed, and many of its other sheets demonstrate the endless lexicon of perverse postures that the letter combinations bred. Frank's living words might be a far-reaching, yet literal realization of the Belgian Surrealist poet Camille Goemans's suggestion that "words are not mere signs but, in a certain sense, organic bodies" (Rothman 2000, 162) (this is the same Goemans who provided Frank with a recommendation letter on the eve of her journey to Paris).

In the context of Zionism, the *Boards* were truly an outrage. Frank not only made no effort to water down the scandalous themes of her work in general, but here she besmirched and derided Hebrew specifically; the paintings perform an abject, carnal, and vulgar interpretation of the heroic Zionist miracle of the resurrection of language. Even the forging of the grounds (paper simulating wood) has a negative connotation, displacing the letters from their natural locus and moving them into the realm of fabrication and deceit, where they serve as stages for perverted lingual orgies. In her documentary film *The Angel of History* (2000), Israeli theorist and curator Ariella Azoulay claims that the poem "Hebrew" by the celebrated Israeli woman poet Yonah Wallach, with its line "Hebrew is a sex maniac," is a homage to Justine Frank.

The *Boards* compose a viable cultural action: an artistic criticism of Zionism (although hypothetical, since the works were never shown). Frank's disavowal of Hebrew in her daily life, on the other hand, was senseless, infantile, and highly destructive. As an immigrant and a spinster, a woman whose profession was eccentric at best and morally dubious at worst, and as a person of no means or contacts, she was expected to demonstrate gratitude and humility. To those around her, Frank's attitude was an expression of arrogance.

Over the years the question of Frank's use of Hebrew in her work has become a source of debate among scholars. It is crucial to remember that while Frank introduced Hebrew letters into her artwork, it cannot be unequivocally determined that she actually spoke the language. Only some of the *Boards* drawings and their drafts in The Stained Portfolio feature correct Hebrew words; some are linguistically meaningless amalgamations of letters. Some scholars have taken this as testimony of Frank's ignorance (an ignorance she seemed avid to preserve, as both an ideological statement and a wall defending her sovereignty). Others have gone to the opposite extreme, linking Frank's appropriation of the alphabet to esoteric Jewish traditions. In this analysis the seemingly meaningless or indecipherable characters are bearers of mystical meaning and secret codes. All this does not change the fact that, in real life, refusing to speak Hebrew was a blatant expression of separatism.

Because Frank immigrated of her own free will, it is difficult to interpret her defiant stance toward Hebrew as part of an anti-Zionist worldview, and it is doubtful that data will ever be uncovered to clarify her precise attitude toward pre-Israeli nationalism. But it is interesting to note how the array of Jewish signifiers Frank employed in Paris altered in meaning in Tel Aviv. In Palestine menorahs and Stars of David were nationalist symbols, and Frank's work that perverted them was read as debasing Zionism, an intolerable aberration in the eyes of the Jewish Palestinian community. Frank's hermaphrodites, clad in traditional religious attire, were especially offensive: they were not only sexually intimidating but echoed the personification of the diaspora – the effeminate, over-intellectual, urban, and ailing Jewish man that Zionism set out to eradicate, fabricating in its stead the new Israeli: proudly independent, resilient, virile, and rooted in the earth.

Justine Frank, from The Stained Portfolio *(55), 1927–28*

Justine Frank, from The Stained Portfolio *(54), 1927–28*

Justine Frank, from The Stained Portfolio *(56), 1927–28*

Justine Frank, from The Stained Portfolio *(61), 1927–28*

Frank's unmitigated animosity to Zionist society was channeled not only in her rejection of Hebrew, her persistent visualization of diasporic Jews, her stance toward Zionist culture, and her audacious art. During her first few years in Tel Aviv, Hissin exerted considerable effort to win for Frank a place among her circle of friends. The artist's behavior in these social gatherings oscillated between intentionally embarrassing and shrill histrionics, including insults, and morose descents into an almost catatonic introverted state. Hissin gradually isolated her friendship with Frank from her other social relations.

Fanja Hissin with Justine Frank, 1938

Her effort to familiarize Frank with the country's landscape was an even bigger fiasco. Frank's general attitude toward nature was far from romantic (as her laconic description of the scenery of southern France at the beginning of *Sweet Sweat* makes abundantly clear), but the landscape of Palestine evoked real loathing in her. A week-long trip to the Galilee region triggered a few sardonic quips that Frank was all too eager to reiterate, given the chance. The Sea of Galilee was, to her, "the puddle." The blinding white sunlight, which was to preoccupy generations of Israeli painters, did not mystify her, and she compared the colors of the land to a "khaki uniform faded by sunlight." Behind this verbal facade is the shock she suffered upon her arrival to the Middle East, faced for the first time with the insufferable heat and the dust that disagreed with her lungs. Hissin, at any rate, did not offer any more such journeys.

Frank lived in a third-floor studio apartment on Herzl Street, on the southern side of Tel Aviv. It was one of the points where Hebraic Tel Aviv met the Arab neighborhoods of Jaffa, an area abuzz with craftsmen and small businesses, a cultural patchwork of Palestinian bakers and greengrocers, Polish Orthodox immigrant families, and Zionist entrepreneurs. Frank felt equally alienated by them all.

Urban development in Tel Aviv was focused on the northern part of town, and in Frank's neighborhood the old buildings were expanded rather than replaced with modern housing, worsening rather than alleviating the overcrowding and other problems. Frank's living conditions were particularly dismal. Water ran from her taps at a mere trickle, the suffocating smell of mold stood perpetually in the air, and mouse and rat infestation was a perennial problem. The roof had no insulation and the apartment was a hothouse in summer and leaky in winter. During the extraordinarily heavy rainstorms of 1935 an accumulation of rainwater led to a partial collapse of the ceiling. Many of the artist's works were destroyed; Frank was luckily spared additional damage when the landlord allowed her to use the cellar as storage space for what was left of her paintings. Frank was eating alarmingly little, either because of the weather or because she could not get accustomed to the local cuisine. Going out of the apartment was a torment for her, and she avoided buses altogether; her visits to Hissin, who lived on Gordon Street in northern Tel Aviv, involved strenuous walks. But Frank's situation would have been much worse were it not for Hissin's resourcefulness. By securing Frank's apartment – as modest as it was – she spared the artist the hardships endured by the waves of impoverished migrants who settled in makeshift shacks. In 1933 there were five thousand permanent buildings and one thousand wood shacks in Tel Aviv, reflecting the massive scope of immigration (Brur 1936, 306). Despite her relatively good situation, Frank felt in those years as if she were trapped in a surreal nightmare from which she could not awake.

It is hard to say what was it about Fanja Hissin that enabled her to make an intimate bond with a woman whose behavior verged on the psychopathic. Hissin was born to the Litvak family, which emigrated from Saint Petersburg to the Jewish town of Rehovot in Palestine in 1911, when she was two years old. The family mythology was rich with tales of the great fortune they had left behind and the accomplishments of family members in old Russia, despite the raging anti-Semitism (achievements of which no material trace remains). Hissin's mother was her private tutor. Propelled by the conviction that she must compensate for the superb European education the child had been denied, she taught her daughter to speak and read several languages. Hissin also became a competent pianist; throughout her adulthood she played from time to time at friends' houses, but she never owned an instrument of her own. As a rule the

Litvak household had an air of displaced nobility that likely seemed a bit ridiculous to outside observers.

Circumstance and her own choices forced this woman of many talents into a dull, tedious life. Her petit-bourgeois existence as an adult was a web of wasted potential and thwarted prospects. Tamar Biniamini, her daughter, remembers her talking in her old age of the novel she planned to write, which, she said, would win her universal fame. This bragging was less an expression of real intent than of ironic self-regard, a trait Hissin shared with Frank and which gave them hours of mutual amusement.

Samuel Hissin, Fanja's husband, passed away at the age of forty-two, several months before Frank arrived in Palestine, leaving his young widow a single mother of a three-year-old child. Samuel was an awkward, introverted man. He was considerably shorter than his wife, but in photographs he projects both power and tenderness. Samuel was industrious and inventive but disastrously inept in business matters. He intended to invest the small fortune he inherited in a large cake bakery, but over time his plans shrank along with his bank account. He finally settled on the kiosk on Alenby Street, whose distinction and pride was the comparatively large selection of local alcoholic beverages he sold. Later on he tried his luck as a founding partner of a brandy distillery in the town of Zikhron-Yaakov. The project was a fiasco and drained what was left of his savings.

Samuel Hissin admired his wife, whom he had wed when she was barely eighteen years old, much to the chagrin of her parents. Fanja's individualism and her bond with Samuel alienated her somewhat from her family but did not create a major crisis; his initially superior financial standing did not affect the condescension with which he was viewed by the Litvak family.

In the late 1920s, encouraged and supported by her husband, Fanja made several journeys to Europe alone. These trips were in equal parts hedonistic escapades and searches for self-fulfillment (and unbeknownst to Fanja they brought the family deeper into debt. The venues of young Fanja Hissin's self-exploration always had a cosmopolitan bent. For a while she worked at translating legal documents from and into Russian, English, Hebrew, and French. While on a relatively long trip to Berlin she became engrossed with the possibility of working in an organizational capacity in theatrical production. Once she journeyed to Florence expressly to take an intensive three-month-long course in the restoration of ancient paintings – perhaps the most deluded vocational move imaginable for a young woman from Palestine, where there was not a single ancient painting to be found.

Hissin befriended Frank on a trip to Paris with her husband in 1930. They met at Studio 28, a theater, after a screening of two comic shorts, a cartoon, and *L'Âge d'or*, the scandalous Surrealist film by Salvador Dalí and Luis Buñuel. The Hissins were not film buffs, but they had read in the newspapers of the upheaval Buñuel's film had caused in the theater the night before: the place had been turned into a battleground by members of two right-wing extremist groups, the Patriots' League and the Anti-Jewish Youth League, who sprayed the screen with ink, threw stink bombs and tear gas, and destroyed furniture and equipment. The authorities were not as harsh with the anti-Semitic hoodlums as they were with the filmmakers: days later the police confiscated all copies of the film and prohibited its screening – a verdict that would stand for fifty years (Polizzotti 1995, 355). Samuel and Fanja Hissin went to Studio 28 that night out of curiosity and as a show of defiant support for the film. Frank came as a matter of habit. She had been present at every screening since opening night.

When the film ended the audience lingered outside around the theater and engaged in passionate arguments late into the night. Somehow Frank and the Hissins began talking (the fact that Samuel immediately liked the eccentric artist attests to his exceptional character). As a result of this new acquaintance Fanja dallied in Paris for another month after Samuel returned to Palestine.

Samuel Hissin died of a heart attack in 1942, en route from Zikhron-Yaakov to Tel Aviv after a meeting with his creditors. Her husband's sudden death dramatically changed Fanja's circumstances. But the burden of breadwinning, the sole responsibility for her child, and the abandonment of her dreams for the future did not make her bitter at all. Despite her relentless individualism, often perceived as naiveté or pragmatic ineptness, she devoted herself to the daily labor of survival for herself and her daughter. She was determined to maintain her autonomy, despite her circumstances – and in that she was very similar to Justine Frank.

The bad manners Frank displayed upon her introduction into Hissin's milieu obliterated any chance of alleviating her loneliness; her antagonistic and unbending attitude toward local cultural circles guaranteed that her own artwork would be shunned. Although Tel Aviv's intelligentsia abhorred Frank and generally ignored her, she was the subject of an unremitting buzz of ill-willed gossip. It is impossible to disprove the claim that Frank was an alcoholic; the slanderers also maintained that she neglected her personal hygiene and had a terrible stench and that she should be banned from public places because of her inclination to strip naked. Another rumor, which became more frequent as years went by, was that Frank suffered from a degenerative venereal disease and her days were numbered.

Tamar Biniamini, who was generally cooperative throughout my interviews with her, even when asked about knotty aspects of Frank's persona, was insulted and angered when I inquired about the artist's bodily hygiene and purported disease. I mention Biniamini's adamant refusal to respond to these questions only in order to offer her a sincere apology in writing. The fact that Frank's legacy has so often been tarnished is reason enough to approach these issues gently and with great caution. And yet it is impossible to truly tell the artist's story without dealing with rumors that had a direct impact on the course of her life and without seeking the perspective of someone who knew her personally.

Hearsay about Frank was further fermented by the artist's worsening financial situation. In 1936, according to Biniamini, the envelopes that Frank had received from Belgium bimonthly since 1925 stopped arriving; they had been her only stable source of support. Frank, who by all accounts had never held a steady job, was completely dependent on Hissin's support; she herself was barely sustained by the profits of her Alenby Street kiosk.

Even if stories of Frank's self-neglect are untrue, it is easy to reconstruct from Biniamini's childhood recollections how such rumors may have evolved. Frank's appearance was extraordinary and her habits extremely eccentric for the time and the place. She preferred to dress "in a revealing fashion, usually in comfortable, slack cotton clothes" (Biniamini's words) with a deep décolletage and high cut. To understand how audacious such attire was in Tel Aviv society at the time, it should be borne in mind, for example, that when the first lady of Hebrew theater, the actress Hannah Robinna, exposed her thighs on stage while acting as a prostitute in Mordecai Langer's play *The Far End of the City* (1932) at Ha'Bimmah Theater in the early 1930s, it was felt to be an obscene and shocking spectacle.

The show closed after a major public outcry. Still, we know for certain that Frank's way of dressing was not provocative for its own sake. She was allergic to certain fabrics, a syndrome that worsened with time, and eventually her Parisian dresses wore out. Hissin offered her clothes from her own wardrobe, but Frank did not accept them. Furthermore, the artist did not shave her armpits or legs, and Biniamini remembers that during the year she lived in her mother's apartment Frank did not comb her hair very often. In addition, her fingertips were stained orange-brown from her habit of crumbling her cigarette stubs with rapid, circular movements so quick that they inspired in the child "a sort of awe, or admiration." Overall, Biniamini's testimony paints a picture of a somewhat idiosyncratic woman, whose odd habits grew to monstrous proportions in the collective imagination of the small provincial and puritan community that was Tel Aviv in the late 1930s.

The origin of the rumors regarding Frank's venereal disease is documented. She had a severe intestinal disorder that was never competently diagnosed, a chronic illness that emerged in 1937 and quickly worsened. Every several weeks Frank suffered fits that lasted three to five days, during which she had searing pains in her lower abdomen, severe diarrhea, and – as a result – headaches, general weakness, dizziness, and, on several occasions, blurred vision. These symptoms could indicate long-term damage to the kidneys or the liver as a result of malnourishment or immoderate alcohol consumption. In August 1939 Frank was hospitalized for a couple of days after she fainted on her way to the grocery store. Although Hissin told the doctors at the hospital about Frank's complaints, they opted not to embarrass themselves with diagnostic speculations. It was noted in her medical record that she had suffered from dehydration and was treated with fluid transfusion for twenty-four hours.

Biniamini is convinced that Frank's illness and her allergic reaction to certain fabrics were psychosomatic and associates them with the almost intolerable hardships of her life. In the second half of the 1930s Frank's days were clouded by ever-growing anxiety. Apart from the social banishment, health problems, and financial difficulties, which grew ever more devastating, she began to have fits of horror in reaction to the dawning war in Europe. She hardly slept, and when she did she had nightmares. She was convinced that Germany would achieve a sweeping victory within a few years, bringing total devastation to the entire world. Her feverish doomsday scenarios were so intense that during the two air bombardments Tel Aviv actually did suffer she was, paradoxically, almost completely calm and indifferent, despite the deaths and panic they caused. For her these were negligible prologues to the horrors waiting at the gate.

During her last years Frank found the persistent disregard of her art especially exasperating. She still had hyperactive outbursts of creative energy and days of euphoria; the realms of fantasy in her art still, at times, defied her harsh realities. But despair gradually seeped through all the tissues of her being. The room Frank shared with Hissin in the last year of her life was crammed with paintings that had never been shown, representing almost three decades of unwitnessed creativity. In the past she had consoled herself with the thought that her isolation was bound to end, that there would come a day when her work would gain recognition, context, and appreciation; this hope gradually withered, leaving the artist with memories of past achievements too feeble even for the modest purposes of nostalgia. Frank aptly called their modest bedroom "a paintings cemetery." She felt as if her entire lifework had never existed and that she herself was a mere apparition, passing her days by waiting to fade out completely. But she still had her most aggressive confrontation with the world up her sleeve.

5. "WHERE IS THE WINGED CAMEL?"
TEL AVIV, 1940–1943

The rage Justine Frank provoked in Tel Aviv society was not caused by her personal hygiene, her lascivious wardrobe, nor her purported sexually transmitted disease – it was mainly the result of her scandalous public behavior. Toward the end of the 1930s complaints abounded of Frank stalking and harassing artists, poets, and at least one of the town's gallerists. Her behavior followed a regular pattern. She would position herself in embarrassingly close physical proximity to her victim and either mime his gestures or disrupt his socializing at a café with belittling comments, mocking questions, and outright slurs about his latest paintings or poems. Initially this behavior merely prompted contempt and dismissal, embarrassment and derision. But in 1940 a dramatic shift occurred in the ostracized artist's manners, a change that would lead to the worst and final crisis of her life.

That year Marcel Janco, the Romanian-Jewish artist, arrived in Palestine. Like Frank, Janco was a new immigrant and a seasoned member of the avant-garde – in his case, Dada. Like her Janco had been associated with radical artistic circles in the role of provincial foreigner, spent extended periods in Paris, and left the movement with which he had been identified. But unlike Frank, who had been a marginal if not negligible member of Surrealism, Janco had been a key figure in the core group of Zurich Dada. Even if in retrospect it is clear that he was quite removed from the anarchism and radicalism of the group, no chronicle of the movement can be considered comprehensive without him. This achievement in itself, we can guess, made Frank terribly jealous.

The difference between Frank and Janco in terms of social aptitude and adaptability was striking in the Jewish Palestinian arena. Janco arrived six years after Frank, but he was able to quickly adjust his artistic agenda to suit the demands of the time and place. He became a formal member of The Hebrew Artists' Association and was soon offered a comfortable position on the city council. A one-person exhibition at the Tel Aviv Museum followed shortly after. The aura of his avant-garde past did not intimidate the local artists for the simple reason that Janco was no longer an avant-garde artist. After cutting himself off from Dada and returning to Romania, Janco had devised a fairly conservative painterly style – a sort of post-Cubist geometric articulation of figurative subject matter. This visual language was easily digestible and highly suitable for conveying nationalistic themes. In Palestine Janco began employing his painterly style to articulate his own Zionist vision, persistently representing the country's landscapes and its inhabitants. His international prestige just gave his patriotic paintings even more clout and made locals feel that Janco was conferring honor upon the budding Hebrew culture through his work.

Analysis of the paintings of the artist's later years reveals that his art was enlisted to constitute archetypical visual tropes for the local Zionist identity. It is interesting to observe, for example, how Janco naturalized the Zionist claim to the land and the Jewish will to imagine their community as indigenous in the different ways he painted groups of men: Palestinian Arabs, Yemenite Jews, and Hebrew warriors heroically echoing the mythic past. Arabs in a painting such as *An Arab Café in Majdahl* (1947) are shown enjoying their idle pastime, portrayed with a paternalistic sympathy and a tinge of patronizing grotesquerie. Here the Arab Other is not dangerous and frightening but is subjected to the more tangled manoeuver of suffocation by affection. To my mind, in its emotive impact this imagery is akin to the stereotypical representation of African Americans in contemporaneous American culture through the trope of blackface: the Other as a gay and ridiculous mask devoid of autonomy, or even as a white man cheerfully made up and assuming the role. Janco's Yemenite Jews in the painting *Yemenite Study of the Torah* (1942) are a bridge between the Orientalism projected onto the Arabs and the figure of the Zionist Israeli. The Yemenites are treated as remote relatives of the Arab group, but they do not waste their time sipping coffee, and the general atmosphere is somewhat warmer, if still tinged with ridicule. Finally, in his famous painting *The Maccabees* (1952) Janco asserts the analogy often made in Zionist rhetoric between the defiant war of the Jewish few against an overwhelming multitude of enemies in the grand ancient past and the present campaigns of the Israeli army.

The distinctions between the three groups in Janco's work are abundantly clear, but the similarities are no less significant: the common denominators are the bases for the visual codification establishing the Israeli monopoly on the homeland as "natural," or self-evident. While the Jews are presented as more active and connected to their land, the Orientalizing of all three groups, Arabs, Yemenites, and ancient Jewish warriors (the Maccabees) alike, links the Zionists with those who had been living in the Jewish homeland for many generations. Similarity is also established in the paintings through stylistic unity (geometric figuration accentuated with thick black contours). The fact that the three groups are masculine firmly grounds them in the symbolic patriarchal realm as the makers and the definers of culture.

After the foundation of the state of Israel, Janco merged his nationalistic and artistic visions by founding the artists' village Ein-Hod, appropriating the houses and land that made up the Palestinian village Ein-Houd and expelling the original residents. Many of the villagers remained nearby in temporary houses, hoping to one day reclaim what is rightfully theirs.

As I write this in 2001 they are still political nonentities, still unrecognized by the state of Israel. From nearby hills they have witnessed the chilling sight of a mosque being converted into a restaurant. In a painting as in a village, appropriating the visible traces and signs of the Other enables his negation and erasure.

Marcel Janco swiftly became the primary victim of Frank's pestering, and his complaints about her behavior have been substantiated. Biniamini remembers heated conversations between her mother and the artist about Janco's accusations. It is easy to understand the strong emotions the artist evoked in her: jealousy, anger, and intense hostility, exacerbated by the fact of their cultural common grounds. Frank's petty persecution of Janco was a performance of aggression but also, perhaps, an expression of her desire for recognition and acceptance. Stalking Janco seemed to reflect an inner debate Frank was having concerning ideology and morality, belonging and deviation, communal pacts and aesthetic agendas. Janco's stance could not be dismissed as a simple case of regression or conservatism. As a member of the Israeli art movement New Horizons he was not a separatist Zionist but one of those who aspired to find a "universal" context for local nationalist art. For Frank, though, this distinction meant little. The vehement expressions of Zionism in Hebrew culture were not even worth her regard, Frank felt, but she saw Janco as no less than a traitor: a fake avant-garde artist who exposed his true colors in producing institutional kitsch. She would have been appalled had she seen Janco's work featured beside that of five other artists in a Tel Aviv exhibition titled *Surrealist Paintings* only a couple of months after her death.

The animosity between Marcel Janco and Justine Frank reached its peak in a violent public row on April 22, 1942, at the Ohel-Shem Theater's hall on Balfur Street in Tel Aviv. The event was the opening reception for a group exhibition titled *Desert Light and Light unto the Nations*, the name of which unequivocally states the organizers' aspirations – a spectacular display of local visual art, emphasizing its patriotism. The goal was to build a bridge between the age-old endeavor to produce indigenous Hebrew arts and crafts, beginning with the opening of the first Hebrew art academy, Bezalel, in Jerusalem in 1906, and the latest trends in international art. This effort was supported by an improvement in the status of the visual arts in Tel Aviv that had begun 1936, when the city's first municipal museum was founded at the residence of its first mayor, Meir Dizengoff, with an exhibition of paintings by the celebrated local painter Reuben Rubin. The title *Desert Light and Light unto the Nations* would suggest – the organizers hoped – that Jewish culture stood tall and proud against the horrors of war.

On opening night it was clear that *Desert Light and Light unto the Nations* could at best be described as a partial success. For unknown reasons – probably personal grudges and quarrels – several important artists had declined the invitation to participate. Local collectors had refused to lend work by older artists, and communication with American and European collectors was virtually impossible because of the war. The curators' hope to splendidly and comprehensively showcase the brief history of a "revival" of Hebrew art was frustrated. Artistic production of the recent past was represented by nothing more than three popular prints by Ephraim Moses Lilien (one of which was his famous portrait of Zionist leader Theodor Herzl), and two paintings by Tel Aviv painter Naum Gutman, who was one of the exhibition's initiators, in addition to works by Aaron Cahana, Abraham Naton, and a few others. As the reception progressed, pomp and circumstance were dampened by glum apprehension that turned, as the hours went by, into dejection. The tension and disappointment were exacerbated by the fact that the mayor had failed to arrive, sending a courtesy telegram instead, and other dignitaries had avoided the event. The almost complete absence of cultural personae from the fields of literature, poetry, and theater was especially irksome and humiliating, as Israeli culture had modeled itself early on as a culture of text with an expressed antagonism and willful ignorance of visual art, following the iconoclastic spirit of Judaism.

According to most accounts Frank arrived at the Ohel-Shem Theater hall, an uninvited and unwelcome guest, long after the speeches and salutes were over and most of guests and some of the artists had left. She quickly paced to the center of the lobby, tore off her dress, and – stark naked and shouting slurs – ran toward Janco and tried to pound him with her fists. Several men restrained her, and someone rushed to call the police. Frank was forcefully evacuated and arrested. Tamar Biniamini insists that, like so many other accounts on Frank, the Ohel-Shem story has been maliciously twisted. She says that Frank had indeed arrived at the opening uninvited and did goad Janco and several other artists using rather coarse language. But Frank told Biniamini later that she had neither cursed Janco and the others nor removed her dress, but had only shouted loudly in Yiddish, *"Der camel mit di fligl! Avoo is der camel mit di fligl?"* (The winged camel! Where is the winged camel?). This single public utterance of Yiddish in Frank's life mirrors the appearance of a single sentence in the dialect in *Sweet Sweat*.

This theatrical provocation was a Frankist encore to a long tradition of public scandals incited by Dadaists and Surrealists (a fact that probably did not escape Janco). But in Palestine in the early 1940s at the Ohel-Shem Theater hall Frank's use of Yiddish was heard as a battlecry against Hebrew culture.

When Frank shouted, "Where is the winged camel?" it was clear to all present (as it would have been to any Palestinian Jew at the time) that she referred to the winged camel that was the logo for the Fair of the East, a spectacular event held annually in Tel Aviv. To Frank the flying camel was a ludicrous icon, typical of Zionist Palestinian culture in its mendacity, the epitome of the nationalist pride that antagonized her so, a figure feigning regional authenticity in a preposterously blatant way toward which she felt utter contempt. Her invocation of the desert behemoth in the language of the diaspora was meant as a travesty of the title *Desert Light and Light unto the Nations,* to denigrate the exhibition's pretensions and reveal them as little more than crass propaganda. Furthermore, Frank considered the Flying Camel logo to be a degenerated, parasitic, nationalist appropriation of Surrealist imagery, a misuse of her own artistic legacy, that is. Perhaps in her delusion – in which megalomania and paranoia predominated – she took the popular emblem as a personal offense.

It is highly doubtful that the artists and guests fully understood Frank's message. They were, however, enraged at her actions, and according to Biniamini Frank quickly went from assailant to assailed. A ring of men tightened around her, and it was they who removed her dress, she said. Some of the men's frustration at the failure of the exhibition found an outlet in violent anger, and they lost their self-restraint and beat her severely. When the police arrived Frank was naked, bruised, and unconscious. Janco himself was not among the assailants, and perhaps he had already left by that time. Frank's impression, as mediated by Biniamini, was that her aggressors had a sexual intent, and were it not for the policemen's arrival she would have been raped.

The incident stirred Tel Aviv's artistic circle, but it was immediately hushed up and not reported in the press – save for one grotesque exception. The brawl and the arrest were described in the pages of the weekly newspaper *Itton Me'yuhad*, the very first Hebrew tabloid in history. It was subtitled "An independent report of public criticism" and offered its readers a plethora of sex scandals and supernatural scoops, such as the item economically headlined "Dead Warsaw Merchant Lives in Tel Aviv." The owner and editor of the tabloid, Alexander Zauber, printed this front-page headline: "Promiscuity Instead of Culture: Naked Madwoman Attacks Worldly Artist in Public: Story on Page B." The story does not appear on page B, alas, quite a common mistake in that publication but one that nevertheless seems almost cut to order for Frank's peculiar biography.

Itton Me'yuhad's credibility must have been quite limited even in the eyes of its most avid readers. More important than the story's inclusion there, Biniamini believes, is that the reputable papers avoided any mention of the incident; she construes this as an attempt by the real aggressors to cover up their wrongdoing. To a large extent, however, Biniamini's version is Frank's own, and should not be embraced without reservations. That such an extraordinary incident did not win Frank a page in the local papers may not indicate an attempt to silence the truth but simply reflect the all-embracing boycott enacted against her. In this sense the attitude of parochial Zionist society did not differ much from that of older, religious Jewish congregations who ordered outcasts to lie on the synagogue's doorstep to be spit upon by the congregation.

The violence of the event, whatever it had been exactly, shook Frank. Apart from the trauma of physical brutality and collective hatred, she endured more than a day under arrest. Frank was already physically and mentally unstable before this humiliating, frightening experience. By the time Hissin bailed her out of jail she was a wreck. From that day on she lived with her friend.

Frank had started painting in Hissin's home as early as January 1941, when she finally had to evacuate her modest apartment on Herzl Street, five years after the termination of the financial support she received from Belgium. The landlord let her stay in the small, windowless cellar of the building, but the space was far too dark, damp, and unventilated for painting and so she moved the tools of her craft to Hissin's Gordon Street apartment.

The move of her studio across town had added a taxing walk to Frank's day and necessitated the adjustment of her schedule to accommodate the habits of Hissin and her daughter. In this agonizing situation Frank labored, against all odds, on relatively large canvases. Biniamini, custodian of Frank's estate, still has five big rolls of fine-quality cotton canvas and a thick roll of paper with a French watermark. Frank was fortunate enough to have purchased a decent stock of painting materials in advance, perhaps with her bimonthly allotment or with the help of Samuel Hissin.

After the incident at Ohel-Shem Theater in April, Frank crammed the rest of her belongings into Hissin's two-room apartment. The bedroom served as storage space for the paintings and as a library, and the living room was both the child's bedroom and Frank's improvised studio. A strong stench of cigarette smoke, paint thinner, and oil paint permanently hung in the air. Young Tamar grew accustomed to sleeping with the electric light turned on while Frank painted at night. Biniamini remembers well the frequent clogging of the sink and toilet in which Frank cleaned her brushes. The artist herself almost never left the house. If we add to all that Frank's possessive demand for attention from Hissin (who returned home in the late evenings after her long workdays), tension and confrontations between the eccentric artist and the girl seem inevitable. But Biniamini says that despite her age she felt more mature than Frank and had a feeling of maternal responsibility for her. It is astonishing to hear Biniamini, a woman in her seventies, expressing feelings of guilt and personal failure because of sporadic quarrels with Frank when she was an eleven-year-old child deprived of privacy and tranquility.

Frank's physical condition had been continually deteriorating. She was always very thin, but she began to look emaciated. Her smooth complexion, which she had been very proud of, was creased by deep wrinkles at the corners of her mouth. Her hair was still black and abundant, but after years with neither brushing nor trimming the dark fan in her early Surrealist photoportrait had turned into "a prickly, cartilaginous brush," like Rachel's in *Sweet Sweat.* Biniamini says that Frank alternated in appearance between a woman much older than her actual age and a young girl. She has no recollection of Frank's alcoholism, but she does, however, describe her own panic at once witnessing Frank's physical weakness emerging from under her veneer of resilience and energy. One day while Frank was painting, the child lightly patted her back; the artist crumpled forward, sprawling on the wet canvas as if her muscles had no remaining power of resistance.

The paintings of Frank's late period, 1941–42, are characterized by broad, abstract expanses and the persistent presence of paint drips. Of her entire oeuvre, it is the late work that is relatively serene, poised, and airy. Most of the canvases were executed in a meticulous technique, and at least three depict nothing but cloudy skies. At first glance these paintings appear to lack the confrontational imagery of the artist's early work – but a second look reveals that Frank's work remained as erotic and morbid as ever. In all three sky paintings the clouds create a symmetrical formation that may be read as a big, rather grotesque face. The nose clouds are shaped like Stars of David, and grinning mouths double as streams of ejaculate shooting from the erect organs of two hunchbacked cloud figures bracketing the face, whose profiles are reminiscent of fairytale witches' or those of Jews in anti-Semitic caricatures. The skeletal quality of the bodies and the two large circles protruding from their skulls – part coiffure, part animal ears – make them seem displaced and capricious yet engaging and humane.

The color scheme in these paintings is odd. In one, pink and dark-brown drips stain realistic skies. In the two other works the skies are silver-brown, and the drips, again, are pink and dark brown. The titles – *Sick Heaven*, *Shit Heaven*, and *A Portrait of Thieving Skies* – leave little doubt that the colors were not chosen purely on aesthetic grounds. The brown drips pollute the heavens with bodily secretions while pink bodies liquefy and mix into the sky – Heaven itself is incarnated in an ethereal mixture of manure and decaying bodies. Frank's late preoccupation with the sky suggests that the artist was aware that death was drawing near, and they express her willful detachment from her mundane, earthbound being. But the abject, somatic character of the works grounds them nonetheless, thwarting any attempt to eke from them an experience of spiritual exaltation or a renunciation of corporeality.

In the early afternoon on April 12, 1943, Justine Frank left the Hissin apartment after asking for – and receiving – all the cash Hissin had on hand. Biniamini was not home at the time. We shall never know if Hissin tried to stop Frank or if they discussed her intention. Justine Frank was never seen again.

The Jewish Palestinian community was too small for a member to disappear within it without leaving a trace. Frank's poor health and scarce means would not have allowed her to perform an extravagant delusional exploit like returning to Europe in the middle of a raging war, if she had entertained

Justine Frank, from The Stained Portfolio *(75), 1927–28*

such an idea. It cannot be determined unequivocally that she committed suicide, but it seems that the sad aporia is not whether she took her own life but why her body has never been discovered.

Frank's pathetic condition on the eve of her disappearance should preclude any romantic speculations about her end by those aiming to add grandeur to the Frank enigma. In any case, if the bizarre conclusion of her life is considered in the context of Dada and Surrealism, it does not seem quite so enigmatic: a mysterious vanishing act was the last chapter of several life stories in those circles, among them those of Dadaists Arthur Cravan and Julien Tormé (and Cravan, it should be noted, is mentioned in *Sweet Sweat*). Like Frank they performed a dangerous balancing act between following the spiritual promise of liminal states and blatant self-destruction. Frank's life and her death reveal an unresolved tension between misery and a radical act of will to create a personal myth of the sort so dear to André Breton's heart.

The portrait of Justine Frank we have drawn here is strongly colored, and its most basic contour lines are clear. The setting is rich and familiar, and we even have a pathway – Frank's paintings and her own words – to follow straight into the artist's innermost thoughts (supposedly). And yet the most that scholarly research can reveal about Frank is that we can learn nothing more about her. Observation of Frank's life and death is blindness, study is ignorance, and memory is oblivion.

Unknown photographer, Justine Frank, *1933*

Sweet Sweat

Justine Frank

Translated from French by Joanna Führer-Ha'sfari

1. A RUBBING CHILD

In Southern France, a few kilometers from Baron de M's castle, west of the border of Provence, rolls a charming range of hills. The vineyards and cowsheds of the small villages give way to the natural flora and fauna. The gaps between telegraph poles grow wider.

The hills are perfumed with the smell of the region's typical plants: trees, bushes, weed.

Alluring insects live there (beetles, for example), as well as beautiful birds, of those genera that inspire poets to apply metaphors like "pounding heart," or "resplendent love"; yes, indeed – pretty birds, flying and chirping birds.

The soil is black and damp. The leaves are green and damp. The sky is blue and damp.

The hills glow with that idyllic French light that has captured the heart of many an obnoxious landscape painter. The hills exude pastoral grace perfect enough to make one sink into glum sleep, or run amok.

And yet right there, smack in the heart of this loathsome flawlessness, the wanderer who strays from the regular routes will encounter a real surprise. Here – in the middle of nature's tedious splendor – stands an ugly village! And not merely the characteristic ugliness of local poverty (which has also won itself devout painters), but the absolute wretchedness of a dismal Jewish village that seems to have been transported whole, complete with shacks and their inhabitants, from the filthy snow fields of whorish Poland to the haughty mounds of France!

Not only does the shtetl's locale seem wrong, but its date as well: this village frog-leaped into the twentieth century from days long gone. A car has never driven its muddy, narrow roads. There is no electricity. Hunchbacked women draw water from a stingy well. Men sweat profusely under the long and heavy black wool overcoats they wear in spite of the terrible heat. Death rattles of chickens and cows being slaughtered mingle with the groans of a collapsing mule, the bubble of manure in the sewer ditch, and the hoarse whines of a tubercular cantor.

In short, the village looks like the film set for a delusional spectacle; as if a mad American producer had joined forces with a German Expressionist hysteric to create an epic film about the miseries of Eastern European Jews, all the while sipping fine French wine.

There, in that village, lived a milkman and a milkman's wife, a shoemaker and a shoemaker's wife, a tailor and a tailor's wife, a hat-maker and a hat-maker's wife, a rabbi and a rabbi's wife, three butchers, three butchers' wives, and ten butchers' children, a bachelor teacher, a lame woman beggar, a tough woman who kept an inn, a stuttering peddler, a busy gravedigger, and several young men working hard at their studies. All were devout, righteous, industrious, humble, hungry, and ceaselessly delousing and squashing fleas.

The most creative person in that miniscule village was

the hat-maker. He burdened the men's pates with traditional Jewish hats, made of soft, shiny disheveled fur. Even the softest breeze transformed these hats into hallucinatory wild beasts, convulsing in obscene heat.

Oh, thrilling hairiness!

All the perverse passions of the pubis and all the fancies forbidden by religion were lumped and hollowed into unholy halos! The women side-eyed the lewd hats and licked their lips. So sensual were those hats that the men seemed merely mobile holders for unreal pudenda!

The Jewish hats merit further rumination – but this book is not about hats.

Among the downtrodden, stinking shacks, a modest red-brick building stood out in its relative neatness – the synagogue. There an old widower, fragile and sad, labored day and night, serving as treasurer and janitor both. Since he was busy and poor, his only daughter, Rachel, who was twelve years old, spent most of her days wandering aimlessly outside [. . .]

Moldy potato peels, rotten crusts of cheese, dust soaked in sweat and coagulated into oily mortar, all this stuff accumulated in her thick black mane, making of her hair a prickly, cartilaginous brush. A gray layer of slime veiled her cheeks. Her young skin shimmered underneath with the mute glow of a gas mask.

Her face was a garden of filth, but underneath its grove of grime a keen observer could detect the white blossoms of her eyes, the pure twinkle of her lovely teeth, and especially the moist lips, rising red from the sewer of her face like a juicy, quivering, blushing squirrel, skinned and cooked alive in *sauce Provençal* [. . .]

The constant hunger gnawing in little Rachel's belly never clouded her cheerful expression and actually made her more alert and sensitive. An amusing story was told in the village: one day the milkman's wife observed Rachel bent over the sewer ditch, kissing a green pebble and carefully laying it on the grass. It seems she pitied the pebble, which rested on the road, and so saved it from the cruel stomps of uncaring pedestrians. This was naive compassion, not to say imbecilic; yet the result of such compassion was that it engendered another: the warm compassion the villagers themselves felt toward Rachel. And for that they were grateful. It is well known that no emotion is as uplifting and jolly as compassion.

Compassion is a known remedy for constipation and other digestive disorders!

Compassion is excellent for strengthening the soul and fortifying one's self-love!

Sometimes a compassionate person will shed tears perceived as tears of compassion. But they are not so: most often these are tears of self-admiration. The compassionate person is overwhelmed by the fact that even though he is the center of the universe his heart is big enough to accommodate the object of his compassion.

This book, however, is not about compassion. Hence, we return to Rachel. Her behavior had a single flaw, an inexplicable and disturbing mental aberration (as there was no local expert in the secrets of psychology). Little Rachel would rhythmically and vigorously rub her genitals against tables and chairs. She did not abstain from those obscene strokes when she was outside: she always found rocks, tree trunks, or fence posts on which to massage her nervous Venus mound. Even while walking she was inclined to perform intricate wiggles meant to quench her insatiable groin, her buttocks drawing odd aerial ellipses with each and every step. The problem was serious: Rachel was a rubbing child.

And so in the musty classroom the bachelor teacher warned his pupils time and again against the treasurer's daughter.

The pubescent yeshiva pupils, their skin peppered with

pimples and dandruff, their backs hunched over harsh books, could feel their fettered penises swell in sad silence, constrained by the prison bars of their stifling trousers. Their teacher warned them yet again not to come nearer to little Rachel than was absolutely necessary – and to never, never give in to her sweet pleas.

Never let her rub her body against their own. (pp. 1–4)

2. SMELL EPIPHANY

The peaceful routine of Rachel's life is disturbed when Count Charles Urdukas, a handsome, refined, and awe-inspiring libertine, invades the shtetl:

[. . .] Decades devoted to the deadly sins had done the Count good. Wild orgies had buffed his muscles, flexed his limbs, and thickened his silver-tinged hair, which was always combed back with artistic rigor. Though he was a big man and no longer young, he had the fine, smooth complexion of an adolescent maiden: his secret was a prolonged ritual, each morning, of rubbing his skin with an ointment based on goats'-milk cream.

Urdukas was as proud and pampered as a Catholic chapel. And how witty were his fashion fancies! He wore, for instance, red silk underwear under his semitransparent, light-blue riding breeches – thus giving his privates a stupendous purple aura! His yellow shirts fastened with magnificent ivory cufflinks, with miniature reliefs of yawning vulvas. The lips of the almond-shaped clefts, their inner folds, and their hairy tufts were executed with such ingenious realism that they could have aided an anatomy student!

Time will not suffice to describe the gloves, the coat's lining, the collar, the ties, the crocodile-skin boots. But one item, of which Urdukas was extremely proud – and which he considered his talisman – should be mentioned: a cherry walking stick with a bird-shaped silver knob. He had purchased the stick years before while still a student in England, the morning after he succeeded in smartly seducing a virgin of a good family into accompanying him to a brothel and then left her there locked in the bathroom chamber, bleeding and crying [. . .]

[Urdukas was en route] to buy a female slave in the secret pirate market held annually in a hidden forest clearing in the Pyrenees. Even though this was the liveliest fair in all of France, it was not mentioned in any edition of *Michelin*. This was a human dunghill all abuzz, where pimps crossed paths with bankers; retired generals with corrupt judges; eunuchs pale with despair with little gypsies whose tongues had been cut off to keep horrendous truths hidden; the degenerate descendants of noble families with Satan-worshipping parsons [. . .] (p. 6)

Urdukas arrives at Rachel's village escorted by an extravagant entourage of servants and concubines. He perceives the Jewish village as an amusing curiosity. After a gluttonous feast at the dilapitated inn the Count and his people take to the streets and amuse themselves by assaulting the villagers with whips and clubs. In the ensuing turmoil Urdukas notices Rachel, and she is quickly seized at his command.

The Count intends to rape and murder Rachel that night. She waits on his travel bed, bruised and scratched from his servants' foreplay. But when Urdukas is about to tear her hymen, her bodily odor overwhelms him and prompts a dramatic change in plans:

[As he hovered] over the skinny body, his nostrils were filled with the aroma of horror-sweat that poured from Rachel. He was swept by the scent. His breathing became a guttural purr and his eyes glazed over.

Oh, shrewd liqueur of tropical fruits!

Ah, venomous crème de cassis!

Hurrah, distilled, tyrannical sweetness, tainted neither by a salty tint nor sour hint!

Never had the Count been caught by such a fire as was ignited by this sweetness [. . .] a carnivorous perfume, as seismic as epilepsy [. . .] A smut potion worthy of the sacred nostrils of the Pope!

"A great future awaits her – she who secretes such waters," exclaimed the Count inwardly. "A great gift has been revealed! And as for me – who would have thought I would find a calling as tutor and patron!"

He shoved his snout hither and thrust it thither. An orchestra of sweetness responded to his digging. Sweet as what? It was impossible to say. The aromas were so rare that even metaphors, those shameless, ignoble jackals of poetry, even metaphors paled with shame and silently scurried away.

The olfactory harmony emanated from the armpits, welled from the womb, steamed from the roots of the hair, and sifted as thin white smoke from the cringing sphincter, which emitted merely a hint of its wealth of smelly secretions. And all those odor instruments joined in one sublime smell song.

The sweet smell kneaded, molded, and remodeled Urdukas' body into an improved, more condensed, and pragmatic form.

Now, he had only two organs – a nose and a cock – patched together with some tendon glue and tissue paste.

Cock and nose shaking and huffing like steam engines.

Nose and cock rising like telegraph poles.

Cock and nose swollen and stiff like gas tanks.

Two happy meat lumps, intoxicated and flushed. (pp. 8–9)

3. *KNOWLEDGE AND ITS SPOILS*

Urdukas cancels his trip to the pirates' market in order to bring Rachel to his castle on the outskirts of Paris. He draws up an ambitious study program, designed to introduce Rachel to the most exquisite of carnal desires and to train her for her future as an arch-criminal. The first part of her apprenticeship lasts four weeks and takes place within the castle's walls. The second part will involve practical tenure in far-away Turkey. A strict timetable drawn with "mathematical precision" regulates meals, bathing rituals, physical experiences, and theoretical learning.

During her first days in the castle Rachel takes preliminary studies in fornication techniques, then moves on to the culinary study of bodily fluids and secretions. Finally, she is acquainted with pleasures involving humiliation and pain and research regarding bizarre, exotic perversions. Her learning is aided by rare aphrodisiacs, ancient torture instruments, thorough analyses of artworks, tutorials with pimps and whores, an arsenal of sex toys, and a troupe of "teaching and demonstration assistants" of every age, sexual orientation, and physical attribute – a few volunteers, some paid workers, but mostly forced laborers.

The promise of the gifted protégé's sweet sweat is fulfilled. In a number of wild orgies (scenes missing from existing copies of the book), the bashful child is revealed to be a prima ballerina of the arts of desire. Furthermore, she is miraculously transformed:

[. . .] It was as if her bodily orifices had been sealed with corks, which now popped out, propelled by the pressure of inner fermentation. Jets of carbonated juice gushed from between her nether lips, as if her womb was a depot of outlandish desires, a laboratory of esoteric essences and orgasmic gnosis – while her upper lips discharged rhetorical pearls and precious knowledge, the origin of which was no less enigmatic. Within a few weeks the gray rural mouse had transformed into an erudite, noble nymphomaniac. Her bashful rubbing evolved into sublime convulsions. Shy silence gave way to lyrical logorrhea.

What was the meaning of this transformation? Was it a great gluttony for obscenity and wisdom? A swindle? An evil transmigration?

Rachel's extraordinary talent is demonstrated in an advanced exam she takes toward the end of the study program's first term, shortly before her journey to Constantinople. She is faced with a a person gilded from neck to toe. The stiffened body rests on its back, its arms spread in a cruciform. The only exposed part of this human sculpture is the right armpit, which is visible through a circular opening in the metal armature. The figure's head is concealed by a sack, tightly knotted at the neck, and its mouth is stuffed with rags to prevent coughs and groans from helping Rachel in her task – to discover the person's identity on the basis of a single armpit.

[...]

—judging by the hair quality and the skin texture – a female, fifteen or sixteen years old.

—Very well.

—Her Northern origin is immediately evident in the hair's honey hue. Excessive perspiration and breathing difficulties caused an allergic inflammation, but the speckled, flushed condition of the skin is not the result of her trials, but rather another mark of her Northern descent. The hair is thin and sparse, betraying hereditary flaws: the girl is the daughter of a long lineage of affluent city folks. A degenerate yet law-abiding family. The mother is enchanting, complex, yet so shriveled and desperate! The father has the gout. He is effeminate and oversensitive. His sperm is watery.

—Indeed. What else?

—I will have to smell.

—Go ahead.
(Rachel bent toward the armpit and filled her lungs with the perfumed air of the little valley of flesh. Her nostrils consumed its secretions of distress. Her eyes were shut. She concentrated. She wavered. Charles urged her:)
—Well?
—Slowly ... Slowly ... The pleasure is too great ... mmmm ...
—And now?
—A strict diet has certainly been enforced for quite a while. The aroma bouquet is quite economical in its tones ... I must extend a compliment ... You are an artist when it comes to concocting living smells ... The odor is so round and intricate, with a nuance of grapefruit and a resonance of the fetid private parts of an obese, sexually excited man.
—Rachel! You flatter me too much! Nevertheless – can you guess her menu?
—By the viscosity of her sweat and the slight dryness of the pores, she is obviously thirsty. She was only allowed a sip of sweet wine over the last few days ... Pardon my ignorance in the secrets of wine ... I am not certain ... Perhaps Muscatel ... In any case – no more than one glass in the evening hours. Apart from that, warm, earthy food: bitter roots and dense dark bread ... barley?
—Rye.
—Rye. I can stand it no longer ... the pleasure is too intense ...
—Slow down, you are close to your reward. Would you care to lick?
—Oh, yes!
—Salute! But don't forget your task!
(Rachel stretched her tongue toward the hairy cranny. The armpit seemed to respond to the invasive touch of the tongue

by contracting into itself, like a snail retreating into its shell. Then the tongue expanded, softened, and grew comfortable. Saliva mixed with sweat, and it was difficult to divine one flesh from the other. With great effort Rachel bestirred herself, and resumed her dissertation:)

—Oh! Superb! She is marvelous, Charles! The sweat tastes sublime! What a sunny zest! I feel a tickle in the depths of my womb ... She ferments champagne in my cunt! My clitoris is so swollen it might combust! I feel tipsy! One can spend an entire summer with one's nose nested in such an armpit!

—Composure, Rachel! Your mission is not complete!

—Yes ... Yes ... Well ... even though the taste is misleadingly childish, I clearly sense that she is not a virgin. Neither does she suffer so much from the recurring, coerced copulations, although she convinces herself that the loss of her virginity is a disaster. Her nerves are irritated, and she is scared ... The aftertaste of the armpit porridge is bitter indeed ... I infer that she longs for someone dear to her heart. Holy Satan – why on earth does she feel so guilty? And there is something else here, in this cocktail of bodily flavors ... Something more mature, more vile ... One second ... You scoundrel! I can taste it now! She recently gulped a hefty dosage of sperm, and I can recognize you even with a sour tongue! Even when you are secreted from the glands of a dehydrated lady!

—Rachel! You excel! You are too good for me! Her name, by the way, is Juliette, and she is the daughter of Monsignor Baron Charles de Vasivierre, the Bishop of Po. This slave of God will probably not last long, now that his beloved daughter has disappeared. "Oversensitive" and "watery sperm"! Come, come here, my dear, and claim your prize! Unleash your desires with the armpit slave.

With quivering, greedy fingers, the proud victor peeled off the felt panties constricting her sex. Then she plucked the sack off the wrapped maiden's head. Juliette's fearful eyes blinked in the blinding light, her thin, long nose purple from want of air and glazed with greasy perspiration.

As Rachel took the rag out of Juliette's mouth, the tortured throat spat twitters of suffocation; a whimper was abruptly smothered as Rachel violently pressed her twat to the girl's lips, looming over the golden mummy while gripping her ankles. Tyrannical thighs were tightened around the Baron's daughter's temples, squashing her ears; Rachel's ass enfolded her noble forehead, enshrouding her eyes, crushing her nose.

With circular grinding movements Rachel forced the thirst-chapped lips to open, the aching jaws to stretch, the delicate tongue to stand at attention and be flooded by the fluids flowing from her sex cave.

Rachel's pelvis whirled, a gear rotating on the axis of an all-but-torn tongue, trapped in cunt.

Rachel's vulva revolved like a tribesman dancing for rain. She chafed against the weary woman's skull as if she were trying to spark a flame.

And while deep in her depraved dance, she devoted her attention to the naked armpit; in her own way, she courted the curly cleft.

She sucked and gnawed, scraped and scratched.

She sweet-talked the armpit and terrorized it with threats.

She gently petted it and viciously plucked its hairs.

Her chin pecked at the sweaty niche as if trying to open a secret door.

Urdukas – beholding the sights, hearing the sounds, whiffing the smells – was rabid with lust, his erect organ bobbing up and down like a praying Jew. He edgily searched for someone suitable to molest.

Alas, all of the castle's prisoners and its servants were locked in the basement chambers. The only woman at hand was also the single person in the Count's residence whose body had never been defiled: the fat matron, a Prussian spinster of sixty. She was an artwork the Count had been diligently refining over many years. Urdukas had bailed the woman out of the Berlin jail into which she had been thrown after assaulting the old banker whose house she kept. Since Urdukas acquired her she had been intentionally maintained in a state of harsh purity. Her white uniforms were as stiff as planks of wood. Underneath them a biting linen corset constricted the ripe flesh – from the folds of her waist to the top of her ribcage – with pigskin laces.

The matron spent her free hours engaged in laborious physical exercises based on the training routine of Napoleon's army.

Every night she soaked her mammoth form in a bath of spirits.

Before bed she whipped herself and recited prayers to the Devil, beseeching him to grant her the composure and cruelty she needed – she who was overseer of slaves, overseer of choice fillet cuts, overseer of the brass lavatories and their daily evacuation, overseer of the latrines' contents, which keenly interested her master.

She was a cruel crocodile, a trampling tank, a white human lump of hygiene and solitude.

Urdukas credited himself for her miraculous mixture of excessive body fat and engorged muscles.

He was the one who had painted her religious fancy black!

He was the one who had molded her delusions and glazed the fresco of her viciousness with layers of pigment and yolk!

A precaution against his fits of lust, he had fitted her with a chastity belt!

He had even planned an ingenious death, just for her!

Yes, she was a work of art – but in the heat of battle, one destroyed even works of art!

The Count summoned her with a growl. He emptied a drawer and found a jagged knife with which to saw a hole in her bandage of clothes, releasing her rump. The matron, nipples pressed to the tiles and buttocks pointing up, rolled her eyes in exaltation.

And so Charles joined Rachel: she pounding a mummified maiden, he shoving his swollen semen hose into a spinster's sphincter.

The shrill, horrifying hollers of ecstasy that rose from both directions would have curdled even the blood of de Torquemada, the great inquisitor [. . .] (pp. 20–26)

Rachel, who has not completely rid herself of compassion, asks Urdukas to have mercy on Juliette. He consents. The armpit maiden is cleansed in a bath of goats' milk (in the merits of which the Count is a true believer) and given a warm meal. She assumes a new status as Rachel's puppy, sleeping at the foot of the Jewish girl's bed and spending her days in a cage. Because Juliette is infatuated with Rachel, she perceives her metamorphosis as a blessing. The German matron is not as lucky. It is rumored that she lost her sanity and was then expelled, empty-handed, from Urdukas's castle.

4. A NEW LEADERSHIP

Urdukas devotes himself to Rachel and soon considers her an equal. Before they embark on their journey to Turkey, they take vows in a formal ceremony. The witnesses – two old whores and a pair of midgets – sign the contract with their blood. According to the pact the Count's estate and wealth will remain his alone, save for the left half of his body, which will henceforth belong to Rachel; the two thus become partners in the libertine's flesh. The scene ends with an orgy in which the witnesses partake. This chapter is missing in the existing copies of the novel, except for the following sentences:

[...] In the ceaseless turmoil of her escapades [Rachel] could not find the peace of mind to properly reflect upon Charles's cock – a magisterial organ that certainly deserved concerted attention, gratitude, and contemplation. His prick was a busybody, in constant movement. Consequently, it was difficult to measure its precise circumference and length. But it was clear to anyone who spent the shortest time in its company that this member defied both gravity and the anatomical location assigned it: it extended perpendicularly from the groin like an uplifted elephant's trunk, leaning leftwards slightly as if it were a horseman ready both for frontal attack and a cunning flank assault.

Its wide-open urethra surveyed the horizon like a Cyclops's single eye, a tear of sperm always hanging at its tip. The glans itself, tinted Prussian blue by a plethora of blood vessels, was forged like the helmets of the Prussian artillery battalion.

With what speed did this penis regain its upright position once it spewed its sauce! And how abundant and dense was that exquisite elixir! Even after six and seven ejaculations, the sperm retained its rich, porridgelike consistency. This testicular soup had the hue of whipped yolks and caramel custard – in other words, the color of sweets – and its taste was reminiscent of a spicy, cognac-laced mustard dressing.

The foreskin was no ordinary envelope but a magnificent mantle, constantly dripping tantalizing mucous. When the prick stretched out, this prepuce did not simply retreat, it contracted and hardened in the shadow of the cock's thick tendons, like an autonomous organ – a masculine clitoris hung upside down.

The testicles were a pair of heavy iron weights, swelling and receding like the cheeks of a mad frog; the shiny, hairless scrotum was abnormally elongated by its burden of jewels, and it hung like Buddha's earlobes.

It was then, with this prick lodged deep inside her, massaging the walls of her uterus, that Rachel clenched the left testicle – the one that now belonged rightly to her – and squeezed. The cock responded with a sharp upward leap, as if to tear her belly and spring out through the navel. Her rectum cringed, her nostrils flared – she was overcome by a great excitement. Notwithstanding the intense pain caused by the member's grinding against her internal organs, she felt she had won a crucial battle. She had become the new cock commander. A deckhand made captain, the steering wheel securely in her hand [. . .] (pp. 29–30)

5. THE ROMANIAN COOK

On their way to Turkey, the Count, his young mistress, and her bitch, Juliette, stop in Bucharest to visit a master chef who is a dear friend of Urdukas. The chef's messengers meet them late at night in a side alley; they are blindfolded and hoisted into a small horse-drawn cab. As they bounce about on their way to the restaurant, Urdukas tells Rachel about the chef and explains why these exceptional cautionary measures were taken:

"My friend is devoted to his gastronomic fantasies. He has no interest in politics. But like many great artists he is misunderstood and misinterpreted. The farmers' party that governs Romania sees his restaurant as a dangerous anarchistic enclave. The potency of his platters petrifies them. They fear his stews as a source of terrorism, his broth as a cause of instability in foreign diplomacy – why, some even think his food might stir a revolution. If he's caught they'll throw him in a dungeon from which he'll never emerge. Hence he insists on absolute secrecy, and even I, his intimate friend, and you, my dear Rachel, of whose merits he has received epistolary accolades, and Juliette, who being a human canine cannot even speak – even we must not know the whereabouts of his establishment."

"But what on earth makes ministers and generals dread a cook?"

"A cook, yes – but Nikolai is no ordinary chef. He was always a passionate man. While still a youth his mind was confused by the Catholic fever; he was ordained a priest and became a missionary. The gospel virus carried him to the *terra incognita* of Oceania and its cannibal tribes, where he vanished. We were all certain the primitives' molars had minced his flesh. But after a few years he suddenly reappeared in Europe, spat in the holy-water basin, and committed himself with the same ecstatic zeal to the natural sciences. He was brilliant. He could distill poison from potatoes and improve gunpowder with cucumber extract. His secret pills transformed cowardly rodents into combative carnivores. He became the darling of the court. He was knighted. Yet his achievements were nothing to him. He strove to change the world. And then he began grafting plants –"

"A priest, a biochemist, and a horticulturist!"

"Horticulturist, yes – but no ordinary agronomist. More like an alchemist, only not the sort that strives for trivialities like transmuting base metals to gold. He wanted to produce vegetative monsters, floral dragons whose leaves would turn green by a photosynthesis involving absinthe rather than chlorophyll, whose fruit would act like a sword thrust, or like an oracle's fateful prophecy [. . .]" (pp. 32–33)

Urdukas tells Rachel how Nikolai finally combined his diverse talents to realize a culinary vision of mystic proportions. He himself witnessed one of the early experiments of the gastronomic genius – a dish that affected its consumers in one of two extreme ways: continuous sexual ecstasy or severe nausea with spells of delirium. A small and loyal clientele worshipped the Romanian cook's recipes, revering his creations as holy delicacies that reveal inner truths through their consumption. In time, rumors began to spread that the scandalous behavior of the exiled crown prince, Kroll, was the result of his addiction to Nikolai's food, and his restaurant went underground.

Urdukas's story excites Rachel. Juliette, on her knees, is summoned to provide Rachel with cunnilingus until they reach their destination. Urdukas prefers to save his energy for dinner.

The Romanian restaurant is concealed in a deep rock cleft. When they arrive, the chef and the libertine warmly embrace. Rachel is surprised by Nikolai's appearance:

[She had expected] an updated incarnation of Rasputin: a hirsute, broad-shouldered giant with electric eyes, surrounded by a red halo; a man whose engorged organ was his literal, physical avant-garde; a wild, messianic Titan with a thunderous voice, whose most nonchalant gestures were a magnificent dance, whose fingernails curled, whose flowing gown was shit-stained. In fact, Nikolai was small, slim, and frail. His thinning hair was liberally greased with brilliantine. Dark-framed spectacles pinched the root of his beaklike nose. His voice had the nasal twitter of a little girl's, sick with influenza, and his attire was that of a conservative, strict, uniformed government clerk of the middle rank.

Rachel's surprise turned to amazement as she drew near him, sniffing intently with her wonder nose to decipher the text of his glands.

His body had no smell!

He had managed, she concluded, to vaporize all his natural odors for professional reasons. (p. 33)

Another, rather aggravating surprise awaits Rachel. Unbeknownst to her, it had been agreed that Juliette would be bartered for their meal. Urdukas tries to appease Rachel. He explains that the price is quite reasonable, that the establishment's clients are accustomed to sacrificing family members and some even subject themselves for a few years to the chef's whims. Urdukas had resolutely refused to exchange Rachel herself for the feast and bargained the chef down to Juliette. Besides, it would be a great honor for Juliette to serve Nikolai's lofty designs. Urdukas promises Rachel that Juliette's life is quite safe: the chef abhors cooking human flesh. He uses his subjects instead as sources of secretions, keeping them in hothouses. And so Juliette, who had already been demoted from human to canine, assumes a new ontological rank as farm animal, or plant.

Once Rachel is pacified, Nikolai honors his guests with a guided tour of his establishment. They observe the laboratories where exotic grains are grafted and secret potions are concocted and distilled. They pass by cellars of spices and herbs and linger in the rare-insect hatchery. They express keen interest in the human hothouses and the human dairy, where urine and dung, sperm and milk, blood and menses, and tears and saliva are drained and collected in exemplary order and silence.

They are barred from entering the kitchen, but they view it through a glass wall; inside, the chef's assistants are equipped with gas masks and gloves to protect them from the extreme effects of the food and its odors. The tour's last stop is the garden of criminal plants, their host's special pride:

[. . .] "This is a new, carnivorous variety of mandrake," chirped the tiny man, gently caressing the dark, hairy, densely creased leaves of a low bush. "And believe me when I say that the legend claiming that the mandrake sprouts from the last ejaculation of a hanged man is absolutely genuine – although true only for a very, very rare subspecies of the plant – not the familiar *Mandragora officinarum*."

"[Can it really be that men have their necks broken at the] scaffold merely to provide the restaurant with a regular supply of seeds?" asked the curious Jewish girl.

Nikolai exploded in rolling laughter, the likes of which Rachel had never heard. Gone was the nasal soprano of the eunuch, and in its stead surged the roaring fanfares of an evergreen forest. Those awe-inspiring reverberations were not emanating from the heights of Nikolai's larynx, but from the depths of his belly; belly blasts were interlaced with the gurgle of digestive fluids. This was the laughter of a great visionary of desire, a retarded stable boy, or a sick god!

The bubbling echo of the chef's barks seemed to unravel the enigma of the cosmos: its meaning was nothing more, it turned out, than a blind marten roaming hither and thither in an intestinal maze, lost midway between the dental doorway and the rectal gate of guts.

Still convulsing in laughter, the chef waved his arm forward, pointing his guests in the direction of the dining room – the most expensive, exclusive, miraculous shrine of nourishment in the world. (p. 35)

6. INTESTINE DUMPLING

Holy Satan!

Order had been turned on its head! The kitchen – spacious and luxurious, its workers handsome and in festive apparel; the dining room – a small, slimy prison cell, its ceiling lower than the height of an average human. The air smelled like a stale soup kitchen. The coarsely chiseled walls were black with a thick veneer of grime, and instead of comfortable padded chairs and smartly set tables, the diners were offered filthy, low pine stools and coarse, misassembled planks for the plates to be put upon. A single waiter stood at the door, indifferently eyeing the patrons, his arms crossed over his bare, hairy chest.

Nor were the establishment's clientele appetizing: a naked man of sixty, well preserved (save for the scarred, cracked crimson crust of his ass hide, attesting to an excessive fondness for the whip), was staring at his own erection and hitting it with all his might, as if it were a dangerous, outlandish parasite. His elderly wife scurried around with surprising speed, sweat sprinkling from shriveled breasts, torn dress hanging from her hips. Only the third patron, a dark-skinned man whose beard was squarely trimmed in the ancient Assyrian fashion, seemed to be relishing his dish, sprawled on his back, completely enervated save for his belly, which was jerking up and down. His face was aglow with the elated, unadulterated bliss of idiocy.

The ghastly leftovers of the entree these three had consumed were congealing on the floor: a puddle of green beans *ragoût,* in which dark, toe-shaped lumps were floating.

But Charles and Rachel were oblivious to their surroundings. Their attention was centered on the plates that had been rudely thrown under their noses.

Indeed, a quick glance sufficed to confirm that the impresario of the stove had earned his reputation justly.

No prophet had ever envisioned food like the hulking, sulking dumpling they had been served – a veritable dough hippopotamus slouching in a muddy sauce lake, its shores covered to the edge of the plate with basil leaves. Threads of quivering brown matter were interlaced in the porous dough shell, simulating veins. The dumpling's lips were caked shut; their fleshy, tight texture foretold a palpitating plenitude hidden within.

We read in the New Testament that the Messiah's chest wound looked much like a meat pie. His disciple, doubting Thomas, dipped his sausage of a finger into the bleeding gash to taste the sauce. In much the same manner, Rachel plunged her shaking finger into the dumpling's aperture, gently pushing apart its folds, which were as flexible and moist as the nether lips of a woman in the thralls of ecstasy.

A menacing, steaming brown blob peeked from the slit; the glutinous stuffing seemed like a living being, about to emerge from a womb of dough, a food infant whose sublime, stupendous stench softened Rachel's skeleton and stiffened her muscles.

What ingredients produced such a putrid, rich, tempestuous malodor? Bull's kidneys pickled in apple vinegar? Mud sautéed in blood? Dung of the young and horny? Foam of fermented fuck fruit? Purée of trout testicles? Brain pulp of a suffering fir?

Suddenly Rachel grasped the stuffing's philosophical import. It was a body without body, neither solid nor liquid, immaterial matter extracted from the stomach midway through its exhilarating metamorphosis from food worm to shit butterfly! The dumpling's entrails were a simulation of half-digested food! All the finesse of the bowels, all the commotion of somatic transformation, all the subtleties of utter gluttony, and all the riddles of mortal fear – in short, all the powers of shit – were epitomized in a single, spectacular gesture of mimicry, deceit, sculpture!

The cook was a God – a Jewish God, no doubt – who created living food!

A theological question was served on this plate. What true believer, no matter how zealous, would dare hope for a second coming of food?

And here, in the zone between absorbing mouth and emitting anus, an ontological query presented itself. Consider, if you will, the thrilling glide of a living oyster down the esophagus – is not the existential titillation caused by the life of the food? And yet even the inspiring quivers of swollen shellfish are merely the fleeting vivacity before the death of the delicacy; even this gift donated to the diner by the selfless oyster is merely a candle's last flicker, extinguished in its terminal intercourse with the stomach. But here, within the Romanian intestine dumpling, life itself had been offered! The digestion of digestion!

The epiphany of the dumpling brought tears to Rachel's eyes. She was about to reflect further – maybe to muse upon her desert fathers' renunciation of food as it related to prelapsarian

Adam; perhaps even to reassess the great iconoclastic controversy in light of this graven image of shit – when a horrified scream came from the corridor:

"Soldiers! An attack! Run for your lives!"

Poised and confident, Rachel clinched the lips of the miraculous dumpling shut, lifted it with both hands despite its considerable weight, and unceremoniously shoved it down her décolletage. A third breast materialized on her chest, bulkier if somewhat less wholesome than the other two.

Mayhem ensued. Apprentice cooks stabbed gendarmes' thighs with meat skewers; hacked-off arms flew through the air; precious dishes were destroyed; wails; blood: the entire fatiguing affair of fighting and dying. Rachel and Urdukas surreptitiously departed. (pp. 35–37)

7. PEASANTS' SUPPER

[. . .] They were lost. The landscape was impoverished and oppressive: vulgar soil, puritan plants, and thorny air, stingy with its oxygen. A fence delineated a secluded farm, and beyond the fence – the shadow of a shack.

Breaking open the door, they woke up a pair of peasants. The wife's body was an uncommon anatomical aberration: a deflated windbag of a torso with four lanky limb-pipes and a miniscule nut-head.

The husband was much smaller: a sea urchin with the head of a titmouse.

Both were ill with poverty, drained from labor, and mute with horror in front of Urdukas's black pistol.

They were directed to the yard, still in their nightgowns, to hitch the melancholy horse to the despairing cart and ordered to drive the affluent tourists back to Bucharest.

The woman served as coachman, the man as hostess.

Spirits rose as they neared the Romanian capital. The unsavory devastation and carnage at the restaurant were forgotten. Now Charles and Rachel could pay more attention to the farmers. They fondled the stout man's slumped shoulders. They sniffed the earthy reek of the woman's armpits. What a fastidious, dim-witted model of existence they had stumbled upon – and the colorful Romanian language to boot! And why not? Why not add a folkloristic flair to the frolics that would follow their dumpling dinner, which, after all, had almost cost them their lives?

Back in their hotel room the excitement grew. Charles and Rachel decided not to bathe. The stench, the nervous agitation, the yearning for their feast, their hunger for fucking after such a strenuous day were complemented handsomely by their chance meeting with the proletarians. In a moment of witty inspiration Urdukas invited the pair to take the first bite of the dumpling Rachel had pulled from between her tits. He did not anticipate that they would attack the food with feral fury and devour it with a couple of impolite bites.

Ah, haste – your fruit is bitter!

The villagers' gray cheeks reddened at once. For a moment it seemed that the intestine dumpling had agreed with them, like a sip of brandy or a vigorous massage. But soon their blush darkened further and their arteries blackened and began palpitating in a furious gigue, as if their bodies were being grilled from within.

The windbag now resembled a leg of lamb.

From all his apertures, the sea urchin secreted his own dressing.

They staggered and fell to the floor, their lips twisted in an obscene grin of pleasure and horror.

Urdukas was infuriated by the impolite egotism of these human animals, and at the same time he craved the wantonness they reeked of. He stripped off his trousers, grasped the peasant man's bony thighs, and shoved his sperm spear to the depths of his hairy asshole, inundated with its fluids of internal grilling.

The puny man vanished entirely under the brutish bulk of the Count; Urdukas enveloped him like a thick, tight layer of dough, teeth gnawing at the farmer's neck, fingers mauling the tiny male tits. It was a bloodletting, terrorist cock thrust – but the peasant seemed oblivious to Urdukas's presence. The mincing of his dung tunnel should have had him screaming in agony or groaning in ecstasy, but instead he kept muttering in bewilderment, as if to himself:

"I'm being cooked! I'm almost ready! Don't stir! I'm being cooked! From inside! Cover the pot! Cover the pot! I'm almost ready! Just a little more! I'm being cooked from inside!"

Meanwhile, the farmer's wife, quite lethargic a moment earlier, was aflame, as if overspiced, and she gingerly bit her own arms. Dazed, Rachel sunk into her armchair, hair disheveled, three fingers deep between her thighs, stirring the fluids of her orgasmic broth. In her frenzy, she suddenly exclaimed in the language of the Jews:

"*Woonder iber woonder! Di essers zynen Gevaren essen!*" (An ancient, traditional maxim that means "Wonder of wonders! The mice turned into lions!")

Rachel was overwhelmed, under a spell of food, fornication, and onanism, while Urdukas, upon depositing his seeds of satisfaction deep in the sea urchin's bowels, sobered up and became worried. The government detectives who had invaded the restaurant might still try to hunt them down; they should hurry to the car and be off. From the corner of his eye he indifferently observed that the farmer's wife was no longer gnawing on her bleeding limbs and was now munching on her husband's legs (which did not disturb his exhilarated mumbles: he was still being cooked). When Charles and Rachel locked the door behind them, the couple was still engaged in their bodily business. Their prospects seemed poor.

An hour later, in the luxurious Mercedes speeding eastward, tears suddenly welled in Rachel's eyes.

"I miss my daddy," she said.

Urdukas was so amazed by this statement that he momentarily lost his balance, slamming his head against the bird-shaped knob of his walking stick. (pp. 37–40)

8. AFGHAN MONKEY

A couple of weeks after their arrival in Constantinople, already immersed in their orgiastic crimes, Rachel and Urdukas bring six child beggars to their inn. "The typical enthusiasm of Oriental youngsters," their "cappuccino complexions," the "pricks [that resembled] miniature blood sausages," the "tight slits into which the prying finger could barely fit," and the variety of sexual positions enabled by "the acrobatic flexibility" of the children – all these result in an exhausting night, complemented by immoderate consumption of "dates and pomegranates, Turkish delight, hashish, and cognac."

The morning after, they leave the naked children in their room, and roam the street market, dizzy with fatigue:

They were unmoved by the rare rugs, the sticky sweets, and the hallucinogenic herbs. Even the torture devices, with their arabesque ornamentation, and the Persian and Mongolian sex instruments offered to the connoisseur in the dark side alleys – even these marvels did not restore Urdukas's flabby, flaccid member to life. His shriveled, apprehensive testicles winced in his underpants. Rachel's ailing vagina coughed profuse sexual phlegm, like someone dying of tuberculosis.

And then they noticed it.

A tightly tethered miniature monkey of an unknown subspecies. It had a large flat skull, shiny, honey-hued fur, and a pale, bald, protruding ass. The monkey's big eyes had a poet's expression of disconsolate longing that brought to the educated mind the famous portrait of Charles Baudelaire.

The animal's prick was erect and stretched up to its nipples. The personable peddler explained that this rare creature was the last of the virtually extinct Afghan Oasis primates. These monkeys, he said, are a scientific enigma. Their very existence defies Darwin's theory of evolution, as they exterminate themselves: if the monkey were unfettered, it would exhaust itself to death in a compulsive fit of masturbation. The miniature Afghan's self-corruption knew no bounds.

Without hesitation Rachel removed her father's wedding ring from her middle finger. Of all the items Urdukas had robbed from the old Jew this had been dearest to his heart: it was the only memento left of the man's beloved, deceased wife. Rachel bartered the ring for the fettered monkey, and they hurried back to their room.

shook their cocks up and down like street market greengrocers proud of their stock. But Rachel did not want to be bothered. At her order Urdukas crammed the six agitated little bodies into a big wooden chest. It took some time, but their screams eventually grew softer and then stopped.

The Count and his mistress released the arms of the miniature Afghan. The rowdy pawing started at once. (pp. 43–44)

Rachel and Urdukas intently observe the monkey and masturbate as well, degrading themselves in a human reflection of animalistic autoeroticism, aping the monkey. After fourteen hours the drained animal collapses. Its eyes are wide open and it convulses uncontrollably:

[. . .] Was it dead? And if so – why did it move? Perhaps it had already found a cage in Hell in which to dwell and had come back merely to play its last encore and bid adieu – a five-minute Lazarus.

The Afghan shuddered on the crimson silk sheets. The sperm, sweat, and saliva he had secreted during his long hours of onanistic frenzy circled his tender body in a damp, dark mandorla, smelling of things burnt: sugar, hair, flesh.

Rachel waved her hand in front of the little creature's eyes. When it failed to respond, she concluded that it had become blind. (p. 45)

9. THE INTERCOURSE OF DREAM AND REALITY

This exceptional scene occurs the night before Rachel and Urdukas return from Constantinople to Paris. It is a turning point in the book, after which supernatural events become an integral part of the narrative.

Every toddler knows that Dream and Reality are unclean, irate beasts in heat, imprisoned in neighboring caves. Iron chains prevent Dream and Reality from merging in corporeal filth. But that night the sublime copulation occurred!

Rachel was sleeping that tranquil, deep sleep that only villains enjoy. The perfect conditions for Dream and Reality to fuck were attained. Slowly her naked body stiffened and began exuding a thin vapor. Her thighs' ligaments stretched almost to the breaking point. She clutched the bedposts. Her torso arched upward. Her vagina opened to the heaven like an upside-down umbrella.

Skin pricked and distended; the body's armature was a net of nipples; the skin a dense fabric of erect feelers, with humid, narrow tunnels wide open on each tip.

The skin was a bridal veil of burrows.

The skin was an armor of cavities.

Such was the skin – and Satan was the dermatologist!

Blessed be the Holy Body – transcendent vessel of lust!

Rachel's entire entity was a sex organ, a mercurial, gelatinous mollusk glazing with the glossy crud of *the first liquid*.

Oh, the first liquid! It was a greasy, syrupy white stock; a zesty marinade of kidneys and spleen in which Rachel simmered like a criminal roast. Then her inner anatomy melted and the burble of *the second liquid* ensued.

The second liquid, murky and viscous, was rich in earthy chiaroscuro – like a canvas by Rembrandt or a saucer of shit.

It sprouted up and out, pushed from below by the pressure of *the third liquid*.

The third liquid was a distilled resin of black bile, lethal and sweltering, its color petulant. Its fumes scorched holes in the blankets.

All in all, it was a complicated geological event.

What, precisely, happened to Rachel – that corrupted, villainous soul – when she defied the cosmic prohibition with her impudent cunt? Did her skin dissolve in the lake of fluids that poured from under it? Were her armpits' hairs and nostrils' whiskers burnt to dust? Or were they simply weeded and washed away with the sperm streams of that fuck? Had her Jewish flesh putrefied and gone up in smoke or simply decomposed and fermented, like a dark, puffy fruit in a jar of cannibalistic conserves?

Dream is a boorish rogue.

Dream is a rabid wild boar.

Dream's testes are flying balloons, inflated with toxic gases.

Dream is a kleptomaniac.

Dream was quick to sniff his chance! He sensed that he no longer had to merely guess at Reality – that shriveled, lizard-faced whore – through barriers and bars.

Dream stretched and plunged through Reality's layers into Lake Rachel like a sinking ship, frothing its own seminal fluids. (pp. 48–50)

10. A LETTER

Dear Father –

En route to Paris we stopped in Burgas, on the shore of the Black Sea. The pure air here would have done marvels for your lungs. The sound of the waves here is nothing like the gay jazz of the Mediterranean; it is deeper and more restrained, echoing the ceremonious chants of the Eastern Church. And to think that you – despite your age – have never seen the sea!

The residents of Burgas eat shellfish and other water creatures, whose tastes and textures titillate the entire body. The saltiness of caviar has an acidic sparkle reminiscent of sour wine, and I don't have words to describe the tickle of the eel's soft fishbone as it glides between tongue and gums, gently pricking the palate and melting in the saliva that floods the mouth. I know our religion forbids these foods, and yet I cannot help thinking how pleasant and rejuvenating these transgressions could have been for you!

And since I mention religion – I should dedicate a few words to describe our curious host. His name is André, but everyone calls him the Desert Father, no less! I do not know how he amassed his fortune. His estate overshadows the city and dwarfs its buildings, but he spends his days enclosed in a small cell, sprawled on a narrow, stiff mattress, stark naked even in the coldest days. It is evident that he once had a virile, vigorous physique, but years of fasting and immobility have degenerated him. His frailty verges on a handicap: he cannot stand without support – yet his infirmity projects pomp and pride because it is self-willed. He seems younger than his sixty years, despite his protruding cheekbones, limp limbs, and transparent skin. In fact, he seems ageless.

His home is abuzz with the ceaseless bustle of fishermen's daughters who clean, cook, read, and play. Imagine: an indoor autarchy of maidens! André, a visionary, has fashioned a new society in his enormous home, yet only a faint echo of its magnificent commotion infiltrates his austere, secluded cell.

Strange, is it not?

Are you curious about how this man spends his time? Would you like to read of the desire that dictates his odd routine? André's wife is a fifty-year-old woman whom he calls *mother* and sometimes *my Jewish mother*. She has big, gloomy eyes, but also a persistent arrogant grin. Her globular breasts and the flabby flesh of her underarms remind me so much of the hatter's wife in our village! She spends many hours stooped over the invalid's genitalia. She scratches his irritated cock's head with her ring finger's nail. She viciously pinches his scrotum. Sometimes she inserts her pinky into his urethra, whose sour orifice has dilated with time. Once I even saw her thrust a twig into that maligned hole and threaten to set it in on fire! And despite this manhandling – perhaps because of it – the tormented prick is ever erect; it seems to suck whatever energy the ailing body has left, as if the rest of the Desert Father's body were nothing but a root system designed to nourish the blossoming penis – a new genus of sex flower.

While on groin guard the Jewish mother reads, converses, and dines.

Occasionally, when her husband stirs or groans, trying to alleviate the pressure on his cramped behind, she will spit in his face or slap it.

They love each other dearly.

When the Jewish mother is bored she summons one of the girls. The two women frolic for hours on the carpet in front of André's glaring eyes. At such times a surrogate torturer attends to his miserable member.

André is prohibited the pleasure of plunging into the depths of his wife's crevice, and the other women usually ignore him;

but on occasion, a crotch will embrace his face, his nose will vanish into a vagina, his tongue will be sucked in by a sphincter. The secret of the Desert Father's ongoing agony is in sensitizing the nerves by harsh prohibition, bodily renunciation, and sublime frustration. He is an ascetic freak, a hunger addict.

Especially breathtaking is the Desert Father's feeding sacrament, which entails a remarkable physical contact: his wife grips with her right hand the [. . .] [*a long descriptive excerpt is missing here*]

In all my travels I have not witnessed such lewdness!

André was once a dazzling libertine. Yet he, who committed his life to the sanctity of sexual pleasure, finally became convinced that masculine ecstasy is not the zenith of desire but, in all truth, a fallacy, an impediment, a malicious travesty. For what is man's orgasmic climax? Several silly spasmodic spits of sperm, forecasting a long drought! A miniscule hop that is naught but a dive down a black abyss of carnal numbness. André yearns for feminine dampness, he longs for bodily metamorphosis, for the supreme ideal of continuous ecstasy. True libertinism, according to his gospel, cannot be masculine. Thus – the preaching of Modern Lust Theology disavows ejaculation. And, truth be told, the Desert Father reaps the rewards of his self-denial: a sluggish, thin dribble of diluted semen endlessly oozes from his penis. André might not qualify as a real woman, but his prick, dear father, is a delicate udder, constantly issuing milk as if it were milking itself, a miraculous male udder, an udder that is the center of the cosmos.

The original Desert Fathers, if I understand correctly, ate as little as possible in order to attain the state of prelapsarian Adam, the first man, who, being immortal, did not need to eat and therefore did not defecate. What a shrewd swindle informed their devout diet! For the Desert Fathers did not ignore the body – they adulated it! They did not run away *from* the body but *to* the body: to the perpetual symphony of digestive churns. No libertine had ever exerted as much passion for – and devotion to – food and dung as did the Desert Fathers. André studied the lessons of their lives well; this is clearly manifested when he [. . .]!

[. . .] I am not sure that I will send this letter.

I kiss and hug you warmly,

Your daughter,

Rachel (pp. 52–54)

11. A BALLAD

This lost scene (pp. 55–58) is written in rhymed verse. Urdukas and Rachel, still on their way back from Constantinople to Paris, stop for a short break in the Black Forest in Germany. A band of robbers assails them, and they are amazed to discover that the leader, a thin youth with a blond mustache and goatee, is none other than Juliette, Rachel's former slave, whom they had left with Chef Nikolai. She tells them of the Romanian cook's horrendous death during the raid on the restaurant. Juliette saved herself by seducing the commanding officer, and after his soldiers had looted the restaurant's riches, she persuaded him to defect, along with his troops. Under her leadership the Romanian soldiers became a fearsome gang, spreading terror throughout Central Europe. Her facial hair, she explained, had grown after she ate a salad of the Romanian chef's special greens she grabbed during the band's escape.

The bulk of the ballad describes Rachel and Juliette making love while the men encircle them, collectively masturbating and showering them with semen. The two bring each other to numerous orgasms, and Rachel falls asleep with a smile on her lips. Juliette then invites Urdukas to make love with her. The bearded hoodlum's flexible sex muscles draw five consecutive ejaculations from Urdukas. In the thralls of her final orgasm Juliette ferociously bites his earlobe, ripping a small chunk from it. This bleeding morsel, which she rolls on her palate and finally swallows, is described as the orgy's sweet dessert, and is likened to both a torn hymen and a circumcised foreskin.

Exhausted, Urdukas falls asleep as well. By the time he and Rachel wake up, Juliette and her gang have already disappeared into the thick of the forest.

12. THE ANIMIST

Upon their arrival in Paris the protagonists meet a woman of an extraordinary, irresistible sexual magnetism. Her name is not given, but she is dubbed the Animist. She is broad-shouldered, muscular, and stands taller than Urdukas. Her odor contrasts with the seductive allure of Rachel's sweet sweat:

[. . .] In public places the dense malodor ducked into the folds of the Animist's flesh, like an assassin on the run, hiding in the outskirts of town a few kilometers beyond the reach of the hapless policemen who hunt him ineffectively for years, a few kilometers away from his victims' eviscerated corpses – so the smell recoiled into its concealed sanctuary, deep, deep underneath a cattle shed crammed with emaciated cows, malicious leeches, and a steamy carpet of manure and damp fodder – this is where the smell hid, for the smell is a cunning criminal: it knows that the fumes of the shed, dominating the tunnel, conceal it, the body odor of the odor-murderer, which is, according to pure reason – *ipso facto*, as it were – the smell's smell, the aroma's body, that is to say, the odor's odor, patiently waiting underground in the tunnel dug below the cattle shed, and the cattle shed, pure reason reasons, is the folds of the Animist's clad body, and if the body, in part, is a cattle shed, it stands to reason that the clothes are a dismal farm of herders – toiling, irritable, thick-hipped, disillusioned herders – cursed sons-of-bitches who munch much and wash little; precisely so lurks the killer smell between the folds of its colossal body-host, while she, the Animist, calmly strolls from the neighborhood's old pastry shop to the desolate stores of the arcades, and from there on to the wide avenues that Haussmann built. And the killer smell, that master of disguises, awaits its chance to strike once more!

At the Animist's house, as soon as the door is shut, the smell breaks loose, its reign ubiquitous – from the cellars through the corridors to the attics.

This smell was a reeking cocktail of church incense, jasmine and sandalwood essence, sulfur, life-swarming dung heap, overripe Roquefort smeared on a stale slice of rye, pine resin, rosemary, sage, and the filthy fluids of wild beasts.

In vain did the guests try to smartly sip their digestifs from crystal goblets and cordially chitchat. The smell invaded their throats and stifled their vowels. Smell spoke.

The Animist's complexion had a dark brassy hue. Her chilling gaze pierced the air from under her bushy, black eyebrows. Because of her slanted eyes Rachel guessed that Mongol blood ran through her veins. A magnanimous hooked nose leapt from her face, like Arthur Cravan about to score a punch. Her flaring nostrils and tremendous lips gave the impression that the face was simply too small to accommodate its features. The forty-eight years of her life were etched on the Amazon's countenance and further intensified her awe-inspiring, hypnotic power.

When the Animist removed her sweat-soaked robe, Urdukas and Rachel were staggered to discover an abundance of anatomical marvels. Like daredevil navigators they surveyed her nipples, a pair of gargantuan growths in eggplant-purple, two tropical turfs of crimson capillaries, creeping and climbing on the peaks of her grand chest mountains.

Thick fur covered the amazing woman's legs and upper chest, and pubic hair curled between her thighs in black, moist coils. Thighs! These were solid, glistening oak trunks, interlaced with veins as thick as fingers. From within the pubic thicket a colossal clitoris proudly rose, about nine inches long, gregarious and combative. Both guests would soon experience its mighty thrust and expressive ingenuity on their own flesh.

The Animist's brawny butt was a spectacle of advanced geometry: smack in the middle of each succulent buttock, the monstrous enormity of which exceeded even the rumps of Hottentot females, was a brown mole – sitting high on this pair of overgrown, perfectly circular meat-mushrooms, creating an equilateral triangle with the asshole!

The ass was an imposing face, with the asshole for a mouth and brown moles for eyes! This posterior face aimed its blind gaze at Urdukas, who always felt woozy when confronted by concise sciences. The gaping anus underneath the eye-moles was neither hidden nor shy. This was a charismatic, flamboyant rectal ring, a lower mouth with an eternal song on its lips, a cavernous, fuming nether pharynx, turbulent in its operatic burps and gurgles, melodiously performing in a pitch ranging from alto to baritone.

Urdukas pleaded for a tête-à-tête with that impressive ass-face. He diffidently crawled toward it, slowly disappearing in the shadow of the Animist's superb architecture of flesh. But he had overestimated his stamina: he fainted.

"Fetch me a German gas mask from the armory! I am

responsible for my guests' well being. We shall draw from the lessons of the Great War," commanded the Animist impatiently. While still unconscious, Urdukas was harnessed with the rubber and iron mask, still dripping with machine oil. The Animist, meanwhile, leaned toward Rachel, hoisted her in her arms as if she were a kitten, and carried her to the bedroom. There, without further delay [...] [a *description of an orgy is missing here*] (pp. 59–61)

13. MODERN MAN

Urdukas is compelled to wear the gas mask while in the Animist's presence; for Rachel this facial prosthesis becomes more than a mere safety device.

When the couple retired to their room for an afternoon rest, the convalescing Count's eyes opened wide behind the thick glass, like two assholes about to unleash an enormous enema. A pinch of excitement squeezed Rachel's bladder. The gas mask changed her lover so!

What a hybrid: an automaton and a muzzled pup!

What an imposing fragility the once threatening scoundrel now exerted!

His nose – formerly a nose like any nose, handsome and noble to be sure, but still just a nose – had turned into a hole-riddled beak of metal, extended forth like the snout of a starving hyena in search of cadavers. The black rubber pipe leading to his mouth seemed romantic, valiant, keen – a hidden trachea straining to break loose, even if it meant forsaking the lungs to the cruelties of the world. Rachel even fancied his ears, drawn sideways and out by the leather laces like ludicrous airplane wings: diagonal extensions of a human machine.

In a cuddling, cooing manner she bid him not to remove the mask: "I see you now with new eyes, my love. With the gas mask you are so much more … modern!"

She sat on his belly, kneading his scrotum with her right hand. Her thighs pressed against his tight buttocks. The fingers of her left hand brushed lightly over the ventilation holes above his armored nostrils. She slapped his nipples – they swelled in response. Her body arched with excitement when she discovered that even this slight constriction of his breathing holes, a subtle insinuation of suffocation, was enough to make his prick prick up, his eyeballs roll, his chest shrink and swell convulsively. Rachel's nether lips darkened, engorged, and expanded in astonishment. Desire juices flowed from her vaginal well, while asphyxiation milked vanilla spurts from the count's crotch cane. Wonder of wonders! The swollen penis showed no intention of shrinking when it finished serving up its semen soup. On the contrary – as the dong dried out, it hardened ever more!

Soon she rode him, clutching a buttock, tweaking a tuft of hair, fondling the new face. Her tongue lapped the panes of glass protecting his eyes. Her finger, scented with her rectum's savory secretions, attempted to infiltrate his oral funnel. She committed herself to this tempestuous fuck, partaking in the making of a brave new world.

It seemed to be common, run-of-the-mill intercourse: rhythmic piston pounding of two meat lumps; predictable pricking of nerve ends in response to the rubbing of lust-cud reserves; temporary imbecility and loss of balance; routine erasure of the real world; frothing of sexual biles by reflex. But the glass eyes, with their metal mascara, hypnotized Rachel and carried her into a trance. She became a mystical medium, and a psalm of glory emerged from deep within her soul:

"Oh, my darling Charles, how you've managed to transform into an iron insect blessed with rubber feelers! How you've turned into a magical entity – a machine man!

"You, my love, were born twice: first at your pedigree-parents' castle – a malleable, frail corpuscle, a normal miracle; but your second birth was in Europe's laboratories of evil, you were assembled from components worn in Europe's death trenches, stained with splatters of blood, brain, saliva spat from Europe's convulsing, slaughtered lads. Your second mother is Europe of the Great War; Europe, that shriveled cow, whose body incubated swarms of worms, lewdly wriggling in an orgy of mass killing! You, who began as an evolved monkey cub, have become a charming chimera of chemistry and engineering!

"No one deserves my longing genitals more than you – Knight of Synthesis! Your second birth has demonstrated that nature is outmoded, demoted, and defective!

"Will your sperm, sizzling with the mixture of mechanical past and electric present, inseminate me with your worthy descendants?

"Would the fruit of our love have steel ... nipples? Tubular nails? Would it have a gear soul? A stomach engine? A magnetic liver? A synthetic spleen? Pasteurized bile? Gasoline urine? A spiral tongue?

"Ah, my champion! The air of your breath, acetone fumes; the air of your winds, innovative smoke – be grateful to Chance, the enchanter; say Amen to Fate, the wizard" [...] (pp. 61–63)

During their stay at the Animist's, Urdukas rarely takes off his gas mask. When he does remove it, he discovers that his physical condition has changed: he suffers from chronic attacks of shortness of breath, and he becomes more dependent on Rachel.

14. THE DEATH OF MARAT

The Animist's most thrilling magical ability was breathing life into a variety of inanimate objects and then using them for obscene purposes. The spectacle's arena, her vast bedroom, was jam-packed with torture devices, Rococo furniture, Neoclassical nude sculptures whose proper proportions were corrupted by gargantuan sexual organs, sophisticated automatons, and Fabergé eggs; the decor combined Russian imperial decadence with Piranesi's phantasmagoric prisons. The stable and the dungeons, the dwellings of dozens of slaves, were located in the basements of the urban palace.

After a prolonged evening feast, the guests were guided to the bedroom. The orgy's main attraction was the animation of still objects, complemented by many of the Animist's slaves posing in tableaux vivants during its long hours: frozen reenactments in the nude of historical, religious, or mythological scenes – the conquest of Troy, Danton's execution, the descent from the cross. The spectacle staged that night was the murder of Jean-Paul Marat, hero of the French Revolution, by Charlotte Corday.

Just as in the famous painting by Jacques-Louis David, a big porcelain bathtub stood at the center of the scene and in it the dead Marat, his arm dangling over the tub's edge to the floor, his head drooping, turned to the spectators. Yet the scene as realized by the Animist was much more impressive and comprehensive than that of the old painting, as the gloom and shadows of the dusty canvas had been replaced by the room's brightness, bringing to light many, many more details!

While the painting had shown only Marat, here the murderess, knife clenched in hand, was poised in lethal immobility over the tub, bent like a mother shielding her child. And what inspiration resonated from the perfect realism of the blood trail dribbling from the wound!

The secret of that perfect realism was unhidden: the knife, the wound, the blood – they were real!

The tip of the blade had pricked Marat's chest lightly, just below the left nipple, but because of the thespian assassin's inadvertent trembling, the cut had somewhat broadened. She – the slave posing as Charlotte Corday – was a dark-skinned, heavy-breasted Amazon. Her pubic hair was shaved, the accentuated contours of her naked sex contrasting with the dense, brown brushes of her armpits. The murderess's feet treaded in a puddle of sweat and piss – which was hardly surprising, considering that the historic murder was being endlessly perpetuated! And if all those lovely details were not enough, there were also two armed guards, frozen in the act of rushing to capture Charlotte, and three mourning, wailing women, crouching beside the victim's headrest. Such is true artistic boldness: old David had dared to render merely the revolutionary's pathetic corpse, while here were offered, simultaneously, in three heaving dimensions, both the murderous act and its aftermath!

Only when the visitors drew near the spectacle could they discern its true labor and ingenuity. What refined casting, deciding on a fifty-seven-year-old woman for the role of Marat! The wrinkles bracketing her lips and the sagging, purple rings under her eyes added a dimension of tactile, tangible death throes to her natural beauty. Her open mouth emitted a mute death scream, and though her lips were chapped, a thin thread of spittle projected from within like a frozen stalactite. What a heartrending contrast the Animist attained between Marat's pretty face and the flesh of his body, gnawed by a gruesome skin disease! From the rotting skin's deep furrows rose powdery knolls of mushroom-shaped tumors. Here and there an inflamed abscess tinted the masses in dark vermillion.

Bodily scents fused with the aroma of food; it turned out that the magisterial magnum opus of this disease was also a culinary feat!

"To begin with, we coated Marat with a generous layer of butter," explained the Animist, "from whence comes the lovely, oily yellow glaze. Then we peppered her with white flour, rich in yeast, which provided a fluffy frosting, and funneled it here and there into little mounds the shape of a nipple or a wart. Finally, we sprinkled brandy and heaped blackberry pulp to create the abscesses. The skin malady, my darlings, is a delicacy.

"You will be surprised to learn," continued the astonishing woman, "that 'Marat' is none other than 'Charlotte Corday's' mother! The finest vaudeville and circus acts are family businesses; there is no substitute for the sensual thrill of kinship."

While talking the Animist peeled off her soaked panties and deposited them in the hands of a quivering servant. He fell to his knees in ecstatic gratitude and began to vociferously suck on the steaming fabric.

While Marat and his murderess were both women, a mother and a daughter, the three mourning women were revealed to be three adolescent boys. Hair buds sprouted in transparent triangles above their tender members, but their cheeks were yet devoid of down. A rough rope, pulled tight by a heavy iron weight, callously noosed the scrotums of all three. This simple apparatus not only caused the mourning women great pain but also threatened to castrate them if they abandoned the posture.

From whence the perfect realism of the tears: they looked real because they were real!

"I do not understand how the women's pricks remain erect despite their taxing exertion and pain," said Rachel, turning her bare buttocks toward Charles's free hand (the other was already diligently rubbing his cock, which, judging by its fidgety leaps forward, was an art-loving organ).

The Animist smiled with satisfaction: "Every artist has little secrets she will not disclose, yet I can promise this much: even were the women to faint from exhaustion or lose their sanity from pain, their members would remain useable. My only hint is that the secret is in the prostate."

To demonstrate this the Animist positioned her foot near the diabolic device constricting the testicles of the grieving women. Three pairs of horrified eyes were raised to her in a mute, futile plea. The terrifying woman stalled, frowning in fake compassion. Then she lifted her foot and kicked the iron weight with all her might [. . .] (pp. 65–57)

15. MENORAH AND BROOM

The festive orgy that commenced with the abuse of the actors playing The Death of Marat *proceeds with the animation of several domestic objects and – in honor of Rachel – some Jewish ritual articles. The Animist brings to life a sewing machine, a broom, an umbrella, and a recamier sofa, but also a menorah, a dozen mezuzahs, and several brightly colored silk sheets described as "Jewish burial shrouds." (Here, as is often the case in Frank's book, it is hard to tell whether this ludicrous description of Jewish shrouds made from extravagant fabrics is intended as mockery or whether it reveals Frank's ignorance). The objects, once animated, are restless, hypersexual entities.*

[. . .] Oh, Holy Menorah!

Seven thighs aflame and six brass pudenda in between!

The perverted candlesticks clasped Rachel's breasts and pinched her buttocks. The menorah's vaginas mouthed Urdukas's testicles as if they intended to suckle and swallow the egg-shaped glands. The mischievous flames varnished the noble bollocks in hot, milky paraffin oil. The squeezing movement stretched the scrotum to the verge of ripping, causing searing pain and milking spasmodic ejaculations from Urdukas. How relieved he was when the Animist summoned the menorah with a shrill command, her awesome thighs spread wide and her entire body quivering with erotic rage! The menorah hurried over like an obedient, frightened pup. In the blunt manner of a policeman harassing a drunken bum, the Animist shoved the holy candlesticks into her hirsute sex cave. Could it be true? Was the Count really seeing clay-colored smoke rising from the perturbing cunt? Surely, the Animist would answer fire with fire!

Urdukas gained only a momentary respite – for not only did the menorah fancy him, but the broom did as well!

The broom scuttled on its single leg toward the petrified, befuddled man.

Oh, broom! Oh, super-man!

Solemn Caesar of dust! Indian tiger of spider webs! Mighty wood warrior!

Despite your domestic modesty, you may be the strong-willed being envisioned by Nietzsche, that philosopher with the broom mustache!

The broom shoved itself into the deepest depth, the holiest hole, of Urdukas's ass. So overwhelming was the sudden pain that the Count's jaws clamped shut and his front teeth cut his tongue, a bloody morsel of which – as tiny as a newborn's foreskin – fell to the floor.

But the broom hadn't had enough!

Oh, broom! Oh, super-man!

Filthy Hercules of cleanliness! Hero of sawdust and grime!

The straw coxcomb lashed at the noble back. Then, craving a consummate copulation, the wooden stick dilated and softened itself, crawling and climbing up, up the libertine's bowels. The Count pounded at the marble floor with his fists like a defiled virgin. Tears were jerked from his eyes, the sinews of his pubis ached, his belly swelled and rose, growing and hardening. And yet – lo and behold – his prick stood attentively, like an obedient lackey.

Soon the restless snake had snuggled completely into Urdukas's stomach-womb, stuffing it to the brim. A torrent of blood, bodily fluids, and shreds of semidigested food gushed from the Count's rectum like a swarm of insects fleeing a burning room.

The pretty carpet was stained.

As for Urdukas, his suffering was great – and yet he was granted not only a single, but a double, triple, quadruple miracle! Has there ever been, in the entire annals of sensuality, an intercourse as multifaceted as that between the Count and the broom?

One: the broom made love to Urdukas.

Two: the broom performed taxidermy on the Count while he was still alive.

Three: the broom purified Urdukas with an exhaustive enema.

Four: the broom swelled his belly as if he were pregnant.

Overstuffed Urdukas – a skewered roasting pig, his mind dimmed by overstimulation and inhuman pain – failed to notice how the Jewish burial shrouds, whose splendid embroidery glowed in many colors, first caressed his torso and then wrapped themselves around him, tightening, mummifying his hips and intensifying the pressure on his burdened belly. By the time he had awoken in alarm from the trance caused by his belly torture to the lethal corset's embrace, his internal organs were already bursting.

While his stomachache was driving him berserk, Urdukas's gas mask came alive and sealed itself closed.

Alas, murderous resurrection! Alack, assassin animism! Rubber and iron-clad Urdukas's features distorted in a passionate kiss of terminal strangulation. His ribs curled inwardly – suicidal skeletal pitchforks – and pierced his heart and lungs. Thus the Count was transformed from a full-fledged player in the orgy's ensemble to a lowly role in its stimulating set. Thus died the champion of libertines, killed by the will of a broom, several rags, and a gas mask. Even dead Marat forgot for a moment her own tribulations and witnessed with her sad eyes the Count's demise [. . .] (pp. 67–69)

During the cathartic stage of the orgy, after Urdukas's mummification and death, roles in the sexual theater reverse: the Animist's slaves curse her, urinate on her body, and viciously beat her, much to her delight. Then the house itself is animated by erotic energy:

[Even the walls shook and began] spewing plaster, foaming with stone bricks, secreting brass dribble [. . .] irresponsible, reckless architecture." (pp. 71)

16. RESTORATION

[...] Rachel was completely oblivious to her lover's death. Unlike Urdukas, tormented by heartless objects, Rachel had been surrounded by well-wishing articles: the recamier sofa she sprawled upon became an insulated, cushioned cocoon of pleasures, its bouncy upholstery briskly massaging her neck and ass; a dozen dazed mezuzahs merrily vibrated in her vulva; an enamored umbrella showered her with wet kisses; a sewing machine serenaded her with smut psalms.

Only when the still life fell still and serenity had overtaken the shrine did she learn of the Count's death. She leaned over his wrapped body, weeping. The Count's corpse had been deformed; the fabric wrappings had desiccated and shrunk his body, which looked now like a sculpture of a little girl. (Rachel was reminded of the gilded Juliette.) His head, still encased in the gas mask, was disproportionately big. (Rachel was reminded of the miniature Afghan.) Urdukas – so invincible while alive – seemed vulnerable, paradoxically, only now that he was dead. (Rachel was reminded of a green pebble.)

Then an aggressive, possessive smell filled her nostrils. She felt the Animist's strong fingers on her shoulders and heard her indifferent voice from above:

"Calm down, my dear. Nothing happened. I have seen deader dead than that." (p. 72)

The Animist bids Rachel to follow her to the kitchen. The Count's corpse is laid on a big table. Then and there his body is "repaired" by the Animist in a grotesque operation that can be interpreted either as magic healing, sexual folly, or the Count's own nightmarish dream. (The scene is missing in the surviving copies of the novel.)

17. A CONVERSATION REGARDING A SHADOW

When Urdukas has recovered from his death he feels younger, livelier, and more resilient than before. The following dialogue between the Count and the Animist takes place over breakfast. Urdukas's query concerns a naked fourteen-year-old girl laboring inexplicably under the table.

—Why is this charming lass convulsing and thumping on the floor?
—She massages my shadow.
—Do shadows need massage?
— My shadow enjoys it. The girl tries to pamper and pacify it.
—And why does a shadow need to be pacified? Is the shadow angry?
—The shadow isn't angry now, but if it *gets* angry – its rage is perilous.
—Should I fear your shadow?
—My shadow is a God.
—Does it have a name?
—It is the Jewish God. You should know how to call it.
—I thought God was dead.
—Does my shadow seem dead to you?
—It doesn't seem quite alive.
—Do you want to argue or do you want to eat? [. . .] (p. 74)

18. BUDDING NEW CUNTS

In a gesture of feminine camaraderie the Animist confers some of her magical powers on Rachel. The Jewish girl is still unable to animate the dead, but her hypnotic spell over people is bolstered, and she excels in transforming her own body.

Before a long orgy scene (pp. 87–92) Rachel uses magic to mold two supplementary vaginas for herself, one in each of her armpits. The virginal parts are described in great detail:

[. . .] The tufted clefts hollowed, deepened, and yawned in Rachel's clammy armpit nests. She – poetess of the flesh – became the mother of two baby cunts: fruits of her intercourse with herself.

Ah, peculiar conception!

Ah, lyric pregnancy!

Upon delivery the cunt kids were revealed as nonidentical twins!

Peering out from among spirited sweat glands, the right-armpit cunt's mouth was small, its inner tunnel narrow and muscular. Its lips curled inwardly, their color that of a fine Bordeaux peppered with black spots like the skin of a Dalmatian. An ever-erect clitoris leaped forth from the vulva's tip like a glistening, impudent pine nut. This clitoris – a puny, sharp nose – attested to its quarrelsome inclination. The tautness of the slit's lower fold disclosed to the discerning eye an abundance of immature charm, a naughty, snappish spirit, a soft spot for sport, and some interest in social affairs.

The right-armpit cunt's hairs grew only below the lower creases, flowing thin and silky like boyish chin plumage. Such a natural yet orderly coiffure, combined with the cunt's immaculate cleanliness, was strikingly reminiscent of the refreshing liberty of Élisabeth Vigée-Lebrun's paintings (and thus this cunt earned the name Cunt Élisabeth).[1]

Indeed – here was a cunt that would meet an intruder with a tight, almost painful grip. Despite Cunt Élisabeth's delicateness, its hot, burning pepper odor filled noses near and far with sneeze spray and caused sperm to spill prematurely. This searing smell argued with the sweat's dewy sweetness, which frothed gregariously around the cunt. In terms of nostril philosophy, it was a dialectical armpit cunt.

Cunt Élisabeth's sister – the left-armpit vagina – was soft and malleable, its lips limp, wrinkled, fat, drooping. Labia majora and minora interlaced like a dense skein of ivy. The sagging slopes of this armpit-mouth were not without a certain Byzantine melancholy; this vagina had evidently been molded from rich historical matter. And yet an experienced scientist, versed in the secrets of genital physiognomy, would not have been deceived: classic melancholy, marked by swollen, dwindling lips (such as those, for instance, of a Polish Jew) attested to immoderate carnal hankering. This combination – Byzantium and bordello – raised the question of transmigration: could it be that the soul of Empress Theodora – she whose fornication fire set aflame fair Ravenna, she who had been stuffed stiff in all her holes simultaneously – could it be that the soul of Theodora herself had metamorphosed and been reincarnated between the coils of a modern armpit?

Cunt Theodora was a nymphomaniacal organ. The softness of its dilated door hardly hid its excessive quivering and glandular overflow. This vagina contained a sex gasoline awaiting a single spark from a penis match to burst into flame and

1 Élisabeth-Louise Vigée-Lebrun (1751–1842) was Marie Antoinette's gifted and beloved court painter. The hairstyles in her paintings reflect the "natural" look favored by the queen: free-flowing curls and intentionally simple coiffures.

burn a forest. Beware! Address such a slit sweetly – and it will spit viscous juices in response!

The skin of all four lips had an orange hue, and a bulbous clitoris hung down over them like a monkey cub on its mother's nape. The smell, astoundingly, perfectly simulated a steaming *coq au vin*, awaking a tremendous desire not merely to lick and lap the armpit cleft, but to gnaw and chew its flesh! A thick shrubbery of frizzy hair grew wild all around the lips. Who could have guessed that Rachel's bodily soil would bear such agriculture!

Holy, Holy, Holy! A holy trinity of cunts materialized when Rachel opened her legs and raised her arms!

And what ensemble of holes was revealed when Rachel opened her mouth, forming a silent O, and jutted her buttocks into the air! A mouth that is an upper cunt, a cunt that is a nether mouth, two rare sex tunnels underarm and the sweetest rectum in the world! A licentious quintet of cavities proclaimed its challenge for five erect swords. (pp. 86–87)

19. DOUBTING THOMAS

Four lucky men join Urdukas in order to inaugurate the armpit vaginas and realize a pentagonal copulation: Gaston and Phillip, two young law students entrapped by Rachel's charms, and a pair of slaves from the Animist's stables. A sacramental rite precedes collective intercourse:

Rachel raised her arms high: a great orator hushing the crowd; a great priest beginning a ritual; a great whore spreading her upper thighs. She invited the four naked men – kneeling in line before her elevated throne – to lick, each in turn, the armpits of the new clefts and then grope the cunts, insert inside an awestruck finger, and beseech these nascent slits with grateful prayers.

The anxious anticipation milked sultry trails of semen from the stiff penises. Each prick grappled and knocked on the thighs of the man in front, like a blind man in search of an open door. Each finger in turn, as it entered the damp magical cavities, palpitated and extended like a little cock. The two almond-shaped cavities resembled the chest wound of the Christian Messiah, doubled – and the five trembling men were five doubting Thomases.

Soon the succulence of excitement rose within the armpit apertures, yielding flowing falls of feminine fizz. (p. 89)

The unusual allusion to Doubting Thomas turns the insertion of the disciple's finger into Christ's wound into a form of foreplay. When the fingers are pulled out of Rachel's armpit orifices, the men lick and suck each others' fingers. After this thanksgiving ceremony, Rachel's body receives five deposits of sperm simultaneously in an orgiastic-acrobatic spectacle.

20. THE BLIND VAGINA

On the morning after the armpits rite the two law students, enamored of Rachel, are informed that only one of them will be allowed to fulfill his dream and become her slave. Their fate will be determined by a game called the Blind Vagina. During the month preceding this duel, their lives are subjected to a strict training program intended to prepare the victor for his vocation and the loser for his fate:

[. . .] Long spells in steam baths softened each cock, endowing it with a wrinkly, crispy complexion. Their flesh was cured in fragrant essences of oils. Within a week a heavy aura of perfume emanated from them, not unlike the smell surrounding old whores in their glum, hopeless attempts to cover up the stench of syphilis.

They were ordered to be silent. They signaled their urgent needs by rubbing their cheeks on the rug, amusingly aping begging pets, and were most often met with no response. Hairs were daily plucked from their bodies, one by one, a cosmetic supplication inducing screams of pain – and yet they were grateful for it, for the attention and for the resolute nakedness of their bare and chafed skin, far beyond common nudity.

Their pricks were spanked morning, noon, and evening with pig-hair brushes. Their hands were encased in tin gloves. Their feet were constricted in mahogany pillories. Their elbows touched each other behind their backs, tied with ropes. In the end they were completely mummified: the linen shrouds – fibers sharp as glass and crass as a horseman – allowed no movement. Only their nostrils were exposed, gaping to the dark universe like the beaks of chicks.

Negro castrati supervised the advocates' nights, preventing sleep with rhythmic needle pricks to their feet hourly. Thus the night was a time of profound meditation.

Harshest of all was their diet: forest berries, emetic drugs, and emissions from Rachel's bladder and bowels – brown puree hither and golden wine thither – which they suckled straight from the wells of plenty. Frequent vomiting fits weakened them further and prompted further cruel punishment.

By the end of the month Phillip and Gaston were exhausted. Their souls soared to new peaks of sensitivity. They lived in a melancholic cloud. They were perpetually on the verge of crying.

Pride mixed with horror gripped them with the approach of their competition. To give them strength they were force-fed raw animal fat while seated face to face on the tranquilizers of Doctor Rush. (pp. 91–92)[2]

The spectators in the Blind Vagina game include Rachel, Urdukas, the Animist, several male and female slaves, and two "professional consultants" – a priest and a doctor. The law students are informed that their battle will be an "artistic reenactment" of the debate between the Church and the Jewish faith – ecclesia *and* synagoga*:*

[...] The experts found Phillip suitable for the Jewish role: his feet were large and flat, black hemorrhoids ornamented his anus like rubbery wild mushrooms, and he was distinctly prone to hysteria.

Gaston, much plumper, had reacted to his tortures with screams that reverberated not only with pain and dejection but also with anger and arrogance; the doctor diagnosed him as

2 The Tranquilizer, invented in 1811, was considered to be the last word in the production of constriction devices for the insane. The device fixes the patient's entire body and hides the face inside a cube. A bucket underneath the seat serves the patient's natural needs in cases of extended use. The assumption behind such constrictive devices was that in many cases "self-corruption" – masturbation – was the evil root of madness.

suffering from excess yellow bile – a syndrome, the experts felt, befitting he who would play the role of the Christian church.

An iconographic diptych formed, opposing two lascivious maidens: proud Ecclesia, clinging to her scales of justice, and defeated Synagoga, her covered eyes blind to the light of the New Testament.

A black handkerchief was tightened over Phillip's eyes – the blind synagogue. Gaston's arms were roped spread-eagle to a wooden beam with heavy weights at either end – human scales.

A change of sex was publicly pronounced: they were deemed women. The rules of engagement: a merciless war to the bitter end. The victor would thrust his erection to the depths of his competitor's rectum.

The toll of defeat was high: the loser would be expelled from Rachel's entourage and suffer from sexual abstinence until his last day. A chastity belt would be attached to him: an iron diaper welded around his hips and sealed with a heavy iron lock. The key would be entrusted to Rachel, and the loser would be forever denied audience with her.

The two miserable young lawyers-to-be wept and begged each other's forgiveness for the pain and shame they would soon inflict on each other. [. . .] (p. 93)

Phillip and Gaston are given a last chance to withdraw and leave unharmed, but the two have made up their minds and they accept the rules of the duel.

After a long, violent battle it is the blind synagogue – the Jewish religion – that has the clear advantage: her body presses the church down, but due to "clitoral withering" she cannot realize her advantage – she is unable to insert her flaccid organ into defeated Ecclesia's sphincter. An alternative resolution is declared: the synagogue sits on the church's face and smothers her until she faints.

Gaston – Ecclesia – is thrown out, his groin burdened by a heavy weight and his heart by a heavy stone: he has been not only barred from Rachel but also denied his partner in torment, whom he had grown to love passionately.

Phillip's lot, too, is soon clarified: the blindfold is to be worn permanently. The Animist then transforms the anatomy of his primary organ of servitude: the length of his tongue is doubled. To prevent the obscene muscle from lolling out of his mouth, he must roll it up by contracting his jaw muscles and gritting his teeth. His speech is corrupted beyond recognition, and he is subject to endless jokes and impersonations. His chief tasks as slave are to provide oral services and to be used as a human latrine.

But Phillip's ordeal does not end there, since, in spite of his lowly status and worsening mental state, Urdukas is jealous of him: the Count feels that Phillip's servitude creates an intimate bond between him and Rachel, and that the womanly fluids Phillip regularly consumes have rare benefits that he, Urdukas, is deprived of. The Count's treatment of the hapless slave grows crueler by the day. After a while Urdukas demands, during a vocal argument with Rachel, to gouge out Phillip's eyes so that he will truly be a blind vagina. Throughout the long conversation the two ignore Phillip, whose monstrous tongue grazes the Jewish woman's left-armpit cleft (Cunt Theodora). Even though he chose this slavery, torture, and abuse, the enslaved young lawman is horrified by Urdukas's threats. That very night he manages to unchain himself, remove his blindfold, and escape.

21. A WEDDING

Rachel grows more and more restless. She no longer finds satisfaction in acting out her diverse deviant desires. Now she needs "a painful, destructive act through which to be transformed into something else" (p. 111). She makes a sudden decision and leaves the Animist's house, accompanied by Urdukas and a pair of brawny, fearsome slaves.

They head to Rachel's native village, in southern France. Upon her return her old father happily embraces her, and Rachel too sheds tears of excitement. But she is determined to overcome her sentiments and execute her most horrible crime. A grand feast is held that evening at her father's shack. The impoverished, malnourished elder gratefully gobbles the food amassed on his plate: drug-laced pork. His limbs become heavy and his thoughts blurred, but he remains conscious. He gawks vacuously as his daughter's lackeys remove his clothes and pull a white bridal gown out of the travel trunk, precut to his measurements. A union ceremony between the old treasurer and his daughter is performed:

Rachel wore black riding breeches and high, shiny boots. On her head she had a traditional religious hat: flat, wide-brimmed, overflowing with black fur. She stood motionless but seemed to be making a great effort. Sweet sweat was glowing on her forehead and on her naked breasts. Her expression was morose.

A slave in a pink underskirt served as bridesmaid and supported the old, drugged father, naked underneath his snow-white embroideries, his legs flailing freely, the chill air covering his skin with goose bumps. In front of them Urdukas stood on a travel trunk that served as a small stage, Hebrew prayer book in one hand and a goblet of wine in the other. He convulsed with silly giggles, like an intoxicated nun kissed by a handsome man. One could barely make out the matrimonial vows from among his obscene gurgles, brutish burps, and lewd growls.

Despite this clownish conduct he managed to sanctify the marriage of the father-bride and his daughter-groom.

As soon as the ring had been slipped onto the old man's left pinky, the slaves folded his body over so that his arms hugged the multipurpose trunk. They spread his legs apart slightly, raised the long hem of the gown, and attached the fabric at the hips, revealing his shriveled, disheartening buttocks. The treasurer's head slumped to one side against the trunk.

The head and the ass were in breathtaking contrast: on one side of the trunk glared the ancient, macabre bottom, its beady intestinal aperture bracketed by sunken cheeks, veiled by wrinkles of lost memories, framed by mocking muslins; on the other side – wonder of wonders – the head of a newborn baby, with neck muscles too soft to support the heavy skull, lips wide open, and a face smeared with the foggy expression of one who yearns to still hover in a womb of nourishing fluids.

As pale as her condemned father, Rachel clenched in her left fist the monstrous dildo she intended to thrust into the paternal asshole. Little drops of blood trickled from her fingertips: so strong was her grip that the sharp spikes that decorated the surface of the large cylinder had pierced her skin – metal nails ornamenting the artificial prick, that horrible hose which would soon sever the intestinal canal of that old man – obedient handyman of God – who now opened his mouth time and again, gulping quantities of oxygen he had not realized his lungs could contain since the days of his youth, and in spite of the gregarious pumping, and in spite of September's chilly air, he had no voice with which to bemoan this bitter fate – it was once a warm, soft tenor, slightly coarse, but very sentimental – the hapless old man who seemed to have mistakenly wandered into a story not his own, a tale having nothing in common with his private history, the end of which was so unexpected, so alien, that in the wealth of all his experience he could not find a measure by which to reckon the meaning and nature of this pain, so utterly amazed was the treasurer when, several moments later, Urdukas pummeled his head with the silver bird that adorned his stupendously ornate walking stick, the very stick Urdukas had purchased as a young student in England, not merely as a symbol of mastery and dandyish vanity, but as a talisman that would enhance the illusion of stability and certitude in his identity, the illusion of solid selfhood conferred by certain objects, as if an object had the power to soften or delay the deathblow awaiting all men, but in fact it was that very object – that stick – that would with the power of his blow make blood gush from the old man's pharynx, and from his nostrils and from the canals of his ears and from the orbits of his eyes, a liquid moldy with the excesses of decades dense with mistakes and hopes, the blood that would foretell his palpitations of death becoming soon more compliant and soft and his expression suddenly seeming more focused and wise, just a short while before Rachel herself would emit a series of blood-curdling bellows, causing one of the servants to run off, his hairy body still clad in a pink underskirt, losing both his mind and his way in the foreign, sorrow-soaked landscape, falling like a green pebble to the sewer ditch, softly resting his sour cheek against the dung and water-soaked soil, remembering suddenly the only woman who had ever loved him, his miserable mother, a Parisian laundress, crying bitterly as he rolled in the mud, only the warm compassion of his dead mother raising his spirit and preventing him from descending into total madness – for there is a consolation in compassion – and while the overgrown man soils his underskirt, all the villagers hid, silent as mice, in their cellars, like those naive soldiers in Europe's ditches who hoped that by ducking and embracing their heads with their thighs they might avoid the bombs – that is how, it seemed, the villagers intended to avoid the rage – all of them save for the tough innkeeper who had smartly knocked in advance on the front door of the home, several kilometers to the east, on the border of Provence, of the brawny peasant who provided her establishment with beets, fruit preserves, and wine, the peasant to whom she rushed as soon as she saw Urdukas's ominous Mercedes speeding toward the village, that Christian Provençal peasant to whom she offered – in plain words and without hesitation – her asshole forever, and against whom she now rubbed that asshole, as the virile slave continued to rub the mud and the frightened villagers rubbed against each other – all while Urdukas stared, open-mouthed and pained, at the splinters of his beloved stick, refusing to accept that he must pay such a heavy price for the murder of the treasurer, who is busy, very busy, breathing his last gasp, as a cylinder of ivory and nails still juts out of his behind and Rachel herself is hitting her knees time and again against the sides of the trunk until blood begins to flow, trying to crush herself, until the already cold corpse offensively passes wind, the source of which is a mystery – and whether it was a bowel's burble, a tracheal churn, a rectal rattle, or the sound of a breaking bone, it doubtlessly was a fatherly reprimand, admonishing yet gentle, warm and forgiving – after which, finally, a pleasant silence settled, unbroken until sunrise, when Rachel and Urdukas listened to the caressing, cracking sounds of the fire they had set in each of the village houses soon after the murder and which was now consuming the dismal buildings, and all while Charles was poised above the skinny, dew-damp body of Rachel, his nostrils filling with the aroma of horror-sweat that poured from her body, his breathing a guttural purr, his eyes glazed with heavenly ecstasy, his organ beginning to drill in pistonlike motions, in and out of Rachel's original vagina, as if he were trying to extract a treasure, or an internal organ, or a reminiscence, or a little recognition. (pp. 113–17)

22. EPILOGUE

After the assassination of Rachel's father the criminals return to the Animist's house in Paris where terrible news, the only information that indicates the story's time period, awaits Urdukas: his entire fortune was lost in the great Wall Street stock-market crash, and he is deep in debt.

The next morning the Animist wakes Rachel. She tells her that Urdukas, in the folly of his despair, has tried to rob her. She, the Animist, had no choice but to punish him by having her servants crush his knees and "usurping" the erring nobleman's entire entourage. She sends Rachel and Urdukas on their way but adds that if Rachel decides to join her and desert the waning wreck that Urdukas has become, she would be received with open arms and an offer of business partnership and great prospects. She assures Rachel that days of disaster and crisis are coming – the perfect era for the two women's gifts. As a gesture of goodwill she gives Rachel a satchel with a loaf of rye bread and a slice of Roquefort cheese and even equips the Count, already waiting at the gate, with a pair of crutches:

Thus the two trailed slowly from one street to another. The air was cool and agreeable. The sky had a fashionable metallic hue. Urdukas's bandaged knees were as swollen as Bibendum's belly tires.[3] Nothing disturbed the morning's tranquility save for the exhausted Count's groans of pain and angry stuttering.

Two old spinsters, bodies in rags, curled together in an embrace, perched on the pavement, to preserve their meager body heat. Rachel and Urdukas might never have noticed them if one of the pair had not chirped out "Spare something for the poor" and if the voice had not been familiar.

3 Bibendum is the logo and mascot of the Michelin tire company, of France. The Surrealist interest in Bibendum is reflected in Robert Desnos's 1927 book *Liberty or Love!* (Desnos 1993).

"I'll be damned!" growled the Count, "the synagogue and the church!"

And, indeed, the two destitute grandmothers were none other than the two young lawyers! Despite their poverty Gaston had grown fatter still. He was perched on his elbows, belly drawn sideways and legs twisting around Phillip's hips, a posture meant to ease somewhat the bites his flesh endured from the rusty metal straps of his demonic chastity belt, the very belt Urdukas had welded to his body.

Gaston was the one who spoke. Phillip merely stared in phlegmatic apathy, his chameleon tongue rolling in and out of his mouth between his lips, greenish and chafed from dryness. Beside them was a shabby beret with several coins thrown in by passers-by.

The sight of these coins brought back a healthy blush of hope to the Count's cheeks. With a greedy grin he leaned toward the treasure. But Phillip recognized him and cackled a medley of enraged syllables, parched and hysteric.

A passion for revenge rejuvenated the human wrecks. They snatched the Count's crutches and pounded him with them. They did not even glance at Rachel, perhaps out of shame, perhaps out of a lover's bashfulness lingering in their tormented hearts, or perhaps out of the absorbing joy that battering Urdukas afforded their entire beings.

And Rachel? Rachel stared at the events through the veil of her thoughts. Her mind was absent. Arms crossed, she stood with her fingers reflexively sunk deep into her wet armpits: her little finger gently stretching the pits' slits downward, the ring and middle fingers flightily plucking the always-eager lips, the index fingers caressing each of the upper clitorises, the thumbs stirring and burrowing to and fro in the soft hair, like the hand of a meditating grandfather caressing his beard, waves of ecstasy sending shivers through the arm and shoulder muscles, spurts of sex wetting the silk shirt.

Clouded by the veils of her reflections she noticed how her lover's silver hair, which had always been pedantically pulled back, was becoming increasingly disheveled by the beating, poking, and plucking fingers. The thumps of the crutches had made a new hairdo for the Count and dyed it a crimson hue no orgy had ever given it. But for Rachel the sound of his tearing sinews and breaking bones was devoid of drama, like the sound of cinders in a far-away fireplace.

Would the Count be killed by the synagogue and the church? Or might the three have a future as an ensemble of geeks?

She, with her sweet scent and flooding fluids, was already moving in other realms. She turned her back and walked away. (pp. 120–22)

Glaat-Kosher Surrealist Smut

On Justine Frank's Sweet Sweat

Roee Rosen

1. PORNOGRAPHY, MORALITY, AVANT-GARDE

Is *Sweet Sweat* a pornographic novel? If pornography is a distinct literary genre, distinguished by certain stylistic and narrative conventions, than the answer must be affirmative. In Justine Frank's book, orgies are set within a rudimentary, at times incongruous, story line. Lust assumes fantastic proportions and is never quenched. Characters are crudely rendered: rather than compelling human beings, they are mere bodily conduits through which destructive sexual energy is funneled. All of these are common characteristics of literary smut. Pornography is also defined by its purpose – erotic, most often masturbatory, arousal – and by this utilitarian definition, as well, *Sweet Sweat* is a pornographic (although somewhat eccentric) novel. And yet labeling the novel as pornographic sheds little interpretative light on it. Even a quick glance at the variety of cultural products tagged as pornography prove that it is neither a stable, static category nor a universal, timeless concept – but rather a plethora of different phenomena in constant flux.

The word *pornography* originated in ancient Greece, but the modern concept was born during the Renaissance (Hunt 1993a, 11–12). Until the middle of the nineteenth century no legal, moral, or aesthetic distinction was drawn between visual or textual depictions of sex and transgressive political publications. Both were considered obscene and dangerous, inseparable manifestations in a single, subversive, hybrid category. Thus, for instance, the numerous lewd illustrations in which Marie Antoinette is viciously rendered as a nymphomaniacal monster were an integral part of pre-Revolutionary propaganda (Hunt 1993b). It follows that both definitions of pornography invoked above, the formal (prescribing its aesthetic traits) and the utilitarian (designating its *raison d'être*), while seemingly self-evident, are in fact neither timeless nor immanent; rather, they reflect a relatively recent cultural development.

It was only during the Victorian era that pornography became an industry focused exclusively on sexual desire. The representation of sexual desire as separate from the rest of life has resulted, Lynn Hunt claims, in contemporary smut devoid of the creative edge and political and ideological viability that premodern pornography has. I believe, however, that even if we agree that modern pornography's quintessential purpose is erotic arousal, there are still substantial ideological and political differences between the diverse products in this complex field. Contemporary porn, far from being the cohesive, static, and politically inane category Hunt claims it to be, is in fact a heterogeneous array, perpetuated by diverse forces and desires (often antagonistic to one another) and charged with incommensurate social and cultural meanings and ramifications.[1]

1 A preliminary exploration of the spectrum of the supposedly stable "genre" of pornography begins with women who channel their professional experience in pornography into artistic and educational venues (Annie Sprinkle, for example); queer pornography provides alternative models of smut, aimed solely

at gay communities (the multifarious production of author and pornographic film producer Susie Bright, for instance). Compared to mainstream straight pornography, these subgenres not only target a different audience but entail different perceptions both of desire and its representation. Add to this smut geared toward more marginal sociosexual groups (see, for example Laura Kipnis's fascinating chapter dedicated to transvestite pornography [Kipnis 1996, 64–92]) and the simplistic picture of pornography as a homogenous genre begins to collapse: these different, at times transgressive fields of production and consumption are distinct from the mainstream smut industry, and they are consciously generated and consumed as such. In other words, within the vast field of pornography there exist a variety of subgenres in which masturbatory pleasure does not exclude politics and ideology but, on the contrary, is inseparable from culture wars and perpetuated by specific political and community agendas.

But even anonymous, mainstream, heterosexual, conventional, and commercial pornography is far from being a unified, static field. There are four distinctions to be made within it: first, differences in ideals of desire (I place these on a "lust axis"); second, differences between desire models that have evolved over time (the "temporal axis"); third, differences that result from divergent national cultural contexts (the "territorial axis"); and fourth, substantial differences in sexual representation as a result of evolution and revolution in technology and media (the "mediation axis").

Diversity along the lust axis is demonstrated by comparison between "soft-core" and scatological pornography. Soft-core films and still shots are stylistically premised on hidden and blurred genitalia, avoiding masculine erections at all cost and doctoring the images to achieve the appearance of "flawless" bodies. These images often have a literal softness, or blurriness ("Vaseline lens"). Too direct an encounter with "the real thing" (exposed genitalia) would corrupt the purist, synthetic, rigorously coded fantasies this subgenre caters to. In stark contrast, the coprophilic lust for representations of excretion is premised on an opposite desire, to be engulfed by the body at its most abject, odorous, and repulsive, as defined by social codes (by normative diagnostics coprophilia is classified as perversion). The distinction between these opposite poles of the lust axis is multifaceted: it points at a gap between a craving for a fabricated, hygienic, and synthetic ideal (related to social conformity and legitimacy) and the search for transgressive sexuality. These two poles bracket a vast range of desire models.

The temporal axis is also loaded with ideological and social ramifications. Chronological development is revealed through details: the hair styling of the feminine pubis, for instance. In American pornography in the late 1960s and early 1970s pubic hair was often a thick tuft, *au natural*. In the 1980s this look was replaced by a geometrically trimmed patch of hair above a smoothly shaved vulva. This shift was clearly informed by political and cultural developments: the ideal body type of the flower children, freed from conservative restraints, was dismissed in favor of a gym-buffed, "enhanced" body in a shift from Hippie to Yuppie. In this context, one should keep in mind the pair of armpit vaginas that grow on the body of *Sweet Sweat*'s protagonist, Rachel; the hairstyle of one is associated with Marie Antoinette's court, that of the other – an abundance of black hair – with the byzantine empress Theodora. Thus, the hairstyles of the armpit pudenda represent two cases of feminine monarchic authority, even as they emphasize the historic and spiritual incongruity between the two (and a common denominator resonates as well:

Sweet Sweat is part of the body of smut produced by the French avant-garde. On its face, *avant-garde pornography* may seem to be a contradiction in terms: the forerunners of "high" art investing their resources in the lowest, most disreputable genre. But elite circles, of course, were preoccupied with obscenity long before the twentieth century. The abundance of Renaissance texts and images representing ancient gods copulating with mortals (from the intercourse-postures illustrations by Marcantonio

both Marie Antoinette and Empress Theodora were vilified through an obsessive, vociferous preoccupation with their exceptional sexual behavior). The new sex organs transform Rachel's very body into a cultural pastiche, and a collagistic hybrid of feminine sexual identities. The territorial axis, designating cultural spaces, denies the homogeneity of pornography. The wide aesthetic and narrative gap separating, for instance, Japanese animated pornography (manga, hentai) from the silicon mounds of West Coast America reflects different regional versions of beauty, desire, and taboo and different relationships between phantasmagoria and fact, between the theater of desire and the arena of the real.

Finally, the technological mediation of smut is dynamic rather than static – to the point of creating representational, social, and sexual paradigms. Think, for example, of the revolution that occurred when domestic video cameras entered the mass market in the mid-1960s, turning video into an integral part of the middle-class household. Video's dominance caused the bankruptcy of the theater-oriented pornography industry and replaced it with a new industry based on television (a process captured in the 1997 movie *Boogie Nights*, directed by Paul Thomas Anderson). This shift in media transformed patterns of consumption: it shifted into the private sphere of the home and out of the public sphere of the theater. Domestic video also enabled the burgeoning of amateur porn, which centers on the domestic and the mundane (serving both narcissistic pleasure and voyeuristic and exhibitionistic drives). The immense popular appeal of amateur pornography nurtures realistic, imperfect bodily models as oppositional desire objects to the professional, synthetic, and unattainable ones.

In the 1990s the Internet became the dominant venue for erotica. This development has had at least two truly revolutionary repercussions. One is the shattering of a rule that had formerly governed the pornography market: namely, that the less mainstream a product is, the more expensive it will be and the harder it will be to find it (extreme examples are varieties of illegal pornography, such as pedophiliac products). On the Internet this rule does not apply. The other revolutionary development in pornographic media fostered by the Internet is the expansion of online chat (and other communication options), in which participants may choose to identify themselves or to assume a false identity, opening up a virtual discourse premised on blurring the line between fantasy and reality. The same development allows for a sexual dynamic that blurs the distinction between solitary, masturbatory pleasure and interpersonal sexual contact.

Raimundi, to Pietro Aretino's lewd poems, to the art of Giulio Romano), crossed the strict theological divide between right and wrong and high and low. This jovial dipping in the well of lewdness was also a subversive defiance of ecclesiastic hegemony.

Inseminating Christian culture with mythological sensuality is just one manifestation of smut's rebellious challenge. In addition, Renaissance and eighteenth-century transgressive literature often renders whores and homosexuals as a third sex – and favorably so (Findlen 1993) – providing a precursor to later attempts at dismantling the feminine-masculine binary model of gender. It would be wrong to dismiss literati libertinism as utter nihilistic hedonism; sexual whims are indeed the driving force – but they are coupled with cultural warfare at a deep level.

Both the polemics of institutional religion and the dismantling of sexual division are essential elements of *Sweet Sweat* and of Frank's self-portraits, in which she is represented, time and again, as a sexual hybrid, with a strong emphasis on facial hair – with everything from an elegant, thin musketeer mustache to the thick beard of a rabbi. Feminine facial hair is associated in the popular imagination with the bearded lady of circus sideshows, as a mutation provoking ridicule and pity. The bearded lady's identity is constituted by her Otherness: she is a freak; her difference solidifies the normative division between masculine and feminine. However, feminine facial hair has a rich heritage of more complex and positive representation; Frank's bearded self-portraits are part of a tradition of female empowerment.[2]

2 Peter Brown has explored several cultural manifestations in which the distinction between male and female is obfuscated in early Christianity, among them the trope of feminine facial hair. As Brown makes clear, Christianity as a new social and religious framework had an emancipating association for women (despite the strict patriarchal foundations it shares with other normative religious institutions). The establishment of monasticism enabled women to avoid a role as breeders and dedicate their time to study, in a period when such

Avant-garde pornography undermines the border between the abject and the sublime, smut and art. This division has been a point of controversy in feminist criticism and in avant-garde

a choice was a veritable existential threat by the community, in light of the enormous rate of child mortality. Brown examines the shift of the image of the bearded woman from its appearance in Roman sources to its expressions in early Christianity. In pagan dream interpretation, a woman's dream of growing a beard accorded to a will to please her husband by properly keeping house. In Christian literature the meaning of feminine facial hair (and of complete transformations from woman to man) was very different: facial hair on a woman was interpreted as a sign of power and autonomy, a sign that she is a "worthy" Christian, as worthy, in fact, as a man (Brown 1988). In the apocryphal Gospel of Thomas, Jesus declares that he will "make Mary male" so that she can enter the Kingdom of Heaven; he performs this feat in response to a manly doubt in the possibility of feminine sainthood. The hagiography of the martyr Perpetua, *The Passion of Ss. Perpetua and Felicitas*, written mostly by the Perpetua herself in second century AD, features several fascinating instances of gender bending instances. In one of her visionary dreams Perpetua is transformed into a man in order to defeat Satan in a battle. Elizabeth Castelli's reading of Perpetua's hagiography focuses on, among other things, the gradual weakening of the saint's father, expressed in increasing signs of performative, "feminine" weakness (Castelli 1991); there is a strong similarity between this process and Urdukas's gradual emasculation in *Sweet Sweat*, which hinges on a continuous transition from grotesquely exaggerated virility to attributes of femininity further on. Urdukas's effemination is reflected in the masculinizing of Juliette, the slave who reencounters the Count and Rachel in her new, empowered position of a bearded female robber.

The emancipatory, protofeminist quintessence of early Christianity is echoed, more than a thousand years after the death of Perpetua, in Christine de Pizan's book *The City of Women* (1405). The pinnacles of this allegorical city, structured and built on the stories and deeds of great women, are the high tower rooms, dedicated to the acts of women saints (Pizan 1983). The breaching of the axiomatic divide between man and woman has found many expressions, always entailing ideological, legal, and cultural conflicts. Yet, as Thomas Laqueur demonstrates, most often in Western culture when woman's virility (*tribade*) or man's effeminacy (*pathicus, mollis*) are diagnosed and classified, they are ascribed as sickening and perverse, and severely flawed in potency and procreative ability (Laqueur 1992, 53). Times of historical transition allow for the challenging of stable sexual categories to be perceived, to a greater extent, as conscious and positive initiatives. In the Christian context, for example, the spread of religion led to the demise of the affirmative trope of the sexually ambiguous woman, replaced with the all-too-common feminine ideal based on attributes such as modesty, passivity, and willful subjugation to either maternal or virginal moral models.

Finally, to return to Frank's own cultural territory, Georges Bataille explained that one of the pseudonyms he used, Dianus, "reunites the appeal of the bearded woman and a dying god with blood trickling down his throat" (Champagne 1998, 21).

cultural movements of the twentieth century – and both fields of discourse are crucial in reading *Sweet Sweat*. Feminist criticism informs, to a large extent, the way we experience and interpret Frank; Surrealism is the discourse *Sweet Sweat* was written to inhabit. A discussion of the novel itself, then, must include a brief examination of the ways that the moral problems posited by pornography are refracted through these two prisms.

Many pornographic and artistic representations are understood to reflect aggression toward women; Susan Gubar has charted substantially different feminist reactions to such representations (Gubar 1987). A writer who argues for the legitimacy of a pornographic product (despite its belonging to an abject cultural category and the fact that in its literal reading it is oppressive to women) may emphasize the product's "artistic" merit. This, for example, is Susan Sontag's approach in addressing the pornography of Georges Bataille, Guillaume Apollinaire, and others. She finds aesthetic reflexivity, textual ingenuity, and philosophical ideas in these obscene texts that lift them from the cesspool of ordinary smut (Sontag 1967). In this approach the dividing fence between decent and obscene remains as solid as ever; the pickets are just relocated here and there to admit into the garden of high culture several plants that were formerly considered weeds. The preservation of the fence can, of course, operate in the reverse manner: a work of high art may be redefined as pornographic, thereby losing its cultural legitimacy.

Yet an all-out negation of the opposition between viable erotic representation and prohibited smut is, of course, no less problematic. On the one hand, sweeping acceptance of all sexual representations would necessitate the collapse of critical criteria and a nihilistic denial of the very existence of the moral problems related to them. By the same token, paradoxically, lumping together sexual representations can also serve puritan righteousness in its condemnation of the erotic as such. In feminist criticism such condemnations (by Andrea Dworkin, most famously [Dworkin 1987]) assault virtually all representations of heterosexual masculine desire as aggressive objectifications of women. There is little wonder, then, that the antipornography lobby in the United States features an unsettling pact between feminists and religious fundamentalists. Two fallacies are at the core of the dogmatic antipornography-feminist position: first, it is premised on a cohesive, essentialist notion of womanhood (which means not only vouching unequivocally for a questionable exclusive division between two sexes, but, in relation to pornography, excluding from the essential category of women those who enjoy pornography or find it unobjectionable.[3] Second, Dworkin uncritically and categorically posits a false causal relationship between pornographic fantasies and real life: heterosexual fantasy features violence toward women; ergo, fantasy causes rape.[4] In any case, it comes as no surprise that Gubar's main study cases are culled from Surrealism. In Surrealist art and literature, violence and sexuality are not hidden: the ethical/aesthetic problem takes center stage.

In the context of the avant-garde, the division between high and low can refer to an aesthetic distinction between worthy and inferior, advanced and regressive, and popular and elitist art, and to social hierarchies and a differentiation between the corporeal and the spiritual. However, I suggest, in a rather Freudian vein, that as removed as any artistic pursuit may seem

3 For ontological and historical dismantling of the acceptance of the division between man and woman as natural or stable, see Butler 1990 and Laqueur 1992. For further critique of medical and social practices that brutally enforce this divide, see Fausto-Sterling 2000.

4 For a critique of Dworkin expanding on these points, see Kipnis 1996. Kipnis examines several genres of smut and also surveys studies of viewers' responses to other cinematic genres (such as horror film). These studies show that it cannot be taken for granted that the majority of male viewers of a scene in which a woman is assaulted identify with the male aggressor rather than the female victim.

from the politics of the body, it necessarily reflects a stance with regard to sexuality.

André Breton's positions on high and low forms of culture are not as unequivocal as they might initially appear. Breton's poetics and politics challenge purist artistic hierarchies by encouraging hybrids of different media, by focusing on mundane objects, and by their enthusiastic interest in pop-culture products and advertising. Still, Breton maintained a critical distinction between high and low and did not believe, for instance, that worthy culture might be produced by the working class.[5] His ambivalence was only heightened when he considered sexuality. Here, the tension lies not only between popular culture and advanced aesthetics but also in the hierarchic valuation of spiritual sublimity and lowly sexual urges. In his work Breton is certainly far removed from sexual puritanism or moralistic chastisement: his call for the exploration of sexuality coincids with a song of praise for the dark, the perverse, and the transgressive. But the assault on Georges Bataille in the "Second Manifesto of Surrealism" (Breton 1972c, 180–86) clarifies that according to Breton, demoting cerebral peaks to the valleys of the groin can be disastrous.

The tension between license and reserve is palpable in a series of group discussions on sex the Surrealists held between 1928 and 1932, enthusiastically seeking to encourage transgressive

5 The political aspect of the division between high and low is tangled for Breton by the need to bridge revolutionary ideology (by which the avant-garde is actively engaged in class struggle) and a sophisticated artistic agenda (anchored in bourgeois culture, consumed by the rich, and exclusive by definition). In the "Second Manifesto of Surrealism" Breton considers the following question: "Do you believe in a literature and an art which express the aspirations of the working class?" Breton does not, and he explains why: "In order to be viable [a work of art] demands to be situated in relationship to certain other already existing works and must, in its turn, open up new paths" (Breton 1972c, 154–55). On this issue there is a surprising affinity between Breton and Clement Greenberg, whose antagonism toward Surrealism is well known. See Greenberg 1993a, 1993b.

sexuality and create a discourse around it. Surprisingly, the conversations exposed some strict moralistic percepts, in particular the extreme homophobia of most participants, disavowed by a mere few (most notably Raymond Queneau and Louis Aragon) (Pierre 1992).

Breton explains his disgust with homoeroticism in explicitly essentialist terms. He forgives the sin of homosexual desire in only two people: Symbolist author Claude Lorrain and the Marquis de Sade. Lorrain is absolved because he was candid and outspoken about his homosexuality at a time when such sincerity demanded extraordinary courage; Sade – more significant to an understanding of Breton's worldview – is forgiven because his homosexual desire was part of a total ideological system calling for the sweeping negation of moral dicta (5–6).[6] Breton's moral conclusiveness thus has an almost oxymoronic resonance – and especially when the conversations address sensuality and erotica directly:

> *I have the lowest opinion of erotic literature [. . .] To give a name to what one is talking about seems to me to be the least one can do. With some difficulty, but even with the woman I love (who doesn't like me to do so) I call a cock a cock, a cunt a cunt, and so on (145).*[7]

6 Mark Polizzotti, Breton's diligent biographer, is hard-pressed to explain Breton's abysmal hatred for homosexuals. He speculates, as partial explanation, that this hostility was a psychological defense mechanism resulting from Breton's own attraction to Jacques Vaché and to the latter's death. Breton met the handsome dandy during World War I, when they were both soldiers, and he epitomized, for Breton, the cold, defiant detachment at the root of black humor. Vaché and a friend eventually overdosed on opium, and their naked bodies were discovered in a hotel room (Polizzotti 1995, 88). The shaken Breton construed Vaché's death as suicide, turning him, in the process, into a Dadaist hero. (Needless to say, Vaché's being dead enabled him to become one of the very few heroes who did not "disappoint" Breton after a brief spell of adulation.) It is doubtful that this speculation, however, fully explains Breton's homophobia.

7 He also said, "[Sensuality] only interests me in a purely cerebral way [...] I am absolutely opposed to any displays of physical sensuality" (Pierre 1992, 64).

This statement should neither be attributed to the jesting spirit of the conversations (as Breton was, of course, a reader of erotic literature and even, surprisingly, admired Bataille's *Story of the Eye),* nor construed as plain timidity. It points, rather, to the wide gap between Breton, who arrived, at the end of the day, to an idealism of purity, and the likes of Frank, early Aragon, and Bataille, whose approach to sexuality and morality was more radical. Walter Benjamin understood Breton's 1928 novel *Nadja* to offer "a profane illumination, a materialistic, anthropological inspiration" (Benjamin 1986, 179). And yet Breton's illumination seems to dim at the instant genitals are called by name; this reveals his anxiety about the destructive power sexuality might unleash, when materialism, in other words, becomes base, as Bataille would have it.

Like Breton, Bataille saw connections between erotica, ethics, aesthetics, and politics – but his version of revolutionary action calls for violence, desecration, and blood. Pornography, for him, is a medium through which to perform desire and destruction: it is a medium that, by its very status as impure, is already, to an extent, an embodiment of the *informe*. Bataille's famous definition of the *informe*, published in 1929 as one of the articles in the collaborative "dictionary" in the journal he edited, *Documents*, also delineates the operation of the entire dictionary, which is to "bring things down in the world;" to defy Western philosophy and undo its percepts. This is why, as Yve-Alain Bois points out, revolution for Bataille is cherished for its revolutionary power, emptied of its utopic content (Bois 1997, 17). According to Bataille, the order of Western knowledge constricts the world in a "mathematical frockcoat." Refusing order and form through the *informe,* the universe would resemble "something like a spider or spit" (Bataille 1985d); by the principles of expenditure and excess, the *informe* challenges the power of the law, which is founded on economy, utility, and logic. It refuses to become a system, as philosophy aspires to be. In this context pornography is an antiphilosophical instrument, resistant to formal order; "excess [surpasses] any foundational basis," Bataille wrote in an introduction to an erotic story (Bataille 1995b, 145).

In Bataille's early theories the hierarchical distinction between high and low resembles the gap between human verticality, aspiring to heaven and the sun, and animal horizontality, remaining close to the ground. This division is foundational to a rationalist worldview, which is premised on the disavowal of desire. The return of desire engenders a series of scandalous reversals: the sun and the eye, seeing and light – the very ideals of enlightenment – are metamorphosed. The sun is described as "the fecal eye" (Bataille 1985f, 85) and "the solar anus" (Bataille 1985a, 5). According to Bataille, the eye preserves the horizontal field of vision; it is thus the supreme object of correlated libidinal and destructive drives.[8]

In a famous footnote to *Civilization and Its Discontents* Freud offers an analogy of the kind he was so fond of between ontogenesis and phylogeny – man's childhood and culture's prehistoric infancy. Freud's scenario is akin to Bataille's: olfactory stimulation, crucial for quadruped animals, lose their primacy when man stands erect. The broader field of vision that opens up when man stands on his feet is attended by shame at the sight of his genitals (which had been unexposed in his former posture). The first victim of this evolutionary process, Freud continues, was anal eroticism (and the distinguishing sign of this repression, according to Freud, is one's disgust

8 This is how Bataille puts it in his definition of *eye*: "It seems impossible, in fact, to judge the eye using any word other than seductive, since nothing is more attractive in the bodies of animals and men. But extreme seductiveness is probably at the boundary of horror" (Bataille 1985b). For a consideration of Bataille's thoughts on vision and the eye in the context of modern French thought, see Jay 1994.

at the odor of the feces of another; the fact that people are unperturbed by the smell of their own excrement shows this repulsion to be a matter of nurture rather than nature) (Freud 1957k, 99–100n1).[9]

In *Sweet Sweat* all erotic hierarchies are based on odor, thus reversing high and low. Anal erotica and the smell of shit return to center stage in the erotic scenes and are celebrated as the acme of desire. The book's most desired dish is a dumpling: "Neither solid nor liquid, immaterial matter extracted from the stomach midway through its exhilarating metamorphosis from food worm to shit butterfly!" (*105; page numbers in italics refer to this volume*). The most desired fate is that of the character Phillip, who is degraded to the status of a toilet. But *Sweet Sweat's* scent is deceptive. The powerful aroma of Bataille's violent revolution is exchanged for perfumes of exaggeration and grotesquerie.

9 Freud's footnote on the role of the repression of anal sexuality in the history of culture is complemented by another footnote, just as famous, on the act of urination. According to Freud, the renunciation of the urge to urinate into the fire (an act with a homosexual erotic dimension) enabled man to preserve the flame and take it home: avoidance and repression of pleasure, in other words, are at the core of cultural progression. Woman's cultural role is also determined by the architectonics of the pubis: since she urinates downward and not forward, into the fire, she becomes its keeper (read: a housewife). In terms of poetics this pair of footnotes – on urination and defecation – seem like a structurally demonstrative mirroring of (literal) high and low in their relation to the body of the text.

2. "CANNIBALISTIC CONSERVES" SMUT AND FEMININITY

1. Lake Rachel

Dream stretched and plunged through Reality's layers into Lake Rachel like a sinking ship, frothing its own seminal fluids.

In 1927 Justine Frank painted a version of Francisco Goya's famous etching *The Sleep of Reason Produces Monsters,* from his *Los Caprichos* suite of 1799. Goya's bats, hovering over the shoulder of the sleeping man and delineating a dramatic compositional diagonal, have been replaced in Frank's work by animated menorahs and an even more capricious entity: a gaping vulva/bird-in-flight with thighs for wings and a pubic-hair head. Frank replaced Goya's two owls peering over the man's shoulder with a pair of wide-eyed pomegranates (a rare appearance in her work of this traditional Jewish symbol), and for the title Goya had inscribed on the front of the table Frank substituted a meaningless combination of Hebrew letters. Finally, in Frank's work Goya's man has been transformed into a woman. But even more striking than the sex change is the fact that the figure has woken up. Goya's print is universally seen as a self-portrait even though the face is hidden; in Frank's work the viewer is confronted with the artist's own frontal gaze instead of the top of the supine man's head. And whereas sleep, for Goya, symbolizes the monsters that come to life when reason is abandoned, the woman's wakefulness does not end the nightmare.

Homage to Goya illustrates one of *Sweet Sweat's* distinctive characteristics: the merging of reality and dreams. Although this convergence may seem all too obvious in a work at the junction of erotic fantasy and Surrealism (of which the focus on

Justine Frank, Homage to Goya, *1927*

dreams is an essential component), dreamlike and supernatural scenes are extremely rare in erotic literature. The goal of pornography is to enable the reader to project him or herself into the scenes depicted, and it typically does not include supernatural events and images: all that unfolds, occurs "for real." This reality, of course, is not the masturbator's actual world, but the reality of the conditions established within the text so as to serve libidinal desire optimally. Thus even as the pornographic depiction becomes ludicrously hyperbolic – potency knows no exhaustion, an erect penis is as thick as an athlete's muscular thigh, women have no longing but to endlessly bathe in sperm – even then objects of desire and acts of sex are anchored in a documented and prescribed lexicon: incest, sadism, rape, coprophilia, and so on. Disrupting this realism might short-circuit desire's electric current. Masturbatory fantasy is willful and controlled; it follows that such fantasies are hostile to dreaming, which is unwilled and impossible to control.[10] Frank remains, in this sense, a disciple of Lautréamont, in whose lyrical realms Maldoror may copulate with a shark or do battle with God (and, indeed, *Maldoror* can hardly be considered a pornographic text of any sexual appeal). The mixture of dream and reality in *Sweet Sweat* injects a surreal serum into the pornographic vein, and it plays a central role in constituting the book's representation of femininity.

10 Roland Barthes distinguishes between dream and fantasy and writes against the former and in favor of the latter: "Dreaming (whether nicely or nastily) is insipid (nothing so boring as the account of a dream!). On the other hand, fantasizing helps pass any interval of waiting, of insomnia; a kind of pocket novel you always carry with you and can open anywhere without anyone seeing anything [...]. The dream displeases me because one is entirely absorbed within it: the dream is monologic; and the fantasy pleases me because it remains concomitant to the consciousness of reality (that of the place where I am); hence is created a double space, disconnected, layered [...] there is an initiation of writing" (Barthes 1977, 87–88). By these terms, Frank's weave of dream and reality would probably be considered a fantasy.

The breaking of the conditions of reality is "explained" in the chapter The Intercourse of Dream and Reality: a rite of passage of sorts for the heroine, since it is the first manifestation of a link between magical events and a feminine protagonist, a link that becomes a leitmotif in the novel. Furthermore, the scene can also be perceived as a rite of passage *for the book itself*, in which the medium leaps to a different sphere of representation. The book is metamorphosed: it is no longer the same book. It is as if a fairytale became, midway, a historic novel.

During the "intercourse of dream and reality" in *Sweet Sweat*, "Rachel's entire entity was a sex organ" (*112*). According to Anne Kastorp, this process of becoming entails a persistent undoing of signifiers of masculinity and femininity:

Frank's textual and sexual blade is double: she employs patriarchal stereotypes and dismantles them from within, and in the process she manufactures a surreal model of desire which is a parody both of Breton's romantic yearnings and Freud's interpretation of dreams [...] since in terms of sexual identity, Rachel's body is an organ too slippery and evasive to be classified. It is "an armor of cavities" (a feminine figure, for those who ascribe to the binary division of male and female), "a net of nipples" (feminine), and "erect feelers" (masculine) with "humid, narrow tunnels wide open on each tip" (feminine). The stiffness of Rachel's body and its very oneness mark it as a phallus, only Frank's phallus is an oozing mollusk that the dream penetrates (and thereby a feminine phallus).

Frank's comic, divergent sexuality operates not only through descriptive accumulation but within a single image, as well – in, for example, the simile of an inverted umbrella for the "vagina opened to the heavens." Inverting the umbrella is converting masculine to feminine, an erect object to a concave vessel, collecting instead of defending against fluids. Umbrellas, upside down and right side up, appear in Frank's Physiognomies series of gouaches (1927–28); there the umbrella is jaw, scalp, or hat. When dream and reality copulate, the cards of sexual attributes are shuffled (Kastorp 1993, 258–60).[11]

Man Ray, Hats, *1933*

11 The umbrella brings to mind Man Ray's photographs of hats (1933), which originally served as illustrations for Tristan Tzara's 1933 essay "Concerning a Certain Automatism of Taste" (Tzara 1990). Tzara analyzes women's hats and identifies them with female genitalia. Enthusiastically employing Freudian terminology, he decodes the sexual messages sent by the hat as a literal display of sexual organs. These messages, mediated by fashion, are legible through distinctions between the variety of folds and creases. Ray shot a man's hat from above, thus emphasizing its vaginal crease, and a woman's hat in the profile, an obviously phallic protrusion. A masculine reading of feminine sexuality is contrasted with images that defy sexual division (at the beginning of *Sweet Sweat* the hats worn by the men of the shtetl are described as "unreal pudenda" [*85*]). For Freud, the umbrella is a distinctly phallic dream symbol, and hats also usually symbolize the penis, often in connection with castration anxiety (Freud 1957a, 360–62; 1957c, 339–40; 1957d, 154). The umbrella as employed by Frank is also an allusion to Lautréamont's famous sentence on the beauty of the sewing machine and the umbrella's meeting on the dissecting table (which some have interpreted as a sexual encounter between a masculine object and a feminine one). Frank was also undoubtedly familiar with Bataille's analysis of Dalí's 1929 painting *The Lugubrious Game*. In his interpretation Bataille notes the little umbrella in the upper part of the painting as a masculine symbols in its complex sexual scheme (Bataille 1985c, n30).

Kastorp's seminal essay is the first to associate the blurring of the divide between dream and reality and between the ego and the subconscious with the collapse of the masculine/feminine distinction in Frank's book. In this framework Frank offers ironic feminist intuitions in relation to masculine Surrealist symbols and images. However, the intercourse of dream and reality in *Sweet Sweat* is replete with clichéd imagery of feminine sexuality, including the traditional association of femininity and fluids, right up to the final flooding, in which the protagonist becomes "Lake Rachel."[12] This rhetorical excess is squarely opposed to Lacanian theory, in which in the symbolic order woman is nothing but phallic absence. Therefore, as the symbolic order is entirely based on the phallus and it constitutes sexual difference from which there is no escape, and as language is dominant in the symbolic order, feminine absence is connected with speechlessness (Lacan 1977, 289–91). Angela Carter describes the archetype of feminine absence in pornography: "The male is positive, an exclamation mark. Woman is negative. Between her legs lies nothing but zero, the sign for nothing, that only becomes something when the male principal fills it with meaning" (Carter 1978, 4).

In pornography a female first-person narrator frequently aids "the male principal." Woman is granted the power of

12 It is hard to determine whether the theme of fluids as a feminine principle is purely ironic for Frank, or whether it reveals a nascent essentialist impulse. The motif of feminine fluidity has a rich genealogy: according to Galen's theory of humors, man is characterized by heat and dryness, woman by coldness and dampness (Nye 1993, 17). This paradigm of masculine heat and dryness and feminine coldness and dampness remained dominant in Western medicine and thought up until the modern era (see Laqueur 1992 for a fascinating and detailed description of this idea in the history of medicine and its historic influence on the understanding of human sexuality and procreativity). In the scene dedicated to the character of the Desert Father, Frank amplifies the trait of masculine dryness, but it becomes evidence of inferiority instead of a signifier of superiority: "For what is man's orgasmic climax? Several silly spasmodic spits of sperm, forecasting a long drought! [...] André yearns for feminine dampness" (116).

speech, but her voice is usually meant to enhance the male reader's fantasy. In rare cases dumbness is disavowed altogether and the female body itself begins to speak. A fascinating example of vaginal speech is Denis Diderot's *The Indiscrete Jewels* (1748). In this erotic Orientalist book a magic ring compels the genital "jewels" – vulvas – to open their lips and entertain the sultan with revealing confessions of illicit carnal affairs (there are, after all, no better witnesses for such misdemeanors) (Diderot 1993). The chatter of the vaginal lips is, of course, disagreeable and detrimental to the women themselves: the oratorical witchcraft belongs to the sultan.

It is interesting to consider *The Indiscrete Jewels* in relation to the infamous 1972 pornographic movie *Deep Throat*, directed by Gerard Damiano. In Diderot's novel the lower "mouth" opens and speaks to satiate a man's desire; in *Deep Throat* the female protagonist is an anatomical freak: her clitoris is in her throat. The cure for her frigidity, her male doctor makes plain, is giving "deep" head. Diderot has the vagina speak, much to the women's discontent, while the "deep throat" of the film opens wide in order to be plugged by the real thing – the penis. The protagonist learns that dumbness (not to mention gagging) is the imperative condition for her sexual satisfaction!

In the "intercourse of dream and reality," Rachel's body arches and stiffens, in a posture clearly borrowed from depictions of feminine hysterics in nineteenth-century psychiatric literature (and one that Frank employed in an odd and graphic manner in some of her drawings).[13] The arching of the body marks the second stage of the convulsive fit – "the clown period."

13 The different stages of the "hysterical fit" were documented by Paul Richer; neurologist Jean-Martin Charcot used his drawings in his work at the Salpâtrière Hospital in Paris. Max Ernst appropriated one of Richer's illustrations for his collage novel *Une Semaine de bonté*. It is the last image in the final chapter, in which the imagery is predominated by convulsing and hovering women (Ernst has Richer's hysteric suspended in the sky). The same drawing is the source

Left: Paul Richer, "Clown Stage" of Hysteria Fit, *1881*
Right: Last page, Une Semaine de bonté, *by Max Ernst, 1934*

As Kastorp comments, this is an ironic arrow delivered at Breton, who found hysteria and feminine madness inspirational (Kastorp 1993, 264). In a short text published in the eleventh issue of *The Surrealist Revolution* – "The Fiftieth Anniversary of Hysteria" – he celebrates hysteria as "the greatest poetic discovery of the late-nineteenth century" (Breton and Aragon 1978).[14]

for a 1936 gouache by Frank, only her hysteric is a man with a disheveled beard and an engorged erection, clutching a Jewish hat. In Frank's gouache the arching of the body serves a perverse sexual act: the hysteric opens his mouth under the buttocks of a Japanese woman, ready to consume the water she'll dispense (and, in another variation from The Stained Portfolio, her excrement). Frank appropriated this second figure from a forceful erotic print by the eighteenth-century Japanese artist Utamaro.

14 Breton's adulation of madness is, in part, an expression of his stance toward institutional psychiatry. But the special spell of female madness is more complex than that. Hysteria is tightly bound with "convulsive beauty," the only possible kind of beauty, according to Breton (Breton 1988, 10). Especially telling in this regard is a footnote toward the end of the "Second Manifesto of Surrealism," expanding on the call for "the veritable occultation of Surrealism." Breton enumerates several spiritual practices (astrology, soothsaying, trance states, and so on). The textual segue from mysticism to hysteria and then to sexually mystifying women is so swift that it is well worth quoting: "Praise be to Hysteria, Aragon and I have said, and to its train of young, naked women sliding along the roofs. The problem of woman is the most wonderful and disturbing in the world" (Breton 1972c, 179–80).

Frank's allusion to the hysteric body acts out a dichotomy: a description of ecstatic lust doubles as a bitter travesty of a masculine Surrealist fantasy. The setting for this idealizing of the hysterical woman was the early phase of Surrealism, in which women were marginalized and almost completely speechless members of the group.[15]

If Frank tackles the problem of phallic order, her stance is, at least from a Lacanian perspective, rather blatant. Frank's symbolic order simply refuses to recognize woman as absence. On the contrary, the vagina is displayed as a super-symbol. Feminine speechlessness is disavowed and replaced by infinite chatter: a veritable barrage of similes, metonyms, and images. Frank's feminine cleft is baroque in its extravagant iconographic excess. While there is no sign in Frank's work of a yearning for "natural womanhood" or a cohesive identity, her orgiastic order refuses to differentiate between the symbolic, the imaginary, and the real. The authority of the phallus is rendered not as an imperative condition but as fiction – dominant, perhaps, but still to be confronted by another fiction. Frank's uniqueness, perhaps, is in her refusal to see a contradiction between self-determination and the comic disavowal of identity. Normative notions of presence and absence are performed in *Sweet Sweat* even as they are subverted and parodied.

The experience of sexuality in *Sweet Sweat* and in Frank's paintings is, therefore, an ironic experience in the profound sense of the word. It may be that this intently marginal book is resistant to interpretation, unwilling to desert the myth it has

15 Regarding Surrealism and misogyny, a theoretical opposition has evolved between a feminist perspective (see, for example, Kuenzli 1991) that considers Surrealism to directly reflect the dominant, patriarchal, and misogynic worldview, and more complex interpretations, such as Rosalind Krauss's. For Krauss, Surrealism's collagistic aesthetic scheme deconstructs the presuppositions of traditional representation (premised on unity and cohesion) and is thereby implicitly transgressive in relation to patriarchal order (Krauss 1986b).

Justine Frank, Utamaro and the Hysteric, *1936*

set out to destroy yet refusing to commit to any clear stance. Perhaps Gilles Deleuze and Félix Guattari's formulation (in relation to the marginal literature of Kafka) of "experiential reading" as an oppositional stance to interpretational deciphering could apply to Frank's work as well (Deleuze and Guattari 1986).

II. Rachel, Simone, Juliette, et les autres

Urdukas pleaded for a tête-à-tête with that impressive ass-face. He diffidently crawled toward it, slowly disappearing in the shadow of the Animist's superb architecture of flesh. But he had overestimated his stamina: he fainted.

Three of the female protagonists in *Sweet Sweat* undergo transformations: first, Rachel is transformed from a bashful country girl into a degenerate libertine equal in power to Urdukas through a crash course in crime; in the second – in the book's "intercourse of dream and reality" narrative – not only the heroine but the book itself is transformed, distancing itself in the process from most of its generic precursors; the third transformation happens under the sign of the astonishing character of the Animist. It is with the Animist that the magical new reality of the book takes over, concurrent with the now-total dominance of its female protagonists.

The Animist has an overwhelming sexual magnetism, diametrically opposite to Rachel's (and to prescribed notions of feminine eroticism): a teenage girl versus a woman in her fifties; virginal fragility compared to a hirsute, Amazonian body; a pure, sweet fragrance as opposed to a suffocating smell. In addition, the Animist has a few masculine characteristics, most importantly her gargantuan clitoris with which she may be the penetrating partner in intercourse.

The reversal performed by the Animist is not only between active and passive, or attractive and repellent. She exploits her alchemical powers to perform another reversal, by animating objects – but the full scope of the emotive and erotic charge, undoing the divide between death and life, is attained by coercing her slaves to act as inanimate objects: sculptural backdrops for her orgies.[16]

The phantasmagoric reversals propelled by wondrous feminine power transform the book. Concurrently, Urdukas, the male protagonist, undergoes a gradual metamorphoses. He, who is depicted at the beginning of the novel as an omnipotent, hypermasculine libertine, becomes enslaved to Rachel and flags sexually (he faints beneath the Animist's buttocks). Later he is raped by an animated broom, a grotesque phallus that is a sexual and mental extension of the Animist. Urdukas's transformation is so complete that he desires more extreme subjugation: he envies Phillip, the young lawyer who serves as Rachel's human toilet. Phillip's and Gaston's lots in the novel are theatrical, exaggerated echoes of Urdukas's gradual change.

In *Sweet Sweat* the collapse of the division between masculine and feminine is inseparable from the undoing of other binary divisions: dream and reality, organic and synthetic, object and subject, active and passive. Textual condensation is one way these diverse sets of ideas are linked. In Freudian dream interpretation, someone appearing in a dream may stand for several different people simultaneously. In *Sweet Sweat* almost every scene is charged with several different layers of meaning that inform each other. Take, for example, the rite celebrating the formation

16 In Sade, similar abuse of slaves takes place at Minski's castle; the giant cannibal uses his male and female subjects as living furniture. But where the Animist's sadistic pleasure lies in the freezing of slaves, Minski's pleasure is derived from *movement*: chairs and tables move on command, chandeliers descend and ascend (as they convulse and palpitate), and tables groan and tremble when hot trays are laid upon them. In Sade pieces of furniture frequently die during meals (Sade 1968, 584–90).

Illustration from Lindner's essay on the connection between thumbsucking and masturbation, 1879

of Rachel's "armpit cunts" (*133–35*). The ceremony is presented as a licentious biblical story, that of Doubting Thomas, and once the fingers confirm the miracle, they are collectively sucked. In the nineteenth century thumbsucking was associated with infant masturbation, especially worrisome in little girls.[17] The men thus provide Rachel with stimulating foreplay, enjoy a homoerotic experience, attain empirical proof of a carnal miracle, and, finally, are driven to a display of infantile sexuality attributed to girls.[18]

17 The association between thumbsucking and masturbation was made by the Hungarian pediatrician Lindner, to whose essay Freud refers several times (Freud 1957b, 179–81; 1957g, 251). For an analysis of the illustration that accompanied Lindner's essay, showing a little girl with a rather detached expression, her right thumb in her mouth and her left index finger between her thighs, see Davidson 1987, 32–33.

18 If the men are Doubting Thomases, Rachel is, of course, Jesus. Leo Steinberg

Only a superficial reader would take the magical power given to Rachel, the wedding scene with her father, and Urdukas's subjugation as literal and direct fulfillments of female desire released from the law of the father. Rachel's perverse lust is too grotesque to stand as a model of feminist sexual utopia. By the same token, the hyperbolic nymphomania of the heroines does not contribute much to the formation of their characters as actual, realistic women. On the contrary: the protagonists do not act out their desires; desires inhabit and possess their bodies. This is why, Kastorp claims, "there is no pretense to be found in the book of either literary realism or psychological 'depth'" (Kastorp 1993, 278). A brief consideration of Frank's precursors in the pornographic field, the Marquis de Sade and Georges Bataille, will illuminate the peculiar performance of desire in *Sweet Sweat*.

There is a clear difference between the modern authors and Sade in plain terms of bulk. Bataille's works of smut – *Story of the Eye*, *Madame Edwarda*, *The Dead Man* – Apollinaire's erotic books, and *Sweet Sweat* are all slim. While Sade wrote in a variety of genres, the quintessential form his work takes is a long, detailed, obsessive text chock-full of repetition, as if the text itself is a machine producing libidinal energy ad infinitum. Consequently, the development of the story is almost cursory, as the goal is a circular scheme of return. This literary order, characterized by exaggeration on the one hand and monotony on the other, has been identified by several critics as the archetypal economy of pornography – only Sade elevated it to an absolute principle. Sade seems to have produced his books according to

has elaborated on the theological reasons for the strong emphasis early Renaissance painters gave to Christ's sex (Steinberg 1983). Caroline Walker Bynum has focused, in a response to Steinberg's essay, on feminine aspects in representations of the Messiah's body; the vaginal form of the chest wound, and Thomas's insertion of his finger play a leading role in her arguments (Walker Bynum 1992).

meticulous, almost didactic, formulas. Even the wildest, rowdiest scene abides by a strict structural scheme. The principle of exaggeration dictates a gradual worsening of perversions and crimes; the principle of monotony dictates an unbending formal framework (Roland Barthes has astutely analyzed Sade's almost arduous, obsessive mathematical order [Barthes 1989]). Because a central recurring motif in the work is the breaking of sexual records and moral dicta, exaggeration does not contradict the mechanism of monotonous repetition. On the contrary – it necessitates that new records be set regularly throughout the book. Male organs, disproportionately big to begin with, attain incredible sizes; the number of victims who are raped and murdered increases from one orgy to the next, and their kind becomes more scandalous (in *Juliette* [1797–1801], for example, first grown-ups, then children, and finally pregnant women). In *The One Hundred and Twenty Days of Sodom* (1785) six story cycles each concentrate on even more extreme sexual stories and acts until the final one, dealing with murder.[19]

The absolute nature of the principle of repetition is demonstrated in Sade's earlier book *Justine* (Sade 1990). Juliette's crimes win her power, fortune, and pleasure. Her sister Justine, the good, righteous, and chaste sister, falls time and again into the hands of cruel tormentors, only to heal from her wounds and be ensnared again in a worse, more painful trap. Justine never learns from her mistakes because these mistakes must return eternally. Her horrible wounds mend because she must

19 The reciprocal relation between repetition and exaggeration is reflected in *Juliette* in several chapters that constitute stories within the story, *mise en abîme*, and autonomous inner texts. Thus repetition is not only a movement forward in a process of expansion, but a flow in every direction, including an inward folding. Such circular movement involves a system and a principle. Bataille describes this circular movement in Sade as a situation whereby nature, in constant movement, substitutes God within an ideological framework resisting the status of a "philosophy" (Bataille 1985h, 110).

be inflicted with new ones. Justine dies at the end of the book, terminating the cycle of torture. But the reader of *Juliette* will find that Justine has been "resurrected," so that she can be killed once more. From one book to the other, even death, the final termination of every movement, abides by the scheme of circular movement and eternal repetition.[20]

Deleuze claimed that Sade was a comic writer and thinker. This assertion about the creator of Western literature's most extreme fantasies might surprise readers who encounter Sade for the first time or who take the crimes and orgies described literally. But of course Deleuze does not mean to suggest that Sade's comic mode is an amusing light-heartedness. The text's violent movement operates against *the law* – both concrete laws and the law as an idea. Deleuze stresses that the law reigns and constitutes everything, including the ways to rebel against the law. Only in the comic mode is a real defiance of the law feasible; in this, Deleuze's notion of the unique potential of comedy is akin both to Freud's perception of humor – as having the sublime power of existential defiance against death – and also the "black humor" championed by Breton.[21] Sade's comic mode,

20 Joan DeJean examines monotony, repetition, and excess as the stylistic traits of the first French pornographic novel, *L'Ecole des filles* (1655) (DeJean 1993, 114). The absolute autonomy of Sade's institutions (such as the castle in *The 120 Days Of Sodom*) and the complete reign of their law of desire help clarify Hunt's claim that Sade's writings are the most extreme distillation of pre-Victorian pornography (writings, that is, in which smut is inseparable from other forms of transgression) and that, simultaneously, they are the prototype for later pornography, which deals exclusively with libidinal desire (and is therefore ahistorical) (Hunt 1993b). The figure of the libertine in Sade has a similarly paradoxical status. In pre-Revolutionary libertine literature, the carnal desires propelling the protagonist's plots are inseparable from an ideological and philosophical worldview, often perceived as transgressive and dangerous. In Sade the radical and transgressive aspects of the libertine are brought to the extreme and it thus, paradoxically, becomes possible to misconstrue the libertine as driven by pure hedonism. Thus an analogy is established between Sade's role in the history of modern pornography and his part in the shift in the figure of the libertine. For the history of libertinism see Feher 1997.

21 For Freud humor is the ego's narcissistic expression of defiance, refus-

according to Deleuze, is that of irony. Irony is expressed in absolute negation, by means of reversal: a negative image of the law is rendered by appropriating the law's procedures, its logic, and its claim for autonomy. At the center of Sade's ironic world is one of the law's foundational tropes: the institution. The institution – a prison, for example – embodies the power of the applicability of the law and its absolute nature. Sade propagates institutions that reverse and thus negate the law. Sade's fantasies are enacted in hallucinatory criminal institutions, well defended and cut off from the outside world: walled castles, wealthy and powerful secret societies, demonic monasteries working under the disguise of holiness, and royal and papal courts.

In Deleuze's model the law and its institutions have a theoretical foundation, a discourse constituting the decent, the proper, and the normal. The pornographic-ironic institution, the law's negation, breeds an obscene discourse constituting the transgressive, the perverse, and the abnormal. In Sade's work, sex scenes are interwoven with "scholarly" monologues that are pseudo-rational apologia for crime. Through this process of reversal and mimicry, the discursive strategies and structures of the philosophy of the Enlightenment are exposed as parts of an ideological institution, power oriented and inequitable (Deleuze 1989).[22]

ing to accept reality's repressive dictums (Freud 1957j). Breton refers to Freud's short essay and attributes the comic expressions he defines as "black humor" with a similar power of liberation and defiance in the face of existential doom (Breton 1997).

22 Deleuze seeks to break the category of "sadomasochism" into two distinct sets of values, both in the sense of the psychological gap between sadism and "masochism" and through examination of the writings of Sade in comparison with those of Leopold von Sacher-Masoch. He considers that the two authors provide two substantially different models of challenge to the law through the comic mode: while Sade employs irony, Sacher-Masoch uses humor. Irony negates the law in an absolute way by positing its reversal (evil is rewarded; good is punished); humor, on the other hand, seems to accept the law, but the masochist, instead of recognizing the law's power to deter, desires the punishment – so much so that the meaning of the offense and the causal relation between crime and punishment become entirely insignificant. Thus, the masochist does not negate

Sadeian desire has been described above as a machine that aspires for endless action, *perpetuum mobile*. Accordingly, the bodies that feed this mechanism's orgies and crimes – victims and victimizers alike – are its fuel. This is, perhaps, the boldest of Sade's transgressions. The humanist novel affirms the human subject by rendering it as real, but Sade's incessantly pounding smut pistons crush the truth value, the singularity, and the integrity of man. The total mechanism negates the autonomy of the human subject as such – including the sadist's. Bataille explains this process:

> *If we start from the principle of denying others posited by de Sade it is strange to observe that at the very peak of unlimited denial of others is a denial of oneself. Theoretically, denial of others should be affirmation of oneself, but it is soon obvious that if it is unlimited and pushed as far as it can possibly go, beyond personal enjoyment, it becomes a quest for inflexible sovereignty (Bataille 1986, 174).*[23]

the law but rather disavows it (the law exists; I am being punished – but I enjoy my punishment regardless of the law). From this difference between irony and humor stems a series of oppositions between Sade and Sacher-Masoch. While ironic negation is dynamic, humorous disavowal results in stasis. Even though Deleuze does not mention Freud in this context, his association of masochism with disavowal is undoubtedly informed by the Freudian claim that disavowal is the psychological mechanism shared by the masochist and by the fetishist to hold on to an image of a phallic woman; each freezes, as it were, an image disavowing her lack of phallus through fantasy (Freud 1957f, h). This helps clarify the masochist's fetishistic preoccupation with fur, shoes, and so on. While irony employs the trope of the institution, Sacher-Masoch focuses on a no-less-foundational legal trope – the contract (which is at the core of law's application, whether between seller and buyer in commerce, state and citizen in civilian life, and so on; in Sacher-Masoch the contract is, of course, the pact between the mistress and her slave). For a detailed reading of Deleuze's model, a few points of critique, and an attempt to apply the model to the work of artists Bruce Nauman and Vito Acconci, see Rosen 1995.

For Freud, by the way, disavowal has an entirely different import for woman: feminine disavowal is ascribed to the destructive refusal to recognize clitoral inferiority in relation to the penis or, in other words, a refusal to reckon with castration. For a mature woman this is the beginning of psychosis, bound with the delusion that she has a penis (Freud 1957g).

23 For Bataille, the idea of the subject's annihilation is returned from the heights of philosophical abstractions to the material world, and the idea of

For Bataille the sexual mechanism of debasing and negating the subject is bound with death.[24] Eros converges with Thanatos, and at the peak of fantasy is the allure of annihilation. In his work this tendency is expressed in an almost opposite textual style to Sade's. The experiences of Bataille's heroines, Simone in *Story of the Eye* and Madame Edwarda, are singular events of horror and exaltation. No stylistic monotony dims the passion. Simone's death (which was to occur in a sequel to the novel) is called for in terms of Bataille's charged perception of the sexual moment as that in which man rises to (animal) life from mundane (dead) existence but also as the moment of recognition of death.

Michel Foucault has asserted that the Catholic ritual of confession constitutes a "subject" in both meanings of the word: a distinct identity on the one hand and a subjugated being on the other (Foucault 1990). In that sense the extinction of the subject, consumed by the mechanism of Sadeian energy, is concomitantly a rebellion against the paradigms by which confession circumscribes subjecthood. And indeed, Bataille assaults the rite of confession directly: *Story of the Eye* ends with a scene in which Simone enters the confessional and masturbates while describing her sins. The priest is then abused and

sacrifice. He writes: "In this destruction [of other human beings] the limitations of our fellow human beings are denied; we cannot destroy an inert object: it changes but does not disappear: only a being similar to ourselves disappears, in death. The violence experienced by our fellow human beings is concealed from the order of finite, ultimately useless things. It returns them to immensity. This was already true in sacrifice" (Bataille 1985h, 122; see also Bataille 1986 and 1989). Both Pierre Klossowski (1992) and Maurice Blanchot (1980) have written in depth on the Sadeian mechanism and point to the notion of a pure principle at its foundation. Both authors recognize that this principle leads to self-negation. For Klossowski, the condition of negation is emotional detachment, apathy (91–98).

24 "Sexual disorder discomposes the coherent forms which establish us, for ourselves and for others, as defined beings – it moves them into an infinity which is death. There is a turmoil, a sense of drowning, in sensuality which is similar to the stench of corpses" (Bataille 1985h, 121).

finally murdered in the middle of a coerced sexual act. One of his eyes is gouged out, and in the thralls of her ecstasy Simone thrusts the bleeding eyeball first into his anus, and then into her vagina. The act that constitutes the self and polices its morality is fully reversed into a catharsis of abjection.[25]

Simone and Juliette thus mark, in very different ways, a rebellion against the human subject. Bataille shares with Breton a degree of adulation for and mystification of uninhibited femininity swept over the edge of madness and even into annihilation (Bataille 1995a and 1995b). But in both Sade's and Bataille's work, the constitution of a subject, including a feminine subject, within a novel would contradict the thoughts that drove its writing.[26] Rachel and the Animist materialize from within this subjective undoing, and in light of it. But despite the immense influence of the work of Sade and Bataille on *Sweet Sweat*, the

25 This ecstatic moment concludes a suite of globular images that rolls through the book: an egg, bull's testicles, the circular hole of the guillotine, and the eye inside the cunt, staring back at the awe-stricken narrator through "tears of urine." It was Roland Barthes who pointed out the dominance of these images and their metonymic relation to the imagery of fluids that is also persistent in the book. For Barthes, Bataille's transgression is first and foremost textual, and he therefore identifies the eye as the true protagonist of the work (Barthes 1972). It is worth noting that even as Barthes's analysis is brilliant and invaluable, his emphasis on the formal texture reflects a willful blindness of sorts to content, the actual import of the acts themselves. Susan Rubin-Suleiman comments on this "blind spot" in Barthes's reading as well as similar blindness in other writers who focus on the textual and structural qualities of the work (most notably, Jacques Derrida). In her essay Rubin-Suleiman juxtaposes these readings with feminist ones (such as Dworkin's) (Suleiman 1995).

26 A rare and interesting attempt at rendering unconventional feminine identities within a Surrealist pornographic novel is Louis Aragon's 1928 book *Irene's Cunt* (Aragon 1996). The second part of the book focuses on two powerful women, the protagonist/narrator's daughter and granddaughter. The sexual excitment of the storyteller, who is constrained in his wheelchair, is tied to his sense of impotence in the face of their extroverted and punishing sexual performance: one is a lesbian and the other – in a reversal of stereotypes – sexually exploits men as objects of her desire. Unlike in Sacher-Masoch's books, the "weak" man does not chose or initiate his condition, the "punishment" is not anchored in a contract, and the feminine protagonists follow their own desires (rather than enacting the role of the powerful woman the slave finds enticing).

novel's investment in the relationship between sex, violence, and death does not seem essential. Kastorp remarks that the "magical" scenes are instrumental here in frequently coloring the book with an almost cheerful tone. She considers the comic modes Deleuze associated with Sade and Sacher-Masoch, and complements them with a third kind of comicality resulting from Rachel and the Animist's actions: the grotesque.[27]

The convergence of the vulgar and the supernatural in *Sweet Sweat* can be read as an exotic spice in a broth cooked for a masculine consumer. But even a reader who downplays the importance of this convergence must admit that superpowers and hallucinatory hybrids are not ordained here by the hand of a god, a father, or a husband but by the will of the female protagonists. True: the pornographic (and the cultural) corpus has shown us all too well that oppression can arrive by winding, indirect routes. This holds true even for an author as complex as Sacher-Masoch; in his writing woman's power is expressed not only in the authority conferred on the mistress by the slave

27 Kastorp writes, "The magical capabilities of the heroines breeds a carnival of vulgarities. But the focus on immoderate gluttony and on excrement is always in a tense relation to a higher sphere, either spiritual or historical. It is crucial that the Animist stages a scene from the annals of the French Revolution (the death of Marat), and that Rachel performs on her very body a theological scene (Doubting Thomas). In the Animist's case, a constitutive revolutionary event becomes a burlesque of multiple desires: transsexuality (Marat is a woman), incest, matricide (Corday is her daughter), and cannibalism ('the skin malady, my darlings, is a delicacy'). Rachel's supplementary vaginas also evoke a burlesque-cannibalistic urge (one of them awakens 'a tremendous desire not merely to lick and lap the armpit cleft, but to gnaw and chew its flesh'). If we follow Deleuze's reflections, we may suggest that the law in *Sweet Sweat* is neither negated (as in Sade) nor disavowed (as in Sacher-Masoch), but rather it palpitates and bifurcates, is eaten and discharged. It is not a coincidence, in this sense, that Ecclesia and Synagoga, the two young man who are infatuated with Rachel, are students of the law, novice advocates; the future of the law – if these are his representatives – is to be subjected to the carnival of woman's body" (Kastorp 1993, 274). Kastorp's emphasis on the cannibalistic quality of desire in Frank's writing brings to mind Dalí's famous statement that, for him, beauty is always edible. Her focus on the grotesque is, of course, highly indebted to Bakhtin's analysis of Rabelais (Bakhtin 1984).

in erotic fantasies, but also by the evidence in the work of the keen interest he had in theories regarding the existence of an Ur-historical matriarchy. An absolute reign of women had, for Sacher-Masoch, a utopian dimension. But in the end of the day, even in masochistic desire the power of woman is masculine wish fulfillment. The initiating subject is punished man, the passive object is punishing woman.[28] And yet if pleasure in *Sweet Sweat* entails losing one's identity through desire, then between the lines of the book rises the claim that womanhood in its normative meanings is an idea founded on a regulatory system – the law. This law, although dominant, is no more necessary, natural, or innate – indeed even no more "real" – than the magical, grotesque womanhood of *Sweet Sweat*.

3. "A BLIND VAGINA": SMUT AND JUDAISM

I. The Double Guillotine – Justine and Jacob Frank

Oh, Holy Menorah!
Seven thighs aflame and six brass pudenda in between!

Justine Frank was a Jewish painter and pornographic writer. Both on the shelf of smut and in the canonical history of painting, Judaism is barely visible. With art, this may be the result of Judaism's iconoclastic spirit, its institutional hostility to visual representation that stems from the harsh rabbinical interpretation of the biblical prohibition of graven images.[29]

28 See, in this regard, the autobiography of Wanda, Sacher-Masoch's wife (Sacher-Masoch 1990).

29 Boyarin (1990) claims that the prohibition of graven images in the Talmud reflects the disavowal and repression of the great ocular desire present in the early phases of Judaism, the peak of which is the yearning to see God. This

And in relation to erotic representations, as a rule Christianity's approach to sexuality is fundamentally negative, but not so Judaism's. The generally positive attitude toward sex in Judaism is the result of the commandment to procreate, which, in Judaism, is not set against a monastic and ascetic tendency as in Christianity; this enables the expansive Talmudic engagement with sex and the body.

The family tree of French pornography is rooted in rich Catholic soil – which it turns into a battle zone. Pornographic texts aspire to extinguish the guilt and fear of the body caused by religion; they imagine transgressions in order to mock the prohibitions of catechism, they concoct licentious farces of the sacraments, they strive to debase the idea of sexual renunciation through descriptions of nymphomaniacal monks. Even Sade's transgressive wedding ceremonies between a father and his children are strongly anchored in Christian thought and consciousness.[30]

Exactly because the creative impulse rebels against its roots, the relationship between abject muse and Catholic inspiration is far more complex than mere confrontational antagonism.

theory does not challenge the fact that Judaism, in its historically and institutionally dominant forms was hostile to visual representation. This hostility, by the way, found an echo – in a secular incarnation – within the budding Zionist culture in Palestine, from its very beginning in the late nineteenth century. While Zionist culture celebrated the revival of Hebrew as foundational and Hebrew poets as national heroes, it slighted and debased an artist such as Boris Schatz, founder of Bezalel Academy of Art and Design, who saw himself as attempting to realize visionary Zionist art.

30 When we think of the scandalous theme of marriage between parent and child in Sade and Frank's books, we should keep in mind that not only women martyrs reserved their virginity for their celestial wedding with Christ: Jesus's mother, Mary, has been considered by several theologians as analogous to the Church, and hence the "bride" of the Messiah. Savonarola, for example, describes Mary's passion for her son (who was issued into the world from a womb whose hymen had not yet been torn) in a rhetoric of ecstatic sensuality (see, in this context, Steinberg's beautiful essay [1970]), in which he suggests that Michelangelo's Pieta sculptures reflect this hidden yet essential erotic-religious symbolism.

Even when the pornographer does not assault the Church head on, theological kinship may find expression in style and structure. Perhaps this explains the surprising affinity between depictions of carnal pleasures in pornography and descriptions of corporeal torments in hagiographies. The devout believer, like the avid libertine, is propelled by desire: to be elevated through death to immortality. Natural essence is metamorphosed through extreme physical acts: torture and murder, frequently of exceedingly beautiful and young virgins. In hagiography as in pornography, endless repetition and wild exaggeration lead to monotony. The drive (sexual in pornography, suicidal in hagiography) is excessive: the drive re-forms and de-forms reality.[31]

The martyr's ascension through torment to divinity perpetuates a reading experience in which pleasure and horror mix. On the one hand, the believer enjoys the seductive perfection of the tortured virgin, whose beauty is often miraculously preserved through ghastly torments, because of her holiness.[32] On the other hand, the horror of physical destruction is emphasized through the ultrasadistic hyperbole of the descriptions

31 Martyrs exist in a twilight zone between documented history and legend and so they easily accommodate changes to personify desired ideals. Thus, for example, Apollonia of Alexandria, a woman in her eighties according to contemporary testimonies, became a beautiful young woman in later stories of her acts. The authoritative figure who persecutes the holy virgins in hagiographies is usually paternal: a Roman leader, a pagan priest, or a king. In many of these stories there is a confrontation between the virgin and her father; thus, there is an analogy between the persecutor and the father, implying incestuous desire. In rare cases, such as the story of the martyr Dympna, this desire becomes explicit. Dympna's father desires his daughter's virginity. She escapes from the house accompanied by her spiritual mentor, but her father hunts her down and manages, finally, to kill her. His success opens an obvious narrative gap: the possibility that he satiated his perverse sexual desire.

32 Many tortures leave no mark on the martyr's body, and certain attempts to kill her miraculously fail. Thus, for example, the fire set on the martyr Lucy does not harm her body, and even the sword that pierces her throat, bringing death, does not prevent her from delivering her last speech in a clear and loud voice (Vorgaine 1969, 34–37).

of torture. This ambivalence between suffering and pleasure, horror and desire is strongly expressed in visual representations of martyrs such as Saint Agatha, who carries her cut-off breasts on a tray while her face is lit with a calm little smile and her posture is peaceful: a heavenly waitress of carnal brutality.[33]

Hagiographies are only one layer of the expansive Christian heritage that nourishes pornography. As a Jew, Frank has no such ancestry. And even though Jewish symbols and images are represented throughout her work in obscene, abject, and comic contexts, the pages of *Sweet Sweat* do not disclose either generic or thematic affinities with – and perhaps not even a profound knowledge of – the scriptures of Judaism. There is no reason to assume that Frank, member of a secular family on the verge of assimilation, was especially interested in the Bible, the Talmud, or the secrets of Kabbalah. I believe that the outrageous attributes and signs of Jewishness in her

33 When the slaughter of the martyr finally occurs, the authors tend not only to pepper the description with an abundance of color and detail but also to amplify the effect by the satellite killing of more people. Thus, for example, in the story of Saint Catherine, either her pagan jailors or the philosophers who debate with her about the true religion and are convinced of her truth find their death before the martyr herself does. In both cases the men convert to Christianity following their audience with the saint and pay for their new faith with their lives. Satellite killing may also engulf the martyr's persecutors: as when the flames set for Agnes catch, instead, her pagan tormentors (Vorgaine 1969, 112). Like pornographic heat, the hagiographic fire does not let go: it expands as the sign of a superior power.

The experiential effect of sacrificial martyrdom is inseparable from its ideological repercussions: it is, after all, the ultimate revolution – the transformation of both earthly and heavenly order. The multivalence between religious impulse and torture and between the "little death" of orgasm and actual death is a central axis in Bataille's writings, sometimes part of broad, quasi-anthropological theories, sometimes focusing on the conflicts in the Catholic psyche, and sometimes part of an anticlerical smut scene (Bataille 1986, 1988, 1989, 1995b). An extreme episode of abjection transports Madame Edwarda to an even higher denomination than the martyrs: she is pronounced "God. But God figured as a public whore and gone crazy" (Bataille 1995a, 155). It goes without saying that the analogy drawn here between martyrology and smut does not exhaust the plethora of links between pornography and religion. Regarding Sade in this context, see the extraordinarily rich and insightful analysis offered by Pierre Klossowski (Klossowski 1992, 99–144).

work hint at her goal to redefine her identity in defiance of dominant European perceptions. She appropriated the tropes of Judaism as part of a defiant stance – within and in relation to anti-Semitic culture. But before I delve into the character of Judaism as shaped, of all places, within a pornographic novel, I will present a contradictory interpretation of Frank's Judaism. Anne Kastorp ascribes Messianic Frankism to the artist in her fascinating essay "Surrealism's Apparition of Messianic Evil: A Reconsideration of Justine Frank's Art and Writings as a Modernist Incarnation of Eighteenth-Century Jewish Esoteric Mysticism" (Kastorp 1997).[34]

In 1935 Frank made two oil paintings of guillotines. In one, Hebrew letters hovering in blue skies form the guillotine – an alphabet scaffold. A diagonal black ן (*noon*) is the blade, while a pink ס (*samech*) is the neck hole. In the second painting the device is rendered in a rather heavy-handed academic style; it features two neck holes. This guillotine can chop off two heads at once, perhaps to execute a pair of lovers or Siamese twins. In a 1936 gouache Frank went one step further, doubling the doubling by painting two double guillotines in one work.

The connection between the alphabet guillotine and the double guillotine is enhanced in a number of drawings from The Stained Portfolio. One features a double guillotine with a plaque underneath each neck hole, both of which are inscribed "Frank," as if the lethal rings were reserved seats in an opera box. Kastorp asserts that Frank's guillotines are not common Surrealist fancies but testimony linking the artist with one of the most fascinating and bizarre stories in the chronicles of the French Revolution and in history of Jewish mysticism.

34 It is almost certain that this important essay will never be published, for reasons explained below. I would like to thank Professor Kastorp, of Brown College, New Jersey, for allowing me to read her manuscript and make public use of it.

Kastorp believes that through these images Frank was hinting at the life story of the German Jacob Dobruschka, a Spiritualist and a relative of the infamous mystic Jacob Frank. Dobruschka's several dramatic changes of identity were unearthed by the scholarly detective work of Gershom Scholem (1982c). In 1775 the Jewish mystic converted to Christianity and bought himself a title, whereafter he was known as Franz Thomas von Schönfeld. In that period, and under his new name, Dobruschka became a poet of a zealously nationalist-Teutonic bent. His poems give voice to the militant muse Siona, who glorified and adulated Germany (the name of the muse, derived from *Zion*, suggests that the poet wanted his readers to be aware of his bond with his heritage). He later became active in an esoteric Christian sect, the Asiatic Masons, distinguished by its reverence toward Jewish mysticism, and in that secret circle he was known by the pseudonym Scharia. As Schönfeld, Dobruschka enjoyed the patronage of Emperor Joseph II, who had a passionate love affair with Eva, Dobruschka's cousin and Jacob Frank's daughter. Parallel to his covert Christian mystic activities, Dobruschka performed the public persona of an affluent man and an amateur writer. Later on he moved to France, accompanied by his brother, Immanuel. There he changed his identity and his name yet again, this time to Sigmund Gutlub Frey, later supplementing it with another name – Junius. This additional name was meant to attest to his patriotism as an out-and-out Jacobin (even though just a few years earlier his Siona had shot fire of contempt and brimstones of hatred at the French Revolution!). Frey and his brother dealt in finance and led a conspicuously extravagant and luxurious life. In the atmosphere of prosecution, fear, and panic in Paris during those years, the two brothers were exceedingly striking in their foreignness and strangeness. Eventually and inevitably they were targeted and charged before the convent with

Justine Frank, from The Stained Portfolio *(79), 1927–28*

Justine Frank, Double-double Guillotine, *1936*

Justine Frank, from The Stained Portfolio *(51), 1927–28*

fraudulence, corruption, and espionage and thrown into jail until a verdict (guilty, as a rule) should be reached. It seems that Jacob Dobruschka, also known as Franz Thomas von Schönfeld, also known as Scharia, also known as Sigmund Gutlub Junius Frey, accepted his fate. Perhaps he wanted to die: he refused to enact the plans for escape his friends devised. After a lengthy detainment and trial the brothers were led to the scaffold. The guillotine's blade chopped off their heads on April 5, 1794, along with that of Georges-Jacques Danton.

Scholem asserts that such astonishing transformations are characteristic of Jacob Frank's school: "We are faced with a person who wears several costumes at once and disavows them all, according to circumstances, and whose intent one can never fully comprehend – the complete person of the Frankist" (Scholem 1982c, 182). The "complete" Frankist, in other words, is a person who embodies the negation of himself as complete, cohesive, truthful.

How did such an eccentric Jewish religious identity came into being? The root of this paradoxical self-negation is the Sabbetaian sect's urgent need to spiritually account for the apostasy of their messiah, Sabbetai Zevi. Belief in Zevi swept entire Jewish communities in the seventeenth century, but instead of bringing redemption, he converted to Islam, causing his followers the greatest shock imaginable. But the momentum of the Sabbetaian movement was too strong to simply halt; thousands had deserted their houses and regular lives, believing redemption was at the gate. Initially the believers tried to explain the paradox of the apostate messiah by arguing that Zevi's conversion to Islam was a necessary stage of the *Tikkun* (the "repairing of the world"). If in the early stages of the cosmic process, during the breaking of the vessels, some sparks of divine light fell into the abyss, the realm of evil, then the messiah surely must dive into that abyss in order to complete the divination of good from evil and bring the world to its perfected state (Scholem 1974, 297). Apostasy was thus perceived as part of the divine mission, an expansion of the theological explanation formerly provided for Sabbetai's psychological peculiarities and outbursts of heretical deeds, which included the saying of God's name, erotic transgressions, and other scandalous actions that were all interpreted within the oxymoronic conceptual framework of "redemption through sin."

If indeed Zevi's apostasy was merely a descent for the sake of ascension, then all the believers had to do was anticipate the divine revelation of Sabbetai's return from the Islamic abyss. But as this yearned-for moment failed to arrive, theological explanations for his conversion gradually shifted. Instead of a dogma of patient anticipation for the apostate's return, a highly complex and labyrinthine dualistic theory of faith and God developed. Torah de'Beriah (the Pentateuch of Creation) was compared with Torah de'Atsiluth (the Pentateuch of Emanation and Divinity). Both of those doctrines are ingrained in the Holy Torah given to Moses by God. Torah de'Beriah comprises the explicit laws and commandments that are absolute and true for the world in its present, imperfect state, embodied in the normative rabbinical version of religion. Torah de'Atsiluth, on the other hand, is a new cosmic order – but under the conditions of exile (understood here not only as the historical reality of the Jewish diaspora but as an internal spiritual state as well), these new laws have to be practiced by the believer in secret.[35]

35 The distinction between Torah de'Beriah and Torah de'Atsiluth had already been made in the Kabbalistic school of Safed (the holy city of Kabbalism), in the sixteenth century. But for these earlier mystics, the distinction had a different meaning: it marked the difference between the comprehension of the Torah in a superior world, the world of divinity, and its comprehension in the world of creation. The Sabbetaians transformed this conception by interpreting Torah de'Beriah as the Torah of a preredemption world, a world of exile. Torah de'Atsiluth, the laws that are revealed only as redemption begins,

Jacob Frank, the messiah who rose in the wake of Sabbetai Zevi's death, realized this condition of exile through intentionally deceitful religious existence. In this sense there is *no difference* between conversion to Christianity or Islam and abiding by the old rabbinical authority. In all three cases the believer consciously acts according to laws he does not believe, he consciously deceives – *and does so out of faith!*

Jacob Frank's doctrine thus entails the debasement of the entire tradition of Jewish moral law. A sin can be a pure act disguised as transgression, and transgression can be sublimated to the degree of godly worship by the power of the passion that engenders it. Similarly, a dichotomy opens up in the relationship between the holy and enlightened elite and the multitudes of common worshippers. On the one hand, collective and willful commitment of sins is perceived as imperative for the hastening of redemption; on the other hand, Jacob Frank's holy – in fact, Godly – status posits him, according to the percepts of Frankism, in a separate moral category than the rest of the human race, "beyond good and evil" (Scholem 1974, 318). These contradictions and tensions enhance a situation in which "just as redemption had so far become only intrinsically real and not yet visible, so the true belief must be held only in secret, while external behavior must conform to the power of evil in the world of *Galuth* [exile] [...] One's heart and one's mouth may not be one" (Scholem 1974, 319). All this clarifies

cancels the Torah of creation, whose laws stand in contradiction to it; thus, for example, "in the world of Atsiluth there are no forbidden forms of sexual copulations." In this Scholem detects the influence of the theory of *Shemitas*, developed in *The Book of the Picture (Sefer Temunah)*, a Spanish Kabbalistic treatise from the beginning of the thirteenth century. According to the author of Temunah, the Torah is eternally true and its laws universal, but it should be read and understood differently in different eras – the *Shemitas*. The present *Shemita* is the era of *Din* (meaning judgment or punishment); its prohibitions and commandments would be cancelled with the dawning of a new era, the *Shemita* of *Rahamim* (meaning compassion) (Scholem 1982a, 37–38).

Scholem's observation that Dobruschka's numerous deceits and shifts of identity are, in fact, the pure expression of Frankism.

To return, then, to Justine Frank. Could it be that the double-eyed guillotines in Frank's art are not only expressions of a typically modern interest in visionary and hallucinatory machines but also concretely historical memory traces with blades aimed at specific necks – those of Dobruschka and his brother? And could the doubling of the name Frank on their plaques point not only to a preoccupation with reflection, self-doubling, and narcissism but also to a highly charged spiritual link between Jacob Dobruschka, Jacob Frank, and Justine Frank? Kastorp does not hesitate:

The guillotine paintings with their abundance of proof leave no doubt that Justine Frank is a descendant of the Frank-Dobruschka family. The double guillotine reserved for two Frank sons is a testimony – intended only for the eyes of those in the know – that the familial cinders of memory have been kept burning. The alphabet guillotine opens the door for an understanding of the painter's artistic and spiritual praxis: astonishingly, she turns out not to be a secular avant-garde artist but rather a modern incarnation of the Frankist faith. In light of this evidence one cannot avoid the conclusion that both Frank's association with the Surrealist movement and the representations of liberated female sensuality in Frank's book and paintings were nothing but a coverup – just as Jacob Dobruschka led a fraudulent life, first as a bathetic German nationalist poet, then as a devout Jacobin. The blatant extravagance of deceit and the heavy social and personal toll it exacts (social condemnation, ostracizing, and death in both Dobruschka's and Justine Frank's cases), all fit the Frankist mold with frightening precision (Kastorp 1997, 12).[36]

36 Kastorp elaborates: "The resemblance between Dobruschka's and Frank's biographies is remarkable even on the level of minute details. For example, Dobruschka's mysterious source of financing is reminiscent of the financial

Until Scholem's scholarly breakthrough, Jacob Dobruschka's life was completely unknown to the public at large. Frank could have heard of it only through an oral history, told in highly confidential and closed circles. Once the step has been made to link Justine to Jacob Frank, what we know of her work and life quickly evolves into a dizzying choreography of speculations. The transformation of Frank and her protagonist, Rachel, into obscene and transgressive personae is now wrapped in a Frankist prayer shawl, connected to the goal of negation of accepted law (Torah de'Beriah), a prohibition against the worshipper revealing his or her true self, and a belief in the holiness of sin). The willful immersion of the Frankists in carnal sins – they had orgies in synagogues – finds a clear echo in Frank's work, and there is also a considerable affinity between the rape of the father in *Sweet Sweat* and Frankist wife-swapping rites and their annulment of the prohibition against incest.[37]

But there is more. Sabbetai Zevi and Jacob Frank were considered to be not merely God's prophets or messiahs but actual incarnations of God. The future, third, and final such incarnation was, according to Frank, to incarnate the *Shekhinah* (the feminine element of God): a woman whom Jacob Frank

support Frank regularly received from Antwerp, and she kept the secret of its source. The only feasible explanation is that members of the family (and perhaps a slightly bigger secret community of believers) had sustained a considerable organization, until the situation in Europe had made it impossible in 1936." (Kastorp 1997, 12–13).

37 The reversal of the Pentateuch's laws from "thou shall not" to "thou shall" originates from the Doenmeh sect of apostates in Turkey, whose radical wing was led by Baruch Kuni, also known as Berahya (Scholem 1982b, 102). From Berahya also came the perception of the spiritual leader as an substantiation of God whom the worshippers celebrate by special prayers, and even Berahya's name among his followers, Signor Santo – Holy Master – was passed on to Jacob Frank (120). Frankist messengers to Thessalonica even claimed Berahya himself beatified Frank (Balaban 1934–35, 109). In the context of this essay it should be noted that Scholem himself has pointed, in a footnote, to the affinity between the demonstrative reversals of prohibitions by these extreme mystic sects and Sade's ideas (Scholem 1982a, 40).

called "the virgin" (Scholem 1982a, 50). Frank's own daughter, Eva, with whom he had an incestuous relationship, symbolized the concept of the virgin. She was to be perceived by the believers as no less than the third incarnation of God. It is tempting to think of the literary character Rachel as an expression of this notion. In the beginning of the book she is a twelve-year-old virgin who later becomes a super-human figure uniting dreams and reality, and in the Doubting Thomas scene, she is explicitly associated with the human/divine image of Jesus.[38]

"I have come to Poland with one purpose only," Jacob Frank declared. "To abolish all religions and all polite manners, and my aim is to bring life to the world" (Scholem 1982b, 128). Dismantling the divide between the Jewish community and Christian society in this manner paradoxically contributed to the association of Frankist descendants with progressive and liberal social circles.[39] Yet "life," for Frank, does not signify anything like humanist idealism. It indicates instead an uninhibited anarchism: the liberation of being from all fetters of social laws, a revolution that necessitates violence: "When the waters are murky it is good to catch fish, and so when the

38 Here, Frank is at the tip of the iceberg regarding sexual tension and copulation between the ten spheres of the divinity (the *Sefiroth* as they appear in the book Book of Zohar, the most important text of the Kabbalah, and especially between the feminine sphere of *Shekhina* (also called *Malkhuth* – kingdom) and the masculine sphere of *Yesod* ("basis" or "foundation") and the divine spheres and the *sitra ahra* ("the other side," the realm of evil). Even though Kastorp associates *Sweet Sweat* with the complex cosmic-sexual scheme of the Book of Zohar, her essay is far from doing justice to this issue.

39 It is worth noting in this context that messianic mystic doctrines often entail an exceptional intermingling with the secular world, but that this practice, in Frank's case and in more recent examples (the Habad Hassidic movement and the school of Rabbi Cook, for example), entails willful duplicity: a different face is shown inwardly (to the worshippers) and outwardly (to secular society). This double-faced quality sheds light on the fact that extremist settlers in the occupied territories can seem simultaneously to accept the law of the Israeli state (and serve in its army), even as they see that army and that state as an enemy. Kastorp attributes to Justine Frank a similar kind of duplicity.

world is flooded with bloodshed, we shall be able to catch that which is ours" (129).[40] Frank was a highly peculiar spiritual leader in that, for him, violence and the breaking of commandments were bound with at over his ignorance – he constantly asserted that he was a simpleton (Balaban 1934–35, 164) – an anti-intellectualism in complete opposition to the archetype of a Jewish spiritual leader.

There is an immense chasm between the violence described in *Sweet Sweat* and the militant aggression of Frankism. Nevertheless, it is in aggression and murder that the most disturbing link between Jacob Frank and Justine Frank lies. Frankist Hassidim played a role in the blood libels the Christian church concocted against Polish Jewry during the second half of the eighteenth century, causing the torture and death of many. Frank's involvement in these atrocities is the reason why many of his contemporaries saw him as, quite literally, a son of the Devil – as he is described in the Book of Shemush: "He has not the image of a human, only his face looks like the face of a devil, and he has no speech or tongue, but rather issues cackles and stutters and chirps like those of the red roosters" (109).[41]

40 Jacob Frank's strong sentiments toward Poland also can be connected to the novel. Unlike several other messianic diasporic leaders, Frank did not long for the biblical country of Israel: his prophecy was that, of all places, Jews would find their territorial autonomy in Poland. "Poland is pregnant with goodness and beauty, and it is to this country that the resurrected patriarchs of the Hebrew people shall return"; Poland, he asserted, is none other than the biblical field of Edom (Scholem 1982b, 122). In *Sweet Sweat*, Rachel's village is described as a Polish shtetl displaced to the landscape of southern France. The import of this description is intensified when one bears in mind the extremely contentious divide between Eastern and Western European Jews in the early twentieth century (more on this topic below). It is conceivable that the description of the village is based on a grain of biographical memory, and the insistence on quintessential diasporic sites, when added to Justine Frank's antagonism toward Zionism, further enhance her commonalities shared with Jacob Frank.

41 Balaban opines that the blood libels are not merely a by-product of the Frankist movement, but the crux of its doctrine (90). Scholem is more skeptical. He explains the tangled situation that resulted in negotiations between Catholic clerics and Frank and his followers and

The critic who hunts for hints of the blood libels and their horrendous outcome in *Sweet Sweat* will likely find them, and not only in the novel's opening (a pogrom of sorts in a Jewish village) or in the end (the murder of the protagonist's religious father). Kastorp detects historical traces of the blood libels even in dialogue between the Animist and Urdukas regarding a shadow, a conversation that can easily be read as an entertaining vignette (*132*). Keep in mind the connection between the shadow as a *doppelganger* and Freud's notion of the uncanny).[42]

concludes that the latter cannot be blamed in this matter (Scholem 1982b, 117–18). The blood libels as such were foreign to the principles of Frankism, and the false testimonies delivered by the mystics were not authored by them but were dictated by the Christian inquisitors. This, of course, doesn't change the fact that the debates orchestrated by the Church between leaders of the Jewish communities and the Frankists served the Church as a highly efficient instrument in its bloody anti-Semitic persecutions (the Frankists, for their part, were in turn persecuted by the Jewish community, and their punishment of death by fire was ordered by rabbinical authorities prior to their actual participation in the debates: the threat of death, in other words, came upon them from both sides of the religious divide [Balaban 1934–35, 128]).

42 The double is one of several recurrent and distinct forms of the uncanny, an effect akin yet distinct from the horror emanating from the twilight zone between the familiar and the unknown, the domestic and the otherworldly, the living and the dead, the organic and the synthetic, the human and the inanimate. For Freud the trope of the double originates from an attempt to cope with fear of death, and the concept of the soul introduced the first double in the history of culture: an entity identical to one's self yet immune to bodily harms and, in fact, to death itself. The double becomes negative and threatening when the irrational foundation of metaphysical faith is shaken. As science replaced religious belief, a gap was created in consciousness that science is unable to explain or fill. What was a consoling extension of the self has been repressed and has returned as a monstrous apparition (Freud 1957c). For an essay examining the development of the uncanny in Romanticism and connecting it with the Lacanian "Real," see Dolar 1991.

In our context – Jewish mysticism – we can point at a fascinating affinity between Freud's reflections on the soul as the double, and an extraordinary mystic idea of a bifurcation in God himself between body and soul. Nehemiah Hayun posited a division in God between God's body, located in time and space, and God's soul, which is the *Ein-Sof* (the endless, infinity) (Balaban 1933–34, 155; the divine division into three and ten spheres is anchored in the Book of Zohar).

Even more pertinent to us is the strong affinity between the Freudian uncanny and the Surrealist perception of the object. On the way the Surrealists related to objects in their experimen-

The dialogue on the shadow is but one of many examples; Kastorp provides detailed readings of additional scenes, pointing to their concurrent connections with Frank's family history, Frankist ideology, and the violent clash between the mystic sect and Polish Jewry (Kastorp 1997, 35–62).

The conclusions Kastorp has drawn have propelled a drastic revision of the general appraisal of Frank. The publication of Kastorp's seminal 1993 essay on Frank paved the way for a new consideration of the artist's work as conveying a protofeminist, transgressive model of female desire. Kastorp, in other words, is responsible more than any other scholar for the renewed legitimacy accorded to Frank's pornographic novel. But the investigation of *Sweet Sweat's* mystic roots has gradually brought Kastorp to an out-and-out denunciation of Frank. Not only did she decline the invitation to participate in the International Frank Conference in 2000, but she has also determined, after a lengthy period of indecision, not to publish any further material about the artist, including the essay cited above.[43] Kastorp writes:

tations, Salvador Dalí wrote: "Every object was regarded as a disturbing and arbitrary 'being' and was credited with having an existence entirely independent of the experimenters' activity" (see Dalí 1968, 418).

For Hal Foster, the Freudian *unheimlich* is the principle idea for understanding Surrealism. He writes: "If there is a concept that comprehends Surrealism, it must be contemporary with it, immanent to its field; and it is partly the historicity of this concept that concerns me here. I believe this concept to be the uncanny, that is to say, a concern with events in which repressed material returns in ways that disrupt unitary identity, aesthetic norms, and social order. In my argument the Surrealists not only are drawn to the return of the repressed but also seek to redirect this return to critical ends" (Foster 1995, XVII).

43 Kastorp's dilemma, as it was explained to me in several conversations, was difficult. On the one hand, publishing her text on the artist's mystic practice seemed to be a reasonable means of exposing Frank as corrupt. On the other hand, any further publication on the subject might intensify the aura of radicality around her. It was not an easy decision to grant me permission to quote the unpublished essay. Kastorp distinguished here, between her personal decision and laudable collegial academic standards.

Justine Frank, Untitled (Self-Portrait as a Black Woman), *1938*

Justine Frank, from The Stained Portfolio *(71), 1927–28*

Justine Frank, from The Stained Portfolio *(72), 1927–28*

Sweet Sweat's depiction of Jewish bloodletting, once read in its relation to the blood libels and to Frankism, can be perceived as willful sinning serving a foggy ideological goal (anchored, in any case, in the tradition of "redemption through sin"). The same depiction can be read as a defiant act against the confinement of law, order, and societal norms, or as a Sadeian variation on a mystic theme. These interpretations, however, are simply not good enough. The violence of one Jew against another is an ugly stain connecting the pornographic text – and, indeed, Frank's entire oeuvre – to one of the darkest historical chapters of Judaism. I am certain that Frank's fictional bloodshed is anchored in a messianic program not only sinister but – from any rational viewpoint – quite insane. The fans of Frank's paintings and pornography must unflinchingly reckon with a hard, solid truth: this Jewish woman artist "personified, in art and life, negative mysticism, a real spiritual hazard. Disregarding this fact is nothing but intellectual indulgence. I can attest first hand to Frank's charisma and the powerful temptation (both academic and sensual) her work represents. Yet surrendering to this temptation is nothing short of cultural bankruptcy [...] (Kastorp 1997, 74).

I do not wish to respond here to Kastorp's sweeping moral condemnation but only examine the substance of her speculations. Her essay puts forward two arguments: first, that there is a substantial spiritual affinity between the artist and Frankism, and, second, that Frank was a descendant of the notorious mystic. I believe that Kastorp fails in both tasks. The explicitly blasphemous spirit of *Sweet Sweat* does not at any point disclose a coherent religious-spiritual program, to say nothing of a mystic or messianic bent. In terms of interpretational coherence and adequacy, it does not suffice to link Dobruschka's real-life willful deceptions to criminal hedonism as practiced by Rachel, a protagonist in a fictive narrative, or with enigmatic objects, however morbid, that appear in Frank's paintings. God's absence (in terms of Jewish mysticism, God's *Hester-Panim*) is absolute in the sphere of *Sweet Sweat*. Despite the supposed plethora of hints linking Justine Frank to Sabbetaianism and to the story of Dobruschka, a skeptical examination of this evidence reveals that it can be reasonably accounted for without fanciful speculations.

Kastorp's claims on the biographical level are even less founded. Toward the end of his essay on Sabbetaianism in Poland, Gershom Scholem describes the crumbling of the Frankist cell that remained within Judaism; many of the believers followed Frank's example in converting to Christianity and maintaining their practice in secret, but they gradually drifted away from the percepts of their original religion; early in the nineteenth century the last Frankist Hassidim belonged to progressive Polish elite circles, and naturally shared that society's widespread anti-Semitism. By the end of the century the very last of the Sabbetaians were observed (or conjured) – like mythological animals – by a few witnesses. The assumption, therefore, that the flame of the Frankist sect was kept burning at the house of Justine Frank's parents in Antwerp and that the radical faith's doctrine was transmitted to the girl so that she could advance a third divine coming through outbursts of licentious and blasphemous deeds goes against all evidence.

II. A Jew, a Christian, and a Monkey

The Afghan shuddered on the crimson silk sheets [. . .] Rachel waved her hand in front of the little creature's eyes. When it failed to respond, she concluded that it had become blind.

"I'll be damned!" growled the Count, "the synagogue and the church!" And, indeed, the two destitute grandmothers were none other than the two young lawyers!

As different as the Afghan monkey scene and the Blind Vagina episode are, both clearly echo the psychoanalytic association of castration anxiety with blindness (Freud 1957e). But here Frank doctors not only Freud but elements from nineteenth-century psychiatry as well. Rachel's grotesque diagnosis – that the animal exhausted from masturbation had lost its eyesight – is a sardonic paraphrase of the medical/moral paradigm by which onanism causes degeneration and blindness. By the same token, the (symbolic?) castration of the characters Phillip and Gaston harks back to the psychiatric thesis dominant in the second half of the nineteenth century by which fetishism and other perversions stem from "inversion" (turning sexual energy inwards – homosexuality, that is). In the widespread diagnoses of this condition, personal degeneration and cultural/national decay were strongly interrelated (Nye 1993); the degeneration of the invert and the fetishist was thought to be a symptom of the malaise corrupting Europe as a whole. Diagnoses were especially frequent and severe among the upper urban class and, in slightly different forms, among Jews.[44]

44 Fin-de-siècle degeneration is embodied in the figure of Des Esseintes, the protagonist of Huysmans's 1869 masterpiece *A Rebours* (*Against Nature*) (Huysmans 1969). Des Esseintes is a pathological incarnation of the dandy (whose prototypical description was written by Jules Barbey D'Aurevilly in 1845 [D'Aurevilly, 1988]). He is the last of a noble family, impotent and of a fragile constitution. His degeneration is made evident in the gradual exacerbation of his inversion – the final frontier of his potency. When this well dries up as well, Des Esseintes dedicates his time to rarified experiences of exotic and convoluted sensuality, premised on the nurture of the artificial in opposition to the natural. The persistent dominance of olfactory sensuality in Frank finds a precursor of sorts in Des Esseintes's "odor organ," little bottles of perfume essences with which their owner may compose smell chords. Frank had undoubtedly also read Huysmans's *Là Bas* (*Down There*), which describes the Black Mass and the cult of Satan, Catholic expressions of the notions of theological inversion and holy sinning.

But the danger of urban decadence was not only personified by rotten nobility and perverted dandies but by the Jew – both in popular imagination and in medical literature (Gilman 1993, 119–21). The scientific community divided between the overtly anti-Semitic explanation of Jewish pathology as heretical and a more moderate approach

Frank's appropriation of the arcane clinical vocabulary of pathologic degeneration is acerbic and grotesque, but it is an ominous travesty: she wrote the book at the very moment it was being rejuvenated by the fast-emerging racism of the 1930s. (Only a few years separate *Sweet Sweat's* theater of degeneration and the exhibition of "degenerate art" in Nazi Germany). The masturbating monkey and the debased lawyers are objects of erotic fantasy; on another level they are literary caricatures of masculine anxieties (castration, homosexuality); they are a programmatic – almost didactic – parody of the diagnostics of perversion; and, finally, the Afghan monkey and the Blind Vagina scenes expose how inversion, perverse sexuality, and degeneration were employed in the clinical construction of the Jew as a pathologized figure.

But there is more. Both scenes contain allusions to Shakespeare's play *The Merchant of Venice* (1596–98). The Blind Vagina game is similar in its outcome to the test faced by the suitors of Portia, the rich heiress of Belmont, in the play. There, as well, a failure in a manly competition overseen by a sought-after, empowered woman exacts a castration measure: each suitor must swear before a choosing game for Portia's hand that "if you chose wrong/ Never to speak to lady afterward/ In way of marriage" (II.i.40–42). The Shakespearean romantic comedy exacts from the failed suitor a vicious lot: a vow of abstinence. Portia and her waiting woman, Nerissa, reminisce

that explains Jewish degeneration as a result of socio-economic and cultural conditions such as a tendency to inbreed, early weddings, and a faulty diet (Richard von Kraft-Ebbing and Charcot were both inclined to accept those relatively liberal assumptions) (Gilman 1985, 1993). Degeneration and the generally high rate of mental illness among Jews were also blamed on excessive intellectual exertion, hence the diagnosis of *dégénérés supérieurs* (Gilman 1993, 163). By most accounts, however, physical and moral decay are interconnected. This science serves not only as the foundation of proto-Nazi anti-Semitism but also as the premise for Max Nordau's urgent call for a new, virile, and muscular Judaism (before Nordau's encounter with the Zionist movement, in which he became a central leader, he was known as a reactionary thinker for whom virtually any expression of "modernity" was a sign of degeneration [see Nordau]).

on past and present failures; as the plot evolves, two more losers, the princes of Morocco and Arragon, will be humiliated before the Venetian Bassanio claims his reward.

Bartering a wedding ring looted from a widowed father in exchange for a monkey is an even more direct allusion to *The Merchant of Venice*. Shylock's daughter, Jessica, robs her father of his treasures and flees with her Christian lover. She sells her father's dearest possession, the ring given him by his late wife – for a monkey. As his friend Tubal informs Shylock, it is a *dancing* monkey, a detail that aggravates Shylock. The dance of the monkey intensifies the comedy's cruel and jeering opposition between the Jew's love and its licentious debasement. A monkey is often a symbol of excessive sexuality, and if the dance of Jessica's monkey is a metonym for carnal abandon, the "dance" of the Afghan monkey is the unveiled obscene deed itself. On the other side of the barter is the ring – a symbol of loyalty and love. The ring is a leitmotif in *The Merchant of Venice*: giving, receiving, wearing, and removing of rings are acts imbued with erotic innuendo and games of sexual power. Concurrently, the drama of the rings serves to underscore the gap between Jew and Christian and, time and again, feminine and masculine switch roles – two divisions enacted as comic elements in the play. Portia gives Bassanio a ring, a masculine act signifying husbandly possession. The gender reversal Portia performs is reinforced when she disguises herself as a judge and succeeds in liberating her lover and his friend Antonio from the lethal grip of the Jewish fiend. Then she demands and receives as reward the ring she herself gave Bassanio and which he swore to never part with.

Parricide also has its counterpoint in *The Merchant of Venice*. Allegorically, Shylock's identity is annihilated by the act of coerced conversion. Portia rules that according to the contract he is allowed his pound of Antonio's flesh, but he may not spill a single drop of blood (a judicial ploy premised on the same ground as the blood libels: the Jew's intention to spill Christian blood). Thus, after Shylock's daughter has disavowed him, his property has been seized, and revenge denied, he is stripped of his faith and compelled to deliver a public admission that he has been granted a righteous trial. His final exit, when he begs to be excused because he is "not well" (IV.i.390), is as piercing an understatement as conceivable.[45]

Shylock's conversion is preceded in English literature by Barnabas in Christopher Marlowe's play *The Jew of Malta* (1589 or 1590). Barnabas is not as complex and conflicted as Shylock: he takes it upon himself to unfold his past as a hideous arch-villain in an autobiographical monologue (how he poisoned wells in order to kill Christians, for example). With Shylock the coerced conversion of the Jew became a recurring comic motif in English literary canon (Ragussis 1989).[46] Frank's allusion to this aspect

45 Antonio and Shylock can be read as figures of ludicrous, botched martyrdom. Antonio is an avid yet erroneous and misguided martyr; Shylock is a reversed martyr. Antonio's mysterious weariness, the topic of the play's opening lines, remains inexplicable until the end of the play. The only instance, however, when he seems to emerge from his depression into a state of enthusiastic action is when he is called to the aid of Bassanio; it follows that the cure for his sadness is tied with the idea of the sacrificial pound of flesh, death by the hands of the Jew, in other words. It well becomes a martyr-in-spirit to be utterly depressed as long as there is no cause worthy of one's death, and his cheerfulness at signing the death contract is quite understandable, even if this is not quite a death sanctifying God's name. But the romantic harmony that is the play's resolution is incommensurate with the martyr's drive; therefore, Antonio, along with his weariness, has to evaporate before the fifth and final act begins.

Shylock, the usurper, is a martyr's negative, son of the Jewish faith who justly suffers and is forced to disavow his religion: the castrated travesty of a martyr. And much like Antonio, Shylock and his suffering have no place in the final act. The princes of Arragon and Morocco are poetic echo of the two botched martyrs: Morocco, like Shylock, is a dark-skinned, Eastern foreigner with strong feelings of inferiority; Arragon is a self-centered European. Both botch the courtship lottery and are driven to castration by their true faith in love.

46 The figure of the converted Jew is reversed in George Eliot's *Daniel Deronda* (1876). The heroic protagonist is brought up as a Christian, learns of his Jewish origin toward the end of the novel,

of *The Merchant of Venice* is thus highly charged. She recycles a dominant cultural formula of the debasement of the Jew but also points at the structural operation of the coerced conversion by an act of superimposition. Through textual condensation, structural interrelations are revealed between the Jew's fate as a poetic device in English literature, the traditional reasoning of anti-Semitic theology, and the psychiatric paradigm by which the Jew is charted as immutably different, defective, Other.

From the nineteenth century onward, Jewish Otherness was no longer ascribed in European culture primarily in terms of religion, but rather in terms of racial difference, as manifested in the Jew's distinct anatomy, inclination to specific diseases, and exceptionally high rate of mental illness. The doctor and the priest who determine, in *Sweet Sweat*, that Phillip fits the role of the Jew reflect something of the contemporaneous scientific compendia of the Jewish body: hemorrhoids and flat feet are Semitic syndromes, while hysteria in men is a predominantly Jewish illness as well. Furthermore, the magical elongation of Phillip's tongue and the preposterous speech it results in stamp the slave's body with one of the quintessential and clearest marks of Jewish identity: *mauscheln,* the Jewish speech defect, which many of the era's scientists believed to be innate and immutable.[47] Faulty diction is proof positive that the Jew cannot really convert: his body does not allow it.

The conversion of Jews was examined, in the nineteenth century, through the prism of a scientific debate on Jewish Otherness. From a progressive vantage point, a willful act of conversion could be interpreted in one of three ways: as a result

and duly returns to the Jewish fold in order to assume a Zionist mission.

47 Among the experts enumerating hemorrhoids as a Jewish syndrome is, for example, Richard Andre, who was considered a major authority on the Jewish body in the nineteenth century (Gilman 1993, 27). Hysteria and leg and foot malformations and especially *mauscheln* are far more common and significant ascriptions.

of a religious revelation (that is to say, as an anachronistic remnant of the age of religion, an irrational spiritual decision); as a dignified pragmatic solution to the Jewish problem (the collective solution entertained by Theodor Herzl, prior to his Zionist conviction); or, from a purely clinical viewpoint, as delusional (since it is mad to disavow the impossibility of conversion in the face of genetic difference). The syndrome of willful conversion was called *pseudologica fantastica* (Gilman 1993, 87, 93): the uncontrollable vanity that propels the Jew who yearns for a higher social status into fallacious self-aggrandizement and therefore pathological deceitfulness (the deception of others and one's self).[48]

48 On Freud's negative attitude toward conversion in general and Jewish conversion in particular, Gilman identifies the stamp of all three approaches. Jewishness is, for Freud, a constitutive mental element, and it is in this context that his attribution of pseudologica to Eastern European Jews should be understood. Gilman writes: "Freud's rejection of Judaism as a religion is made at the same moment when he saw the immutability of the 'common mental construction' of the Jews. Intermarriage could no more obliterate this than could conversion" (Gilman 1993, 93). Freud opposes pragmatic conversion, meant to improve the Jew's ability to function in Christian society, on ideological grounds: he perceives such conversion as debasing, lacking dignity. Finally, Freud sees conversion resulting from a spiritual revelation as a regressive anachronism, regardless of whether the converted is Jewish or Christian. In the Freudian association of civilization's progress with psychological maturation, such religious revelation is considered as regression to an infantile stage (and see, in this context, Freud's famous interpretation of Romain Rolland's religious "oceanic" experience [Freud 1957k] as well as his reply to an American who wrote to him regarding the divine illumination he had experienced and his ensuing conversion [Freud 1957i]). The contemporary Jewish scientist, at any rate, was confronted by a catch-22, since according to scientific knowledge he was both the neutral diagnostician and the pathological exception. Gilman's central argument is thus that Freud's psychoanalytic theory (and those of followers such as Otto Rank) transforms Jewish syndromes into universal ones. It is telling that as bold as Freud's thought was, and even as he was invested in this process of universalization, he maintained a deep-seated contempt for Eastern European Jewry. It is well worth remembering that the attitude of progressive Western European Jews to Eastern European Jews was premised in many ways on the anti-Semitic classifications of racial sciences, with the breach dividing healthy from sick, resilient from degenerate, and debased from dignified shifted and relocated within Judaism itself.

These interpretations of willful conversion are anchored in liberal worldviews. In modern anti-Semitic thought, on the other hand, the Jew's attempt to convert belongs in an entirely different sphere, as an event both macabre and abominable that presents clear and present danger to a healthy society. Of the descriptions dedicated to Jewish conversion in anti-Semitic literature, *The Operated Jew* by Oskar Panizza (1893) has a special place (Panizza 1991). Its protagonist, Itzig Feitel Stern, is a hideous Jew, replete with the entire range of mental and physical aberrations. Through modern science (numerous surgical procedures) he plans to "correct" his body until he resembles a Christian (the transformation entails the substitution of Itzig's blood with pure Christian blood). But the ploy is doomed: soon the stitches of the Jew's surgical and mental operation are torn open, exposing the Jewish monster who cannot, finally, be truly transformed. The Jewish author Mynona responded to *The Operated Jew* with his satirical story *The Operated Goy* (1922), in which the German Count Reshok falls in love with a Jewish maiden and in order to marry her is forced to undergo, among other things, circumcision and psychoanalysis at the hands of Freud himself (Mynona 1991, 81–82). On the Viennese's couch, self-hatred is revealed as the core of anti-Semitism. Like Itzig, Reshok is physically "corrected" in a way that preserves the entire typology of Jewish attributes. He is transformed from an upright Aryan type to the very image of the Jewish intellectual – artificially enhanced flat feet and bent back included. His final lot is that of a rather odd Zionist pioneer: he lives with his wife under his new name, Moyshe Kosher (an anagram of Reshok), in a rustic villa on the outskirts of Jerusalem.

In *Sweet Sweat* Frank, as well, enacts certain surgical procedures to Jewify the Christian man: during his sexual escapades Urdukas twice loses two tiny bits of flesh – from his earlobe and his tongue – and in both cases Frank likens these clippings to circumcision. These procedures in *Sweet Sweat* echo both the Christian phobia of the Jewish man's infiltration into society (the Christian is transformed into a Jew by his Jewish mistress, and his flesh is damaged as a result) and the perception of the Jew's Otherness as associated with excessive sexuality and an effeminate nature. But unlike Mynona, Frank does not employ these motifs in an explicit response to dominant anti-Semitic representations but rather ludicrously transplants them into a sexual fantasy.

The consumption of Christian blood by Jews – a textual family tree on which both Shylock and Itzig Feitel Stern grew – was, from its inception, attributed to Jewish religious rites but also to their illnesses. It was a medieval commonsense that Jewish men underwent cyclical genital bleeding as the result of a Godly curse and that only the drinking of Christian blood could prevent it. From a theological angle, this interconnection between Jew, woman, and Satan was an accursed one. Racial sciences maintained the belief in the femininity of the Jewish man, but only as an additional symptom of his genetic Otherness. In this sense, the theological fantasy and the racist pseudoscience together created a seamless historical continuity in the equivalency of Jewish men with women, updated according to current ideological demands. Masculine menses are the synecdoche of the figure of the emasculated Jewish male, a figure that Jews internalized as well.[49]

49 See Gilman 1993 (96–99) for seventeenth-century sources regarding the connection between libels of the slaughter of Christian children by Jews and masculine menses and note 114 of the same book for its probable clinical origin: illnesses connected with urethral bleeding. In the context of Jewish effeminacy, Daniel Boyarin's *Unheroic Conduct* (1997) is of special interest. Boyarin's claim is not only that the European Christian perception of the Jewish man as effeminate had more than a grain of truth but that, in fact, the Talmudic tradition intentionally championed such a model of manliness, which stands in clear contradiction to the Roman ideal of manliness: instead of the combative, muscular, conquering, and heroic warrior who wanders away from his home and family, the

Sweet Sweat's pornographic conversions have bred a dizzying array of species – both rare and common – from the anti-Semitic corpus. The Jew's femininity and his defective speech appear in this smut novel through a patchwork of iconographic, theological, literary, and scientific traditions. But the roles of Ecclesia and Synagoga played by Phillip and Gaston are revealed as arbitrary (both young lawyers are, in fact, Christian, and contrary to the religious scenario, Synagoga ends up on top – thereby winning the role of a literal bottom, a human toilet). Identity, willfully debased, deceptive, and disavowed – like the symptoms artificially conferred on Synagoga (blindness, tongue malformation, invalidity, hysteria) – is cut to the measures of sexual pleasure. If interpretation wills, it can construe this textual construct as subversively marginal, programmatically destructing its own foundation. Or it can see Frank's effeminate men (and her own transformed body in her work) as attempts at creating new sexual performances, through identities that

Talmud champions the scholar, who has attributes normatively perceived as feminine (he is static, gentle, homebound, etc.). According to Boyarin this figure challenges the dominant, binary heterosexual model because, in absolute contradiction to this model's inner logic, the "effeminate" attributes of the Jewish scholar are in no way associated with castration or sexual insufficiency or abstinence (as in the Christian model of the monk). Boyarin then compares the Talmudic anti-Roman model of man with modern European Jewish types: the *yeshiva bucher* and the *mensch*. He perceives these also to be positive models of manhood within the Jewish community. In the historical reality of Christian Western Europe, however, the correlation of Jew with woman is negative: misogyny and anti-Semitism, hatreds doubly reinforced. To go back to the notion of Jewish menses in relation to gentile paradigms, Gilman surveys the notion of cyclical masculine bleeding as it reappears in Wilhelm Fliess's fanciful theories. Fliess believed that masculine somatic cycles tie the nasal canals with the genitalia – and idea that fostered not only an extensive epistolary exchange with Freud, in which Fliess formulated his speculations in detail but also resulted in an operation performed on Freud's own nose! Even this lofty historical baggage seems to be referenced in Frank's art: in The Stained Portfolio there are several self-portraits, in profile, in which her own nose undergoes a transformation, sometimes into the Jewish nose of caricature and sometimes into a penis. It is highly unlikely, however, that Frank knew of Fliess's theories, not only because these were soon forgotten, but also because Justine Frank herself is a fictional character.

Justine Frank, The Birth of Rabbi Frank, *1937*

do not abide by prescribed cultural roles as masculine, feminine, or Jewish. And if interpretation is mistrustful, it might protest the manipulative whim with which Frank regurgitates racist thought. The "obscenity" of the book, in any case, is augmented when the real histories of the subjects that serve its erotic inventions are kept in sight.

Count Reshok trains his dog to bite Jews. The canine is not misled by Rebecca, the object of its master's love: it smells a Jew (Mynona 1991, 78). The Count knows that this odor, *fœtor Judaicus*, is supposed to be very strong, and as he doesn't smell it, he believes his pet is mistaken. Olfactory deficiency thus leads Count Reshok into the fold of a Jewish bosom. Hypersensitive nostrils, by contrast, lead Count Urdukas toward sexual subjugation to Rachel. Smell transforms, smell governs, and smell derides and decides. *Sweet Sweat* is a book of cultural, religious, and carnal conversions, all with a heavy smell.

Leafing through Montaigne's essay "Of Smells" (1572–80) reveals that Rachel is not alone in her sweat's sweetness: the body of Alexander the Great emanated sweetly as well. Montaigne, though, is unimpressed. To his mind the best odor of all is the absence of odor, and he quotes Martial: "I'd rather smell of nothing than smell sweet" (Montaigne 1958, 228). Smell speaks, but it had better hold its tongue – especially around women. What holds for women's smells holds for their actions as well, reasons Montaigne – they are perfect when they are "imperceptible and mute." For Frank, on the contrary, the Animist's might is bound with her domineering bodily odor. In a world of proper order, it might well be perceived as stench. In the sphere of smut, with its babble of bodily fluids, active glands work marvels, and this olfactory dogma holds for the hirsute witch's overpowering perfume and for the sweetly obscene scent of the Jewish girl. Armpits are the origin of the world. Genitals conquer. Hierarchies sniff. Here, the righteous and the puritan, the anosmic and the fastidious are the *truly* blind synagogues: they are deprived of the pleasure rays of smut.

Justine Frank, Still Life with Pomegranates, *1934*

Chronology

1900 Justine Frank is born in Antwerp, Belgium.

1907 December 14: Fanja Litvak (later Hissin) is born in Saint Petersburg, Russia.

1924 Frank meets the Belgian Surrealist poet Camille Goemans in Brussels and receives a letter of recommendation from him.

1924 André Breton publishes the "Manifesto of Surrealism."

1925 Frank immigrates to Paris and becomes acquainted with the Surrealist group.

1925 Frank meets Georges Bataille and develops a friendship with him.

1927 Frank completes The Stained Portfolio, a group of more than one hundred drawings and gouaches on paper.

1928 Frank completes Physiognomies, a series of ten gouaches on paper. Georges Bataille marries Sylvia Maklès and publishes *Story of the Eye* under the pseudonym Lord Auch.

1929 Bataille edits the first issue of the journal *Documents*.

Frank participates in a group exhibition of Surrealist art for the first time, exhibiting her Physiognomies series. New York gallerist Julien Levy buys three works.

The "Second Manifesto of Surrealism" is published in the last issue of the journal *The Surrealist Revolution*. The manifesto contains a vehement assault on Bataille.

1930 Bataille and former Surrealists publish "A Corpse," denigrating Breton.

A revised version of the "Second Manifesto of Surrealism" is published as a book.

Bataille begins a love affair with Colette Peignot, also known as Laure.

Frank completes the oil paintings *Frankomas* and *The Sisters Frankomas*.

December 3: Members of right-wing anti-Semitic groups wreak havoc during the screening of Salvador Dalí and Luis Buñuel's film *L'Âge d'Or* in Paris.

December 4: Frank meets Fanja and Samuel Hissin after a screening of *L'Âge d'Or* in Paris.

1931 Frank's only book, the pornographic novel *Sweet Sweat*, is privately published under the pseudonym Gregoir Coque.

June 25: Tamar Hissin (later Biniamini) is born in Tel Aviv.

1932 Frank completes *Alchemical Boards for the Study of Hebrew*, a group of four gouaches on paper.

1933 Frank completes two works called *Frank's Guild*, an oil painting on canvas and a gouache on paper.

Samuel Hissin, husband of Fanja Hissin, dies of a stroke.

1934 Frank immigrates to Palestine. She settles in Tel Aviv and rents a small apartment, which she uses as her studio.

1935 Many of Frank's paintings are destroyed when part of her apartment's ceiling collapses during heavy rains that winter.

1936 The financial support Frank had received regularly from Belgium is terminated.

1938 Laure, Bataille's lover, dies.

1939 Frank spends two days in the hospital after a severe attack of an intestinal disorder she had suffered from since 1937.

1940 Former Dadaist artist Marcel Janco settles in Tel Aviv.

Frank completes the oil paintings *Sky-Root* and *The Metamorphosis of a Woman-Assassin*.

1941 Tel Aviv is bombed from the air.

Frank leaves her apartment and moves to the cellar of the same building, where she is allowed to stay rent free. She moves her studio to Fanja Hissin's apartment.

1942 Frank is arrested and accused of exposing herself indecently and attempting to physically assault Marcel Janco. She spends a day in custody before being bailed out by Fanja Hissin.

Frank moves into Hissin's apartment.

Frank completes the oil paintings *Sick Heaven, Shit Heaven*, and *A Portrait of Thieving Skies*.

1943 Frank dies in unknown circumstances.

List of References

APOLLINAIRE, GUILLAUME. 1995 [1907]. The Eleven Thousand Rods, or The Loves of A Hospodar. In *Flesh Unlimited*, trans. Alexis Lykiard. London: Creation Books.

ARAGON, LOUIS. 1996 [1928]. *Irene's Cunt*. Trans. Alexis Lykiard. London: Creation Books.

ARTAUD, ANTONIN. 1976a [1927]. In Total Darkness, or The Surrealist Bluff. In *Selected Writings of Antonin Artaud*, ed. Susan Sontag, trans. Helen Weaver, 139–48. Berkeley, CA: University of California Press.

——. 1976b [1926–27]. Manifesto for a Theater That Failed. In *Selected Writings of Antonin Artaud*, 159–62.

BAKHTIN, MIKHAIL. 1984. *Rabelais and His World*: Bloomington, IN: University of Indiana Press.

BALABAN, MAIR SHMUEL. 1934–35 [Hebrew]. *Le'Toldot Ha'Tenuah Ha'Frankit* (The History of the Frankist Movement). Tel Aviv: Dvir.

BARTHES, ROLAND. 1972. The Metaphor of the Eye. In *Critical Essays*, trans. Richard Howard Evanston, 239–48. Evanston, IL: Northwestern University Press.

——. 1977. *Roland Barthes by Roland Barthes*. Trans. Richard Howard. New York: Hill and Wang.

——. 1989. *Sade/Fourier/Loyola*. Trans. Richard Miller. Berkeley, CA, and Los Angeles: University of California Press.

BATAILLE, GEORGES, MICHEL LEIRIS, MARCEL GRIAULE, CARL EINSTEIN, ROBERT DESNOS, ET AL. 1995. *Encyclopaedia Acephalica*. Trans. Iain White. London: Atlas Press.

BATAILLE, GEORGES. 1985a [1931]. The Solar Anus. In *Visions of Excess: Selected Writings, 1927–1939*, trans. Allan Stoekl, 5–9. Minneapolis, MN: University of Minnesota Press.

——. 1985b [1929]. Eye. In *Visions of Excess: Selected Writings, 1927–1939*, 17–19.
——. 1985c [1929]. The Lugubrious Game. In *Visions of Excess: Selected Writings, 1927–1939*, 24–30.
——. 1985d [1929]. Formless. In *Visions of Excess: Selected Writings, 1927–1939*, 31.
——. 1985e [1929–30?]. The Old Mole and the Prefix *Sur* in the Words *Surhomme* and *Surrealist*. Trans. Donald M. Leslie Jr. In *Visions of Excess: Selected Writings, 1927–1939*, 32–44.
——. 1985f [1930?]. The Pineal Eye. In *Visions of Excess: Selected Writings, 1927–1939*, 79–90.
——. 1985g [1934]. The Psychological Structure of Fascism. In *Visions of Excess: Selected Writings, 1927–1939*, 137–60.
——. 1985h [1957]. Sade. In *Literature and Evil*, trans. Alastair Hamilton, 103–31. New York and London: Marion Boyars.
——. 1986 [1952]. *Erotism, Death & Sensuality*. Trans. Mary Dalwood. San Francisco: City Light Books.
—— [Pseud. Lord Auch]. 1987a [1928]. *Story of the Eye*. Trans. Joachim Neugroschel. San Francisco: City Lights Books.
——. 1987b [1943]. W. C.—Preface to *Story of the Eye* in *Le Petit: 1943*. In *Story of the Eye*, 97–101.
——. 1988 [1950]. *L'Abbé C*. Trans. Philip A. Facey. London and New York: Marion Boyars.
——. 1989 [1961]. *Tears of Eros*. Trans. Peter Connor. San Francisco: City Lights Books.
——. 1995a [1966]. My Mother. In *My Mother, Madame Edwarda, The Dead Man*, trans. Austryn Wainhouse, 23–134. London and New York: Marion Boyars.
—— [Pseud. Pierre Angelique]. 1995b [1941]. Madame Edwarda. In *My Mother, Madame Edwarda, The Dead Man*, 135–60.

Benjamin, Walter. 1986 [1929]. Surrealism. In *Reflections, Essays, Aphorisms, Autobiographical Writings*, trans. Edmund Jephcott, 177–92. New York: Schocken Books.

Blanchot, Maurice. 1980 [1949]. Sade. In *Sade: Justine.* New York: Grove Press.

Bois, Yve-Alain, and Rosalind Krauss. 1997. *Formless: A User's Guide*. New York: Zone Books.

Boyarin, Daniel. 1990. The Eye in the Torah: Ocular Desire in Midrashic Hermeneutic. *Critical Inquiry* 16 (3): 532–50.

——. 1993. *Carnal Israel: Reading Sex in Talmudic Culture*. Berkeley, CA: University of California Press.

——. 1997. *Unheroic Conduct: The Rise of Heterosexuality and the Invention of the Jewish Man*. Berkeley, CA: University of California Press.

Breton, André. 1960 [1928]. *Nadja*. Trans. Richard Howard. New York: Grove Weidenfeld.

——. 1972a [1924]. Manifesto of Surrealism. In *Manifestos of Surrealism*, trans. Richard Seaver and Helen R. Lane, 1–48. Ann Arbor, MI: The University Press and Ann Arbor Paperbacks.

——. 1972b [1924]. Soluble Fish. In *Manifestos of Surrealism*, 49–110.

——. 1972c [1932]. Second Manifesto of Surrealism. In *Manifestos of Surrealism*, 117–94.

——. 1972d [1935]. Political Position of Surrealism. *Manifestos of Surrealism*, 205–78.

——. 1988 [1937]. *Mad Love*. Trans. Mary Ann Caws. Lincoln, NE, and London: University of Nebraska Press.

——. 1993 [1952]. *Conversations: The Autobiography of Surrealism*. Trans. Mark Polizzotti. New York: Marlowe & Company.

——. 1997 [1945]. *Anthology of Black Humor*. Trans. Mark Polizzotti. San Francisco: City Lights Books.

Breton, André, and Louis Aragon. 1978 [1928]. The Fiftieth Anniversary of Hysteria. In *What is Surrealism? Selected Writings* ed. Franklin Rosemont, 320–21. New York: Pathfinder.

Breton, André, and Philippe Soupault. 1997 [1920]. The Magnetic Fields. Trans. David Gascoyne. In *The Automatic Message, The Magnetic Fields, The Immaculate Conception*, trans. Richard Seaver and Helen R. Lane, 39–148. London: Atlas Press.

Brown, Peter. 1988. *The Body and Society: Men, Women, and Sexual Renunciation in Early Christianity*. New York: Columbia University Press.

Brur, Abraham Jacob. 1936 [Hebrew]. Pirkey Geographia ve'Topographia shel Tel Aviv (Chapters in the Geography and Topography of Tel Aviv). In *Sefer Tel Aviv* (The Book of Tel Aviv), ed. Alter Druyanov, vol. 1, pp. 267–320.

Butler, Judith. 1990. *Gender Trouble: Feminism and the Subversion of Identity*. New York: Routledge.

Cahun, Claude. 1999. Heroines. Trans. Norman MacAfee. In *Inverted Odysseys: Claude Cahun, Maya Deren, Cindy Sherman*, ed. Shelley Rice, 43–110. Cambridge, MA: MIT Press.

Carter, Angela. 1978. *The Sadeian Woman and the Ideology of Pornography*. New York: Pantheon Press.

Castelli, Elizabeth. 1991. "I Will Make Mary Male": Pieties of the Body and Gender Transformation of Christian Women in Late Antiquity. In *Body Guards: The Cultural Politics of Gender Ambiguity*, ed. Julia Epstein and Kristina Straub, 29–49. New York and London: Routledge.

Chadwick, Whitney, ed. 1998. *Mirror Images: Women, Surrealism, and Self-Representation*. Cambridge, MA: MIT Press.

Champagne, Roland. 1998. *Georges Bataille*. New York: Twayne.

D'Aurevilly, Jules Barbey. 1988 [1845]. *Dandyism*. Trans. Douglas Ainslie. New York: PAJ.

Dalí, Salvador. 1965. *Diary of a Genius*. Garden City, NY: Doubleday.

——. 1968 [1931]. The Object as Revealed in Surrealist Experiment. In *Theories of Modern Art: A Source Book by Artists and Critics*, ed. Herschel B. Chi, 417–27. Berkeley, CA, Los Angeles, and London: University of California Press.

——. 1998a [1933]. Concerning the Terrifying and Edible Beauty of Art Nouveau Architecture. In *The Collected Writings of Salvador Dalí*, ed. and trans. Haim Finkelstein, 193–200. Cambridge, UK: Cambridge University Press.

——. 1998b [1933]. The Phenomenon of Ecstasy. In *The Collected Writings of Salvador Dalí*, 201.

——. 1998c [1934]. Millet's *L'Angélus*. In *The Collected Writings of Salvador Dalí*, 279–82.

——. 1998d [1936]. Honor to the Object!. In *The Collected Writings of Salvador Dalí*, 302–6.

Davidson, Arnold I. 1987. Sex and the Emergence of Sexuality. In *Critical Inquiry* 14 (1): 16–48.

DeJean, Joan. 1993. The Politics of Pornography: *L'Ecole de Filles*. In *The Invention of Pornography: Obscenity and the Origins of Modernity, 1500–1800*, ed. Lynn Hunt, 109–24. New York. Zone Books.

Deleuze, Gilles. 1989 [1967]. Coldness and Cruelty. In *Masochism: An Interpretation of Coldness and Cruelty*, trans. Jean McNeil. New York: Zone Books.

Deleuze, Gilles, and Félix Guattari. 1986 [1975]. *Kafka: Toward a Minor Literature*. Trans. Dana Polan. Minneapolis, MO: University of Minnesota Press.

Desnos, Robert. 1993 [1927]. *Liberty or Love!* Trans. Terry Hale. London: Atlas Press.

Diderot, Denis. 1993 [1748]. *The Indiscreet Jewels*. Trans. Sophie Hawkes. New York: Marsilio.

Dolar, Mladen. 1991. "I Shall Be with You on Your Wedding Night": Lacan and the Uncanny. *October* 58:5–24.

Dworkin, Andrea. 1987. *Intercourse*. New York: Free Press.

Eilon, Amos. 1975 [Hebrew]. *Herzl*. Tel Aviv: Am Oved.

Ernst, Max. 1976 [1934]. *Une Semaine de bonté*. New York: Dover.

Fausto-Sterling, Anne. 2000. *Sexing the Body: Gender Politics and the Construction of Sexuality*. New York: Basic Books.

Feher, Michel. 1997. Libertinisms. In *The Libertine Reader: Eroticism and Enlightenment in Eighteenth-Century France*, ed. Feher, 10–47. New York: Zone Books.

Findlen, Paula. 1993. Humanism: Politics and Pornography in Renaissance Italy. In *The Invention of Pornography: Obscenity and the Origins of Modernity, 1500–1800*, ed. Lynn Hunt, 49–108. New York. Zone Books.

Foster, Hal. 1995. *Compulsive Beauty*. Cambridge, MA: MIT Press.

Foucault, Michel. 1990. *The History of Sexuality, Vol. 1: An Introduction*. New York: Vintage.

Frank, Justine [pseud. Gregoir Coque]. 1931. *Sueur Douce* (*Sweet Sweat*). Paris: private printing.

Freud, Sigmund. 1957a [1900]. The Interpretation of Dreams. In *The Standard Edition of the Complete Psychological Works*, trans. James Strachey, vol. v, 339–630. London: Hogarth Press.

——. 1957b [1905]. Three Essays on the Theory of Sexuality. In *The Standard Edition of the Complete Psychological Works*, vol. vii, 125–248.

——. 1957c [1916]. A Connection Between a Symbol and a Symptom. In *The Standard Edition of the Complete Psychological Works*, vol. XIV.
——. 1957d [1915–16]. Introductory Lectures on Psycho-Analysis. In *The Standard Edition of the Complete Psychological Works*, vol. XV.
——. 1957e [1919]. The "Uncanny." In *The Standard Edition of the Complete Psychological Works*, vol. XVII.
——. 1957f [1924]. The Economic Problem of Masochism. In *The Standard Edition of the Complete Psychological Works*, vol. XIX.
——. 1957g [1925]. Some Psychical Consequences of the Anatomical Distinction Between the Sexes. In *The Standard Edition of the Complete Psychological Works*, vol. XIX.
——. 1957h [1927]. Fetishism. In *The Standard Edition of the Complete Psychological Works*, vol. XXI.
——. 1957i [1928]. A Religious Experience. In *The Standard Edition of the Complete Psychological Works*, vol. XXI, 167–74.
——. 1957j [1928]. Humour. In *The Standard Edition of the Complete Psychological Works*, vol. XXI.
——. 1957k [1930]. Civilization and Its Discontents. In *The Standard Edition of the Complete Psychological Works*, vol. XXI.
GILMAN, SANDER. 1982. *Seeing the Insane*. New York: John Wiley & Sons.
——. 1985. *Difference and Pathology: Stereotypes of Sexuality, Race and Madness*. Ithaca, NY, and London: Cornell University Press.
——. 1991. *The Jew's Body*. New York and London: Routledge.
——. 1993. *The Case of Sigmund Freud: Medicine and Identity at the Fin de Siècle*. Baltimore, MA, and London: Johns Hopkins University Press.

GREENBERG, CLEMENT. 1993a [1939]. Avant-Garde and Kitsch. In *The Collected Essays and Criticism*, ed. John O'Brian, vol. 1., 5–21. Chicago: University of Chicago Press, 1993.

——. 1993b [1944]. Surrealist Painting. In *The Collected Essays and Criticism*, vol. 1, 225–26.

GUBAR, SUSAN. 1987. Representing Pornography: Feminism, Criticism, and Depictions of Female Violations. *Critical Inquiry* 13 (4): 712–41.

HUBERT, RENÉE RIESE. 1994. *Magnifying Mirrors: Women, Surrealism, and Partnership*. Lincoln, NE, and London: University of Nebraska Press.

HUNT, LYNN. 1993a. Obscenity and the Origins of Modernity. In *The Invention of Pornography: Obscenity and the Origins of Modernity, 1500–1800*, ed. Hunt, 9–47. New York. Zone Books.

——. 1993b. Pornography and the French Revolution. In *The Invention of Pornography: Obscenity and the Origins of Modernity, 1500–1800*, 301–40.

HOLLIER, DENIS. 1992. *Against Architecture: The Writings of Georges Bataille*. Trans. Betsy Wing. Cambridge, MA: MIT Press

HUYSMANS, J. K. 1969 [1884]. *A Rebours* (*Against the Grain*). New York: Dover.

——. 1972 [1891]. *Là Bas* (*Down There*). Trans. Keene Wallace. New York: Dover.

JAY, MARTIN. 1994. *Downcast Eyes: The Denigration of Vision in Twentieth-Century French Thought*. Berkeley, CA: University of California Press.

KASTORP, ANNE. 1993. Repulsive Beauty: Justine Frank's Eroticism as a Feminist Proto-Deconstruction of André Breton's Surrealist Tropes. *Sign & Seal, The Brown College Journal of Critical Studies* 7 (2): 254–78.

———. 1997. *Surrealism's Apparition of Messianic Evil: A Reconsideration of Justine Frank's Art and Writings as a Modernist Incarnation of Eighteenth-Century Jewish Esoteric Mysticism*. Unpublished manuscript.

Kipnis, Laura. 1996. *Bound and Gagged: Pornography and the Politics of Fantasy in America*. New York: Grove Press.

Klossowski, Pierre. 1992. *Sade My Neighbor*. Trans. Alphonso Lingis. London: Quartet Books.

Krauss, Rosalind. 1986a. *No More Play*. In *The Originality of the Avant-Garde and Other Modernist Myths*, 42–86. Cambridge, MA: MIT Press.

———. 1986b. The Photographic Conditions of Surrealism. In *The Originality of the Avant-Garde and Other Modernist Myths*, 87–118.

———. 1999. *Bachelors*. Cambridge, MA: MIT Press.

Kuenzli, Rudolf. 1991. Surrealism and Misogyny. In *Surrealism and Women*, ed. Mary Ann Caws, Kuenzli, and Gwen Raaberg, 17–26. Cambridge, MA: MIT Press.

Lacan, Jacques. 1977. The Signification of the Phallus. In *Ècrits, A Selection*, trans. Alan Sheridan, 281–92. New York: W. W. Norton.

Laqueur, Thomas. 1992. *Making Sex: Body and Gender from the Greeks to Freud*. Cambridge, MA: Harvard University Press.

Lautréamont, Comte de [Isidore Ducasse]. 1970 [1869]. *Maldoror*. Trans. Alexis Lykiard. London: Allison & Busby.

Mitchell, Juliet. 1982. Introduction I. In *Lacan: Feminine Sexuality*, 1–26. New York: Norton.

Montaigne, Michel de. 1958 [1572–80]. Of Smells. In *The Complete Essays of Montaigne*, trans. Donald M. Frame, 228–29. Stanford, CA: Stanford University Press.

Mynona [Salomo Friedländer]. 1991 [1922]. The Operated Goy. In *The Operated Jew: Two Tales of Anti-Semitism*, trans. and ed. Jack Zipes, 75–86. New York and London: Routledge.

Nordau, Max. 1993 [1892]. *Degeneration*. Lincoln, NE: University of Nebraska Press.

Nye, Robert. 1993. The Medical Origins of Sexual Fetishism. In *Fetishism as Cultural Discourse*, ed. Emily Apter and William Pietz, 13–30. Ithaca, NY, and London: Cornell University Press.

Panizza, Oskar. 1991 [1893]. The Operated Jew. In *The Operated Jew: Two Tales of Anti-Semitism*, trans. and ed. Jack Zipes, 47–74. New York and London: Routledge.

Perpetua, Saint. 1986 [100–200 AD]. The Passion of Ss. Perpetua and Felicitas. Trans. H. R. Musurillo. In *Medieval Women's Visionary Literature*, ed. Elizabeth Alvilda Petroff, 70–77. New York: Oxford University Press.

Pierre, José, ed. 1992. *Investigating Sex: Surrealist Research, 1928–1932*. Trans. Malcolm Imrie. London and New York: Verso.

Pizan, Christine De. 1983 [1405]. *The Book of the City of Ladies*. Trans. Earl Jeffrey Richards. New York: Persea Books.

Polizzotti, Mark. 1995. *Revolution of the Mind: The Life of André Breton*. New York: Farrar, Straus, and Giroux.

Ragussis, Michael. 1989. Representation, Conversion, and Literary Form: Harrington and the Novel of Jewish Identity. *Critical Inquiry* 16 (1): 113–43.

Rose, Jacqueline. 1982. Introduction II. In *Feminine Sexuality*, by Jacques Lacan, 27–58. New York: Norton.

Rosen, Roee. 1995 [Hebrew]. Sore Eros Conversions, on Violence and Submission in the Work of Bruce Nauman and Vito Acconci. *Studio Art* 65:40–59.

Rothman, Roger Ivan. 2000. Irony, Melancholy and the Avant-Garde: Francis Picabia, Giorgio de Chirico, René Magritte. PhD diss. Columbia University, New York.

Sacher-Masoch, Leopold von. 1989 [1870]. Venus in Furs. In *Masochism*, trans. Jean McNeil, 143–272. New York: Zone Books.

Sacher-Masoch, Wanda von. 1990 [1907]. *The Confessions of Wanda von Sacher-Masoch*. Trans. Marian Phillips, Caroline Hebert, and V. Vale. San Francisco: Re/Search.

Sade, Marquis de. 1968 [1797]. *Juliette*. Trans. Austryn Wainhouse. New York: Grove Press.

——. 1987 [1785]. *The 120 Days of Sodom and Other Writings.* Trans. A. Wainhouse. New York: Grove Weidenfeld.

——. 1990 [1781]. *Justine, Philosophy in the Bedroom, and Other Writings*. Trans. Richard Seaver and Austryn Wainhouse. New York: Grove Weidenfeld.

Schama, Simon. 1989. *Citizens: A Chronicle of the French Revolution*. New York: Alfred A. Knopf

Scholem, Gershom. 1974. *Major Trends in Jewish Mysticism*. New York: Schocken Books.

——. 1982a [Hebrew]. Redemption Through Sin. In *Studies and Texts Concerning the History of Sabbetaianism and Its Metamorphoses*, 9–67. Jerusalem: Mosad Bialik.

——. 1982b [Hebrew]. The Sabbatain Movement in Poland. In *Studies and Texts Concerning the History of Sabbetaianism and Its Metamorphoses*, 68–140

——. 1982c [Hebrew]. The Career of a Frankist: On Jacob Dobrushka and His Metamorphoses. In *Studies and Texts Concerning the History of Sabbetaianism and Its Metamorphoses*, 141–218.

Sontag, Susan. 1967. The Pornographic Imagination. In *Styles of Radical Will*, 35–73. London: Secker & Warburg.

Steinberg, Leo. 1970. The Metaphors of Love and Birth in Michelangelo's *Pietas*. In *Studies in Erotic Art*, ed. Theodore Bowie and Cornelia V. Christenson, 231–338. New York and London: Basic Books.

——. 1983. The Sexuality of Christ in Renaissance Art and in Modern Oblivion. *October* 25.

Stoekl, Allan. 1985. Introduction. In *Visions of Excess: Selected Writings, 1927–1939*, trans. Allan Stoekl, i–xxv. Minneapolis, mn: University of Minnesota Press.

Suleiman, Susan Rubin. 1985. ReWriting the Body: The Politics and Poetics of Female Eroticism. In *The Female Body in Western Culture: Contemporary Perspectives*, ed. Suleiman, 7–29. Cambridge and London: Harvard University Press.

——. 1995. Transgression and the Avant–Garde: Bataille's *Histoire de l'oeil*. In *On Bataille: Critical Essays*, ed. Leslie Anne Boldt-Irons, 313–34. Albany, ny: suny.

Tzara, Tristan. 1990 [1933]. Concerning a Certain Automatism of Taste. Trans. Michael Palmer and Norma Cole. In *The Surrealists Look at Art*, ed. Pontus Hulten, 201–16. Venice, CA: Lapis Press.

Voragine, Jacobus de. 1969 [1200–1300]. *The Golden Legend*. Trans. Granger Ryan and Helmut Ripperger. New York and London: Longman, Green and Co.

Walker Bynum, Caroline. 1992. The Body of Christ in the Later Middle Ages: A Reply to Leo Steinberg. In *Fragmentation and Redemption: Essays on Gender and the Human Body in Medieval Religion*, 79–118. New York: Zone Books.

Walz, Robin. 2000. *Pulp Surrealism: Insolent Popular Culture in Early Twenieth-Century Paris.* Berkeley, ca: University of California Press.

This book was originally published in Hebrew by Babel Publishing House, 2001.

English language editor: Rebecca Roberts
Coordinating editor: Hila Peleg
Design: NODE Berlin Oslo
Printing and binding: Brandenburgische Universitätsdruckerei und Verlagsgesellschaft Potsdam

Published by arrangement with The Institute for the Translation of Hebrew Literature

ISBN 978-1-933128-66-5

Sternberg Press
Caroline Schneider
Karl-Marx-Allee 78
D–10243 Berlin
1182 Broadway #1602
New York, NY 10001
www.sternberg-press.com

The English edition of *Sweet Sweat* is published on the occasion of the exhibition *Justine Frank (1900–1943): A Retrospective/ Roee Rosen* at Extra City, Center for Contemporary Art, Antwerp, January 9 to March 8, 2009.

Curator: Hila Peleg

Artistic director: Anselm Franke
Manager: Katrien Reist van Gelder
Head of production: Caroline van Eccelpoel
Assistant curator: Lotte De Voeght

We wish to thank Diana Dallal, Zaki Rosenfeld, and Sari Golan

The project is supported by the Israeli Embassy in Belgium, the Brandes Family Art Collection, and Rosenfeld Gallery, Tel Aviv.

Extra City is supported by Vlaamse Ministerie van Cultuur, Jeugd en Sport, Stad Antwerpen, <H>ART, Klara, Bureau Bouwtechniek, Mampaey, Jaga, Zumtobel, Levis, and Koning Boudewijnstichting.

Extra City
centrum voor hedendaagse kunst
Tulpstraat 79
BE-2060 Antwerpen
www.extracity.org

Extra City

Sternberg Press